TUNNEL
VISIONS

TUNNEL VISIONS

KURT KAMM

Published by MCM Publishing, a division of Monkey C Media
www.MCMPublishing.com

Book Cover & Interior Design by Monkey C Media
www.MonkeyCMedia.com

Edited by Denise Middlebrooks

Printed in the United States of America

ISBN: 978-0-9888882-6-5 (print)
978-0-9888882-7-2 (ebook)
978-0-9888882-8-9 (ePub)

Library of Congress Control Number: 2014937234

CONTENTS

AUTHOR'S NOTE 9

ONE – June 24, 1971. 13

TWO – **June 22, 2014, 4:35 a.m.** 23

THREE – November 1992 31

FOUR – **June 22, 2014, 6:40 a.m.** 38

FIVE – May 1993. 49

SIX – **June 22, 2014, 7:20 a.m.** 62

SEVEN – August 1994 72

EIGHT – **June 22, 2014, 8:05 a.m.** 81

NINE – September 1996. 88

TEN – **June 22, 2014, 9:20 a.m.** 97

ELEVEN – December 1998 113

TWELVE – **June 22, 2014, 11:55 a.m.** 122

THIRTEEN – May 2000. 130

FOURTEEN – **June 22, 2014, 12:15 p.m.** 140

FIFTEEN – January 2001 149

SIXTEEN – **June 22, 2014, 1:15 p.m.** 161

SEVENTEEN – April 2008 169

EIGHTEEN – **June 22, 2014, 2:05 p.m.** 176

NINETEEN – September 2010 182

TWENTY – **June 22, 2014, 2:40 p.m.** 188

TWENTY ONE – **June 22, 2014, 3:14 p.m.** 195

TWENTY TWO 198

PHOTOGRAPHIC ARCHIVE. 199

ACKNOWLEDGMENTS 207

ALSO BY KURT KAMM. 208

ABOUT THE AUTHOR 212

In the West, it is said, water flows uphill toward money. And it literally does, as it leaps three thousand feet across the Tehachapi Mountains in gigantic siphons to slake the thirst of Los Angeles....

Everyone knows there is a desert somewhere in California, but many people believe it is off in some remote corner of the state—the Mojave Desert, Palm Springs, the eastern side of the Sierra Nevada. But inhabited California, most of it, is, by strict definition, a semidesert. Los Angeles is drier than Beirut... About 65 percent of the state receives less than twenty inches of precipitation a year. California, which fools visitors into believing it is "lush," is a beautiful fraud.

Mark Reisner
Cadillac Desert – The American West and its Disappearing Water

AUTHOR'S NOTE

THIS IS A WORK OF *faction*, or fact based fiction. It is a novel about the water wars in California and a terrorist attack on the Southern California water system. The book was inspired by an actual event, the Sylmar Tunnel disaster, which occurred in 1971, when 17 men digging a water tunnel were killed in a methane gas explosion.

During one of my numerous fire department outings, I found myself inside Railroad Tunnel 26 in the Santa Susanna Mountains, where Los Angeles County and Ventura County Urban Search and Rescue teams were testing a new technology for underground communications. The man standing next to me began to talk about tunnel safety procedures. That person was Steeve Inagaki, a safety engineer specializing in pipelines and tunnels who had just retired from the Metropolitan Water District of Southern California. (Steeve's father was a superstitious man who believed three e's in a name brought luck.)

I mentioned to Steeve that I was looking for a theme for my next novel and he told me about the Sylmar Tunnel disaster. At the time, I had never heard of it, but soon learned that Steeve is perhaps the greatest living expert on the Sylmar Tunnel (also known as the San Fernando Tunnel) and the circumstances surrounding the 1971 explosion. Steeve is one of the few people to have entered the tunnel in recent years and on one occasion led a Los Angeles County Fire Department USAR team through it on a training exercise. I am very grateful for Steeve's guidance and encouragement

When I started to research the story behind the Sylmar Tunnel, I discovered the contentious history of water rights in California. The unrelenting growth of Southern California in the Twentieth Century is a story of its quest for water. As early as 1913, the Los Angeles Aqueduct was constructed by the Department of Water and Power—the DWP—to divert water to Los Angeles from the rural Owens Valley in the Sierra Nevada. The water, coming out of the Owens Lake at a 4,000-foot elevation, flowed to Los Angeles, a few feet above sea level, by the force of gravity. The diversion soon rendered the lake completely dry and destroyed the area's agricultural base. This led to the first of California's "water wars," when the farmers tried to destroy the aqueduct. The involvement of the DWP and corrupt Los Angeles politicians and developers in this affair was chronicled in Roman Polanski's 1974 movie, *Chinatown*.

In 1928, a quasi-public entity, the Metropolitan Water District of Southern California—the MWD—was created to bring water to the semi-arid areas of Los Angeles and other Southern California municipalities from the Colorado River. The Colorado River Aqueduct was at the time, the world's longest and most expensive aqueduct, designed to move water over 242 miles of mountains and desert to Southern California.

In the 1970's the MWD embarked on a program to construct 700 miles of new canals, pipelines and tunnels and began to draw water from the Sacramento–San Joaquin River Delta in Northern California. A 444-mile aqueduct operated by the Department of Water Resources now transports the Delta water through a series of long gravity flows and abrupt rises at pumping stations on the trip to Los Angeles.

Construction of the MWD's Sylmar Tunnel began in 1969. The explosion occurred just after 1:00 a.m. on June 24, 1971. The tunnel, designed to be 27,000 feet long, was two years ahead of schedule, and only 2,000 feet remained to be completed. The tragedy, and the subsequent prosecution of the contractor, Lockheed Shipbuilding and Construction Company, received wide publicity at the time, but has since slipped into obscurity.

Willie Carter was one of the seventeen miners killed in the disaster. Ralph Brissette, now 75, was the only survivor, and currently lives in Los Angeles.

Today, 25 million people (19 million of which are served by the MWD) in California rely on water drawn from the Delta and the Colorado River, both of which are suffering from diminishing water flows. Recent proposals to divert more water from the fragile River Delta and send it south has resulted in protests and the rise of a new generation of water activists, this time from the Delta area. Anyone driving north on I-5 toward Sacramento can see the signs along the highway: NO WATER–NO JOBS; and HANDS OFF OUR WATER.

The demand for water in California continues to increase—the state's population is expected to grow 50% by 2023—and has created sharp conflicts among the MWD, other water agencies, agricultural, business, and community interests, and environmentalists. While the demand for water increases, California is entering its third year of an unprecedented drought. At the beginning of 2014, the Sierra snowpack, which provides much of the state's water supply, was measured at 12% of its average, an historic low, and state officials have begun water rationing.

***

The depiction of all characters in this book, as well as the dialog attributed to them, is fictional and a product of my imagination. The events described occur in actual locations in and around the County of Los Angeles. The photographs included at the end of this novel are images of the Sylmar Tunnel at the time of the disaster.

This novel is dedicated to the 17 miners who died in the Sylmar Tunnel explosion, and to Ralph Brissette, the sole survivor.

Kurt Kamm
Malibu CA
2014

ONE
June 24, 1971

THE SOUND OF THE ALARM thundered in the dark room. Before Willie Carter opened his eyes, he felt the throbbing in his head. He lay with his face buried in his pillow and when the clock went silent, his headache remained. After 10 hours, Willie was still hung over from drinking at the Watering Hole, the all-hours bar that served the miners working in the tunnel. The blow that Russ Warfield, a miner from the swing shift, had delivered to Willie's chin added to his discomfort. They had traded a couple of quick insults and thrown a few punches, as they often did, but it was no big deal. Willie retaliated, landed a fist in Warfield's gut, knocked him to the floor, and it was over. There were no hard feelings; they were just blowing off steam. Warfield and Willie remained good friends.

But it wasn't over, because Willie's head still hurt and now he had to get up and go to work. He pushed his rank covers aside, sat up on the edge of the narrow bed, and rested his feet on the bare wood floor. The air was thick and stale in his tiny first-floor room at the Osborne Street Guest House, a real dump sandwiched in between a used car lot and a discount liquor store, located on the backside of Whiteman Airport in Pacoima. Willie and many of the miners rented rooms at the Osborne because the boarding house was a cheap place where they could wake up and make it to the midnight shift at the East Portal in less than 10 minutes by car. Aside from its proximity to the dig, the Osborne had absolutely nothing to offer.

Willie struggled out of bed, took three steps across the room to the sink and turned on the overhead light, which illuminated pea-green walls. He felt terrible and knew his hangover would torture him for most of the shift. He twisted the single cold-water faucet, cupped his hands under it and splashed his face, then bent to let it run over his head. He rinsed his mouth twice, but the sour taste of beer and whiskey remained. Willie hadn't even hit 40, but tonight he felt like an old man. He grasped the side of the stained porcelain sink to steady himself. His hands were scarred and damaged. Dirt and grime darkened every crease in his skin. Nine of his fingers had filthy, ragged nails worn to the quick. There was no nail to wear away on his left index finger because it was just a one-knuckle stub, crushed years ago during an accident in a hard rock mine.

He coughed, spit into the sink and leaned forward to gaze at himself in the mirror. His creased face showed three days' growth of black stubble and his eyes were red from the foul air inside the tunnel. Two years ago, when the dig started, the other miners began calling him "the Badger." Most of the men came from the coal mines of Tennessee and Virginia, spent their free time hunting in the woods, and were well acquainted with the animal. Willie grew up on the streets of Chicago and had never seen a badger, but he had learned that they were tough creatures, capable of fighting off much larger predators. Like Willie, badgers had short legs and spent most of their lives digging at night. The description fit him perfectly—Willie was a badger, and he was proud of his nickname.

In the dim light of his room, he stooped to sort through the pile of work shirts, underwear, socks and pants heaped on the floor near the sink. He dug through almost every item of clothing he owned before he found the cleanest dirty sweatshirt and a pair of worn pants. His clothes smelled, but it didn't matter. In the tunnel no one knew the difference—there were stronger odors to worry about. Even so, he knew it was time to do his laundry. Willie sat down on his musty bed and pulled on thick cotton socks and slipped on his shoes. Everything else he needed, including his steel-toed work boots, was in the dry house at the East Portal.

Two meatballs on thick sourdough bread, chips, a banana, a bag of peanuts, and his favorite, a double package of Twinkies, were waiting in the refrigerator, ready to go. Willie knew from years of experience that he could never organize his lunch in the few foggy minutes between the time he awoke and when he left for work. He took his lunchbox from the tiny refrigerator and added a small bottle of orange juice and a Coke to consume at his 4:00 a.m. lunch break. Later, when his shift ended at 8:00 a.m., beer would be available in the dry house for anyone who wanted it.

Willie left a light on in his room and stepped out into the empty hallway covered with peeling vinyl wallpaper. He wasn't sure why, but out of habit he locked his door. A strong shove would force it open, but there was nothing in his room worth stealing. Anyone who wanted his dirty laundry was welcome to it. On the way down the hall, he stopped to knock on his friend's door; Ralph Brissette was a friend who also worked the graveyard shift. There was no response. Unlike Willie, Brissette didn't wait until the last minute to head to work. Brissette wasn't much of a drinker and didn't need the precious extra minutes to sleep off a hangover. He was already on his way to the tunnel.

The dry heat of the California summer night hit Willie when he walked out to his battered car parked behind the boardinghouse. He glanced at his watch—11:35 p.m. When most people in Los Angeles were winding down and preparing to go to sleep, Willie the Badger was awake and going to work at a dig called the Sylmar Tunnel, part of a billion-dollar system of shafts and tunnels being constructed by the Metropolitan Water District—the MWD—to bring more water to the thirsty people of Los Angeles. Willie worked for the contractor, Lockheed Shipbuilding and Construction Company. The project had begun in March 1969, and after digging for 23 months, they were already five miles in and had less than 2,000 feet left to completion. It was a highballing dig and Willie and the other miners loved working on it. Crews worked around the clock, three shifts a day, seven days a week. Willie was proud to be part of the graveyard shift, which was the most productive. They held the record of 101 feet completed during a single eight-hour period. Everyone knew Lockheed would receive a huge bonus for early completion. Every minute and every inch meant money. Willie and the other miners were enjoying it while it lasted.

One of the shifters, a Lockheed foreman named Walters, who wore a spotless white helmet, told the men every week, "If we get a bonus, you'll share in it." They didn't believe a word Walters said, and no one expected to see any extra money from Lockheed. Even so, a paycheck of $42.80 a day plus overtime was damn good. "We're also going to give every man a new Accutron watch," Walters promised. "It runs on a tiny battery and you can hear it hum. Best of all, you never have to wind it, so you'll never be late to work." That caught the miners' attention. A watch that hummed! They talked endlessly about the Accutron. Every man imagined it on his wrist.

Willie rubbed his eyes and tried to ignore the throbbing in his head while he drove the short distance from Pacoima to the East Portal at Fenton and Maclay streets in Sylmar. Tunneling was hard, dirty, hazardous work. There were so many ways a miner could die: crushed or buried under dirt and rock; suffocated by dust or loss of oxygen; dismembered by a piece of heavy machinery; or annihilated in an explosion. Twice in his life Willie had been caught in cave-ins inside soft ground tunnels, but each time he had beaten the odds and survived, while others working with him had perished. Once, when he could have lost his entire arm in a moving piece of machinery, he only gave up two knuckles of his forefinger. He had worked underground his entire life and didn't know anything else; he loved his dangerous job.

Although Willie prided himself on being tough and was accustomed to mining accidents, dying in an earthquake was something else, and that scared the hell out of him. Four months earlier, on February 7, a quake hit Sylmar and the rest of the San Fernando Valley. It happened at 6:01 a.m., while Willie and his crew were nearing the end of their shift. He had never experienced anything like it, but he knew instantly what was happening—what else could move the ground in the same way?—and screamed, "Earthquake, earthquake!" Willie thought the earth shook forever, although he later learned it only lasted 75 seconds. The power cut out, the water pumps stopped, and the Mole—the 225-ton, 140-foot-long excavator—shut down. Willie and everyone else on the graveyard shift froze in the complete darkness, 200 feet below the surface, waiting for the tunnel to collapse on top of them.

When their initial wave of panic passed and the emergency lights flashed on, Paul Badgley, the locy driver screamed, "Get on the muck train!" They jumped aboard the narrow-gauge cars and hunkered down on top of the wet gravel and soil in the gondolas, praying that the cement lining of the tunnel wouldn't come down and crush them. Badgley revved the diesel to full power, but the train traveled less than 500 feet before it derailed on the twisted track, and the men had to run almost two miles to the unfinished access shaft on Foothill Boulevard. Willie's heart was pounding so hard, he thought it would burst. He climbed up the endless metal stairs and emerged into the early morning light, frightened and exhausted, but thankful to be alive.

"It was a 6.6," Brissette later told Willie.

"A 6.6?" Willie said.

"You know, on the Richter Scale."

"Oh," Willie said. He had no idea what that meant, but when geologists reported that parts of the earth in Sylmar rose as much as 7½ feet and the East Portal entrance had shifted upward by almost one foot, that was something he understood.

The good news—the amazing news—was that amid all the destruction in Sylmar and the surrounding San Fernando Valley, along with the death of 65 people, there was no ground shear inside the tunnel and the cement lining remained largely intact. Within days, after replacing most of the rails and the resumption of groundwater pumping, Lockheed engineers told the miners it was safe to continue digging. Willie and the other men were overjoyed to get back on the job—they didn't get paid if they didn't work, and every one of them needed a regular paycheck. Their joy soon turned to anxiety when the miners found out that the tunnel they were digging passed directly through several earthquake faults and was within half a mile of the Sylmar fault zone that had caused the quake. Their unease was compounded by the aftershocks that shook the ground each day and rumbled through the tunnel while they were at work.

The earthquake was only the beginning. Part of the excavation ran under an abandoned oil and gas field and after the upheaval, liquid hydrocarbons and gas from underground pockets began leaking into the tunnel. As they dug through the alluvial fill—water-saturated sand and gravel—the odor became overpowering. One of the Lockheed engineers explained to the miners, "When the quake shifted the earth, it opened deposits trapped for God knows how long. That's what's coming into the tunnel; that's what you smell."

"What about methane?" one man had asked. "Are we gonna be getting methane in the tunnel?" Of all the gases, miners feared methane the most. The threat was not asphyxiation—it was odorless, but highly explosive. Methane became flammable at a concentration well below the level at which it could cause suffocation and the men all knew that more miners died in methane explosions each year than all the other fatal mining accidents put together. There wasn't a miner anywhere in the world who didn't think about the gas every time he went to work underground.

"Don't worry," the people from Lockheed assured them, "we'll monitor it."

As the weeks passed, the smell of hydrocarbons, which some of the men described as diesel fuel and others as kerosene, became stronger. At times, the fumes were so intense that the tunnel became unbearable and the entire shift had to stop work and ride the muck train out into the fresh air to clear their heads. The tunnel was designed to carry water and had no built-in ventilation. A temporary fan line moved along with the Mole and brought fresh air to the area where the men worked, but the flow was weak. The Foothill Boulevard access shaft, which intersected the middle of the tunnel, didn't provide any ventilation either. It only delivered fresh air if you stood directly below it.

When they began to tunnel directly through the Sylmar fault zone, the miners saw puffs of gas erupting at the digging face each time the bucket scooped away the soil. On several shifts, Willie had felt lightheaded, almost nauseated from the fumes, and sometimes he had to stop work and lean against the wall of the tunnel to avoid passing out. The previous week, work had halted more than 30 times on a swing shift while the men waited for a walker—the superintendent of the shift—to test for methane and other gases.

Willie turned onto Fenton Avenue and parked near the floodlights that illuminated the East Portal and the stacks of semicircular pieces of pre-cast concrete used to line the inside of the tunnel. Nearby, the narrow-gauge rail tracks for the diesel locomotives and muck cars ran past bulldozers that worked around the clock, building a mountain from the soil hauled out of the 21-foot-diameter tunnel.

He sat and pressed his hands against his temples, as if to squeeze out his headache as well as his mounting apprehension. He gripped the steering wheel and tried to reassure himself the danger from the underground gas was just part of the job; he told himself it was a risk taken by every miner. He was the Badger, he was tough and fearless, but tonight he couldn't ignore what had happened yesterday on his shift—a small methane explosion and flash fire had ripped through the tunnel and four men from his crew suffered burns. Everyone had fled, bringing the injured miners out on the muck train. Work was suspended and the graveyard shift was sent home at 5:30 a.m., something that had never happened. That was when Willie and several of the others headed to the

Watering Hole to let off steam.

While he was drinking away his anxiety, state safety inspectors, insurance officials, and Lockheed engineers descended into the tunnel to test the air with their Explosimeters. Once the digging stopped, the air cleared and they concluded it was safe. One of the Lockheed supervisors told the miners, "The Mole hit a small pocket of gas and either a spark from the machinery or a welder's torch set it off. There's no cause for worry. We'll resume work with the 4:00 p.m. swing crew."

Willie remained a moment longer in his car and watched the burst of activity at the shift change, as ghostly silhouettes of men came out of the midnight darkness and into the pool of light around the portal. The yellow diesel locy materialized from the tunnel, pulling the man-cars filled with miners. Around him, automobile engines started and headlights came on as wives prepared to haul their exhausted husbands home. Willie thought for a moment about his wife. He missed her and called home whenever he had time. He tried to make the two-hour drive to see her when he wasn't working on the weekend, but sometimes, at the last minute, he decided to go on fishing trips with the men instead. This weekend he was determined to go home.

He locked his car and as he headed to the dry house, he saw Mike Edwards, the walker on the graveyard shift. "Gabriel coming to work tonight?" Willie asked. Hours ago, Ray Gabriel had told Willie at the Watering Hole that he was not going to work their next shift because of the methane explosion. Gabriel said he had a "bad feeling."

"No," Edwards said, "he called in sick, but I think he's bullshitting."

You gotta go with your instincts, Willie thought, and went into the change room. He opened his locker and placed his lunch pail on the top shelf. He pulled on his thick bib overalls and reached for the steel-toed rubber boots that came halfway up to his knees.

Tony Barbaro appeared at the next locker. He worked the front of the Mole on the swing shift, operating the bucket-scraper that scooped the soil from the face of the tunnel and dropped it onto a conveyor belt running back to the muck cars. Dirt and sweat streaked Barbaro's face and his eyes were red and irritated. He dropped his helmet on the floor and slumped against his locker.

"You OK?" Willie asked.

"No, man," Barbaro said in a hoarse voice. "It was hell in there tonight, never seen it so bad. The soil was off-gassing through the whole shift and it smelled like kerosene. I feel awful. My throat was on fire and my eyes was burning. It just don't feel right in there...." He fingered the tiny San Lorenzo medal he wore around his neck, invoking the protection of the patron saint of miners.

Willie and the other miners respected Barbaro, one of the strongest men working in the tunnel. He never complained and he was never afraid of anything. Tonight, Willie was spooked by what Barbaro said. "They test the air?" Willie asked. Different gasses behaved in different ways. Some sank to the invert—the bottom of the tunnel—while methane, which they sometimes called swamp gas, was lighter than air and collected at the top of the tunnel. Using meters was the only way of knowing if the air was truly safe.

"The shifter was running around with his damn Explosimeter," Barbaro said. "After dinner, they told me to stop the digger for a minute after I scooped each bucket load. Man, I could see puffs of dirt where the gas was spurting right out of the face. I'll tell ya one thing; we didn't make a lot of footage." Barbaro patted Willie on the back and headed for the washroom. "I gotta get some rest. See ya tomorrow."

Willie grabbed his helmet, covered with Harley-Davidson stickers, and his frayed gloves and walked outside. He stopped at the board with the brass disks hanging from hooks, each inscribed with a man's name. Willie turned his disk red side face out. Eight hours later, when he finished his shift, he would flip the disk back to the white side, indicating that he was no longer in the tunnel. In a few minutes, it would be a new day, June 24, 1971, but the page of the International Union of Operating Engineers calendar hanging next to the board wouldn't be turned until morning, around the time Willie came off his shift.

He walked out to the portal and was the last to board the man-car. He sat on the stone-hard bench in the front row next to Jose Carrasco and Bob Warner.

"I think Willie Mays is done for the season," Willie heard Warner say to Carrasco. "Number 22 was his last homer."

"No way," Carrasco insisted. "The guy's still healthy. No way is it his last."

Tonight, only 18 men boarded the train. The shift was short five men—four injured in the explosion the previous night and Ray Gabriel, who had decided not to come to work. Just before the locy pushed them into the tunnel, Willie looked up and saw bright stars in the sky. As the train moved from the midnight darkness outside into the perpetual darkness of the tunnel, he stared ahead at the lights strung along the side of the damp concrete tunnel lining, disappearing long before the bend at the California Switch, 2,300 feet in. The snake of the overhead fan duct disappeared almost immediately into the hollow darkness. Willie thought about the miner's rule: a man lost for every mile dug. Despite the earthquake four months earlier, the gas leaks, and the small explosion the previous night, so far there had been no fatalities. With only five or six weeks to go, Willie prayed they could cheat the odds and finish the job without a fatality.

"Ain't no mountain high enough, Ain't no valley low...." Each night as they made the trip to the face of the tunnel, Ralph Brissette sang out in his deep bass voice. A big, strong man, Brissette always had a kind word or an understanding look, and he was well-liked by all of the miners. "Ain't no mountain high enough, ain't no tunnel long enough, to keep me from you," Brissette sang out. "Don't I sound like Marvin Gaye?" he asked in the darkness. No one answered. Each of the miners was deep in his own thoughts.

Willie bent to scoop up a bit of gravel. He worked as a mucker at the back end of the Mole. When dirt and gravel fell off the side of the conveyor belt, his job was to scoop it up and heave it shoulder high into the gondola. It was exhausting work because the conveyor ran fast, the muck was wet and heavy, and a lot of it fell to the ground. Willie was shorter than most of the men, and that meant he had to heft his shovel a few inches higher than the others. Multiply those few inches by hundreds of shovel-loads each night, each week, each month, every year, and that was how much harder the Badger had to work. Joint pain was creeping into his shoulders and he had a continual backache.

The noise from the machinery echoed in the tunnel, and made it impossible to talk. Willie glanced at Danny Blaylock, working on the other side of the conveyor, and saw him point to his eyes, then his nose, and shake his head. Willie understood and nodded. The petrochemical smell in the tunnel was terrible, his eyes were on fire, and his headache was unbearable. The heavy odor of hydrocarbons wafted through the tunnel and Willie couldn't tell whether it was drifting back from the digging face or seeping out of the muck coming off the conveyor. He pushed the filthy sleeve of his sweatshirt back from his wrist and looked at his watch: 12:45 a.m. Was it possible? It seemed like he had been working for hours. Maybe his watch had stopped. He thought about the Accutron and tried to imagine the humming sound, although he would never be able to hear it over the din of the excavation work in the tunnel. This was the shift from hell—it went on forever.

Willie felt a strange pressure in his ears a second before he saw the blinding flash. A burst of yellow, then orange and red light filled the tunnel. An explosion of expanding heat and light came barreling toward him from the digging face. Willie understood what had happened, but it wasn't a conscious thought; there was no time for that. It was a subconscious awareness that came from deep within his brain. The force of the explosion could only move in one direction—from the tunnel face back toward the miners. The blast lifted the Mole and the rail cars from the tracks like toys. When the concussion hit Willie, it forced the air out of his lungs and slammed him against the cement liner at the side of the tunnel. He felt an agonizing pain in his back, and thought it might be broken. The air around him was on fire. His nose and lungs filled with smoke. His eyes burned. Above the high-pitched ringing in his ears, Willie heard the screams from other miners nearby. He saw Danny Blaylock lying motionless on the ground. Willie opened his mouth and gasped for air. His chest heaved. Pain spread throughout his body. He struggled to breathe, but there was no oxygen. Willie felt searing heat on his face and skin. He saw shadows of twisted metal and overturned rail cars. He staggered a few steps toward the East Portal, five miles away. In the last seconds before he fell to the ground and suffocated, the Badger remembered he hadn't done his laundry.

TWO
June 22, 2014, 4:35 a.m.

THE SOUND THUNDERED IN THE dark room. Nick Carter woke up to the emergency ring tone of Cindi's cell phone on the nightstand. For a moment before he opened his eyes, he savored the sweet feeling of the endorphins drifting through his body after their night of making love. He freed himself from the tangled bed sheets and when he lifted her arm lying across his chest, his fingers touched the knot of scar tissue where a bullet had once grazed her biceps. The cell phone went silent, and then started up again.

"I've got it," Cindi mumbled. She reached over Nick and turned on the lamp.

The bulb was small, but to Nick's light-sensitive eyes, the light seemed radiant, and he raised his hand to ward off the glare. His pale blue eyes lacked pigmentation and he suffered from photophobia—light sensitivity.

Cindi pressed her phone to her ear. "This better be important," she said in a low voice.

Nick heard a man's voice, talking fast in urgent tones.

"You lost them?" Cindi sat up in bed. "What do you mean you lost them? You're supposed to be surveillance experts." Her voice rose. "Who had the eye? How long ago did it happen?... Jesus, call the duty agent and ask him to get some more bodies on this.... Yeah, of course I'm coming. Call me back with directions."

Nick watched her. Even in the early hours of the morning, with no makeup and tousled hair, he thought she looked beautiful.

Cindi dropped the phone on the bed. "Dammit," she said. "Do I have to babysit those guys every minute?"

"The Bureau's calling you at four-thirty in the morning?"

"That was someone from my surveillance team. They lost track of our suspects."

"Who are you following?"

"A couple of suspects. We've been working on intel from a CI."

"A CI?"

"Confidential informant. Not one of our regulars, just some kid from Northern California who's trying to trade info to get a drug charge reduced. He called us cold and fingered two guys he said might be planning a bombing."

Cindi lay back against the backboard of the bed and Nick could see that she was wide awake.

"We're trying to figure out what these guys are doing, and if they're working with anyone else. We've been watching them since they left Sacramento in a white van. After three days, they finally get to Los Angeles, I come home for one night, and they get away."

Nick listened to her and realized two unhappy facts: Their night together was already over, and their Sunday plans had just been canceled.

"You know," she said, "ever since Oklahoma City, whenever I see a white van on the street, I wonder if it has a fertilizer bomb in the back."

"Didn't you get a look inside?"

"They've been sleeping in the van so there's been no sneak and peek. We didn't want to tip them off."

"So, who are they?"

"Home growns, as American as apple pie. Get this—they're identical twins, Dwight and Duane. Can't tell them apart. They're farm boys from the Sacramento River Delta, and it turns out, they're water activists."

"Water activists?" Nick rolled over on his back. "What's a water activist?"

"They're part of a radical group, trying to protect their water rights. Know the history of the Owens Valley?"

"Vaguely."

"A hundred years ago Los Angeles bought up all the water rights out in the Owens Valley, then built an aqueduct and drained away the water. The farmers were pissed and tried to blow it up."

"Los Angeles?"

"No, Nicky, the aqueduct."

Nick grinned.

"Now California's in the middle of another water war—this time over the Sacramento River Delta—and guys like this are leading the way. Maybe 'activist' is the wrong word. If they're planning a bombing, they've moved on to eco-terrorism and—" Her phone rang again. She grabbed it, sat up on the edge of the bed, listened and then said, "Rick Daniels? From Explosives?...Sure, he's good, how long will it take him to get there?...Alright, let me know where to meet you." She put the phone down and sighed. "Sorry, I've got to get on this. It's my case. They're somewhere up in the San Gabriel foothills." She leaned into him and gave him a kiss.

Her skin was warm and fragrant and Nick wanted to pull her back under the sheets. "This sucks," he said. "Why does this stuff always happen in the middle of the night?"

"That's the deal." She kissed him again, longer this time. "We don't work regular shifts... like the slugs at the fire department." She tickled him in the ribs.

Nick squirmed, and said, "Right, we're the nine-to-five bunch." There was a grain of truth in what Cindi said. As erratic as his life was as a search and rescue fire captain, Cindi had a crazier schedule, spending 15-hour days dealing with guns and bombs at the Bureau of Alcohol, Tobacco, Firearms and Explosives, the ATF. He understood it was part of the deal, but at this moment, he wanted her lying next to him. He wanted their Sunday together to happen. He had a lot planned.

She threw the covers aside, got out of bed, and mumbled, "Of course, we couldn't use a tracker."

"What?" Nick said.

"We couldn't get court authorization to use a GPS device. Do you have any idea how many white Ford vans there are on the road in Southern California?"

Nick watched her naked backside as she disappeared into the bathroom and closed the door. She looked good. No, she looked terrific; much younger than her 43 years. Cindi had a lean and muscular body. Top physical conditioning for demanding jobs was something they shared. She called him her badger. "They're fascinating creatures," she once said. "We used to see them around the river when I was a kid growing up in Sacramento. They're smart, tenacious and strong beyond their size—just like you."

Nick lay back in Cindi's king-size bed and looked around the semi-dark bedroom. She didn't have much furniture and the big bed was her only luxury. The whole apartment was bare, it had no warmth. She had never really made it hers—it was just a place to crash. He preferred the time they spent together at his condo in Seal Beach. It was small and disorderly, but it was his home—he actually lived there.

The sound of water running into the bathroom sink stopped and Cindi opened the door. Before she could make it to her closet, the phone rang a third time. She came to the edge of the bed, sat down and answered it.

Nick heard another flood of words.

"Just a minute," she said. "I gotta write this down." She reached for a pencil and scrap of paper in the drawer of the nightstand. "Uh huh, sure. Up I-5… What's it called?… No, I've never heard of it…." She scribbled. "Off at Roxford. Left. Half mile to a Chevron station? Got it. I'll be there as fast as I can."

Nick couldn't resist. He ran his fingers across her bare back and reached around to cup her breast.

She leaned back against him for a second, sighed, and then pulled away. "I've got to go. We could have a shitstorm on our hands." Cindi's law enforcement voice had taken over. His lover had morphed into her alternate personality—a special agent with the ATF. "They disappeared near a place called Magazine Canyon."

"I know Magazine Canyon," Nick said. "We've had wildland fire drills up those foothills."

"Did you know there's several tons of movie explosives stored there in shipping containers? And it's right across the highway from the Jensen Water Treatment Plant." She grabbed her jeans from the floor, pulled them up over her slim hips and the tiny red star, the size of a half-dollar, tattooed near her pelvis.

Nick watched her. "No underpants?" he said.

She gave him a look and slipped into a bra and a long sleeve pullover with ATF emblazoned on the back. "This is serious, Nick."

"I've been in Magazine Canyon a couple of times; there's more than movie explosives. Did your guys tell you what's underneath?"

"Underneath what?"

"Underground. The canyon is a major water tunnel junction."

Cindi pulled on socks and laced up her light tactical boots. She looked at him. "Water tunnels?"

"Yeah. It's the end of the tunnel that brings the water south from the California Aqueduct. That's the spot where it connects to another tunnel that runs under I-5 and feeds into Jensen.…There's also the…uh…the Sylmar Tunnel. It ends there."

"The Sylmar Tunnel? Where your father—?"

"That's right," he said.

Cindi scooped up her badge, gun and holster, and keys from the dresser. "For Chrissake, could Jensen be the target?" she said. "Maybe they're after the water supply."

"Can two farm boys blow up the Jensen Water Treatment Plant? It's huge."

"Maybe part of it, if they know what they're doing," She leaned over him and kissed him on the lips. "Close your baby-blues and go back to sleep. I'll talk to you later."

He gave her a mock salute. "Have a nice day, Special Agent Burns. Get out there and save the world—again." Cindi functioned in a world dominated by men and Nick knew she felt compelled to outperform them every day in every way. She was a type-A, over-achieving woman who wouldn't take "no" for an answer. He loved her for it, but sometimes Nick thought he was in some sort of competition with her—without knowing all the rules

She turned off the light on the nightstand and whispered in the dark, "We'll have our day together, as soon as this is over."

"Have I heard that before?"

"I promise. Make yourself some breakfast. I'll call you as soon as I can." A triangle of illumination from the outside hallway lit up the floor before she closed the door.

Nick rolled over in the darkness and stared at the luminous numbers on the clock. Now it was 4:56 a.m., and a long, empty summer Sunday stretched out before him. What a disappointment. This was supposed to be the day. When he planned it weeks ago, they were both scheduled to be off duty. He had wanted everything to be perfect. First, he would take her rappelling on the face of the cliff at Zuma Beach in Malibu. Then they could go body-surfing and have a leisurely picnic with a bottle of wine on the sand. He had picked out a special bottle, which was now chilling in Cindi's half-empty refrigerator. After lunch, he had planned to drive her over to Pasadena to see the 1948 Harley Panhead he wanted to buy. She was no stranger to bikes and he knew she would love it. He planned to roll the bike out onto the street and ask her to sit on the seat with her hands on the bars. As soon as she did, he would pull out the ring and ask her to marry him. Just like that. The culmination of his carefully choreographed day would be his marriage proposal.

After looking at dozens of rings, Nick had selected a one-carat, round-cut diamond with two small stones on the side. The jeweler had shown him marquise cuts, pear shapes, and rounds, and Nick was left wondering which shape would be suitable for a woman in law enforcement who spent half her time working the streets. The cost, $3,700, was an incredible amount, but he decided to go for it. After all, how often did he ask a woman to marry him? He'd had a string of girlfriends and even a couple of live-ins, but Cindi was the first woman he ever felt serious about. They had known each other for a year and a half, and that was long enough. Nick was 43 as well, never married, and had decided it was now or never. He had rehearsed a dozen different versions of what he would say to her, but had finally settled on a simple, no-nonsense, "Cindy, I love you. Marry me." He figured she would laugh, maybe cry, and prayed she would say yes. Now the marriage proposal would just have to wait; it wasn't going to happen today.

He watched the digital numbers on the clock change to 5:02 a.m. By now, Cindi would be driving flat-out, heading north on I-5 in the early morning, her black SUV flashing the little red and blue lights the Feds mounted at the top of their windshields and behind the grilles of their vehicles. Guns and explosives—she was always rushing to the next shitstorm. Several times he had told her he thought she was too old to be chasing down criminals with bombs and guns. Her response to his entreaties was always, "I'm not a pencil-pusher." She had passed up promotions because she didn't want to be stuck behind a desk and detested what she called "law enforcement *administrivia*." They often traded good-natured accusations about which one of them was the biggest adrenaline junkie. She denied it, but she was as big a thrill-seeker as he was. He hoped she wouldn't think marriage was too tame. She was married once before, for a short time 20 years ago to a young FBI agent named Tom Burns. She had described that episode of her life as "a nightmare."

Nick thrashed around on the bed for a few minutes and knew he couldn't go back to sleep. He turned on the lamp again, got out of bed, and took the blue ring box from the pocket of his jacket. He opened it and held the diamond up to the light. As he turned it in his hand, the stone reflected intense blue-white flashes. He thought about how it would look on Cindy's finger. He would be so proud when she was his wife. Except—there was still the problem. He had always known that if they ever planned to marry, she would have to know everything about his father. She was a cop—a cop!—and he would have to tell her the truth about Willie Carter. The minute he told her how his father died in the Sylmar Tunnel explosion, he knew it was a mistake, and every day that went by, it became just that much harder to tell her the truth.

When they had first talked about their families, she had described her father, a police officer. "I guess law enforcement runs in the family," she said.

Nick, in turn, told her how his father, a miner, was killed in a methane explosion in the Sylmar Tunnel. "I was just a little kid growing up with one parent," he explained. "One morning at breakfast, I asked my mother for the first time why I didn't have a daddy. I'll never forget how she looked at me and seemed so sad. She put down her coffee, leaned toward me and said, 'Nicky, your father died a few weeks before you were born. He never even got to see you. He was a miner, working on a water tunnel in Los Angeles. There was an accident, a gas explosion, and he was killed with 16 other men.' I barely understood what she was telling me at the time," Nick had continued, "but she promised she would love me twice as much and always take good care of me. She was as good as her word, until she died of cancer when I was 21." Nick had left it at that. Cindi seemed content with his explanation and thankfully, that was the end of it.

Nick put the ring back in its box and climbed back into bed. He didn't want to get into the quicksand of thoughts about his father, and closed his eyes and tried to distract himself by reliving some of the moments they had shared during the night. He thought about how her body felt, pressed against him. He focused on the moment when she let out the small cries of pleasure and locked her strong arms around him. Just as he began to savor the rerun of their passion, his fire department pager went off. Nick's pulse quickened and he was back out of bed in a second. He was off duty, so whatever it was had to be important. He pulled the pager from the back pocket of his pants.

The glowing screen showed a message from JRIC—the Joint Regional Intelligence Center. A Homeland Security emergency meeting was set for 6:30 a.m. to evaluate information on a possible terrorist threat to the Southern California water supply.

THREE
November 1992

*W*E ARE GATHERED HERE TODAY *to pay our final respects to Ellie Carter....* Nick looked at the plain wood casket suspended above a rectangular hole dug in the dry earth of Mountain View Cemetery, a simple graveyard with a few large pine trees and a cluster of palms surrounding the entrance. Until she became ill, his mother had worked a full-time job at Sun-Maid Raisins. Now the company had rewarded her years of service with a small death benefit and a burial plot. Mountain View was a forlorn place on the edge of Fresno, a poor Central California farm community halfway between Los Angeles and San Francisco.

Nick's mouth was parched and his eyes were dry—he had already cried. At 41, Ellie, his strong, enduring mother who once seemed indestructible, was gone.

Father in heaven, we praise your name for all who have finished this life, loving and trusting you....

Only two days ago, Nick had sat at his mother's bedside in a room at Far Horizons hospice. She lay before him on her bed, propped up with oversized white pillows. Reduced to a fragile skeleton, her chest barely rose and fell with shallow breaths. The faint pain that began in her back and pelvis had become a monster that had taken over her body and had devoured her from within. The nausea and vomiting from the chemo had been almost as bad as the cancer itself.

Nick grasped her hand and felt her cool skin, as thin and transparent as paper. He struggled to hold back his tears and knew she would be gone before the day ended. She weighed nothing. When she passed, she would just float away.

"Mom... I..."

"God is by my side, Nicky. I'm not afraid." Her mouth turned upward in a weak smile. "I'll always be with you. I'm so proud of you. My son, a firefighter."

"Not yet, Mom, but I hope so...."

"In Los Angeles?"

"If I can find a job."

"At home, under my mattress is an envelope with some money. Almost four thousand dollars. It's for you. It's not much, but it'll help."

"Aw, Mom, you didn't have to save your money for me."

"Yes, I did."

Nick bent closer to her, and smelled her sour breath. "Mom..." He hesitated, then went on. "Please, before it's too late. Tell me something about Dad. Anything I can hold on to..."

"No, Nicky." Her voice was faint, her breath a rasp. "We're not going to talk about that now. I'm too tired. It's in the past; let it go."

He looked into her brown eyes, dull with morphine and thought about his own pale blue, almost colorless eyes. "Dad had blue eyes like mine, right?"

"Yes, he did," she said. "Why do you keep asking?" She reached up to touch him. Her fingers barely brushed his cheek before her hand dropped back onto the bed. Ellie sank back into the pillows and her muscles relaxed. Her face softened, the wrinkles dissolved.

Ellie Carter, may you be at peace. May the angels lead you into paradise. May you have rest everlasting.

Nick knew how hard his mother had struggled as a single mother to raise him. She had played the role of both parents, and it worked... until he grew older and began to see other boys doing things with their fathers. He knew nothing about his own father, and had so many questions. His mother had given him just a few facts: "Your father was 31 when he died. We had only been married for two years and he died without ever seeing you. You were born seven weeks after it happened."

Nick had longed to touch something that belonged to his missing parent. He searched their tiny apartment while his mother was at work, opening drawers and looking on the highest shelves in the closets, hoping to find some object that had belonged to his father. "Didn't Dad leave anything behind?" Nick wanted to know when he grew older. "What about a watch or a ring? Didn't he have a favorite hat or a jacket? How about tools or a fishing rod? Did he leave work boots?"

Sometimes she became tired of the barrage of questions and Ellie snapped at him. "I told you, he's gone. Saving things that belonged to him would just make it more difficult. Stop asking me all these questions."

"Why aren't there any pictures?" he persisted. Nick tried to imagine the man he had never known. Willie Carter's face was always vague and indistinct, but Nick always saw his pale blue eyes.

The Lord is my shepherd, I shall not want. He makes me lie down in green pastures. He leads me...

Visions from his childhood passed before his eyes. Nick remembered the many wonderful times he spent with his mother, and he remembered the times when he missed his father. As a child, he tried to imagine him working in the Sylmar Tunnel, and found himself drawn to hollow places in the ground—caves, excavations, storm drains—any confined space that would help arouse imaginary images of his father. In his underground adventure daydreams, Nick's father always accompanied him. When the farmland of Fresno baked, when the blinding sunlight washed over the landscape and grasshoppers filled the fields, Nick and his father went below ground into the cool earth. They crawled, slid, and scrambled down into maze like passages. They squeezed through tight spaces, lowered themselves into deep crevices and explored vast caves.

As Nick grew older, the fantasies faded. Underground spaces still enticed him, but his father no longer accompanied him on explorations below the earth. He also stopped asking his mother questions, but never ceased wondering about Willie Carter's life, and about his death. When he graduated from high school, Nick enrolled in the Fresno City College fire science degree program and planned for a career in search and rescue.

... and I will dwell in the house of the Lord forever.

Nick watched the box containing his mother's body disappear into the earth. He thought he had finished crying, but a sadness—a feeling of hopelessness—descended on him, and more tears came. Now he had no one.

A few ladies—his mother's coworkers—crowded around him, reached for his hand, and offered their sympathy.

"A wonderful woman..."

"Such a tragedy…"

"She will be missed.…"

Through his tears, Nick tried to smile and murmured, "Thank you, thank you for coming."

When the ladies departed, one woman, dressed in black and clutching a small purse, remained. Nick stood alone. She approached him, and said, "Nicky."

He looked up. No one but his mother called him Nicky.

"I'm sorry for your loss."

Her face was unfamiliar. "Do you work at Sun-Maid?"

"No, but I knew your mother. My name is Alice." She glanced at the grave. "We were friends. Twenty years ago, in Bakersfield."

"Bakersfield? I didn't know my mother ever lived in Bakersfield."

"She did, for a short time."

Who was this woman? "Twenty years ago? That was when I was born. What about my father? Did you know him too?" Nick asked her.

Alice looked at Ellie's son, Nick. He looked just like his father; he had the same blue eyes. Had Ellie ever changed her mind? Did she tell him? Did Nick know? She wondered, studying him now. "No," Alice lied. "He died before I met your mother."

"Bakersfield?" Nick repeated. "She never mentioned Bakersfield."

"My condolences," Alice said. "I'm sorry for your loss. Your mother was a sweet woman. She deserved better." She turned and walked away.

"What's your last name?" Nick called after her.

"… opay," she replied without looking back.

"Copay?" What a strange name, Nick thought.

After his mother passed, Nick found the money under his mother's mattress, where she said it would be. When he sorted through her small collection of personal papers, he discovered an envelope containing a page from the *Fresno Bee*, dated June 24, 1971, seven weeks before his birth. The paper was dry and brittle, and beginning to crumble. The newsprint was faded, but Nick was still able to read the five-paragraph account of the Sylmar Tunnel explosion.

TRAPPED MINERS SUFFOCATE NEAR L.A.

SYLMAR (UPI) — A natural gas explosion flared through a water tunnel today, suffocating trapped miners in one of the worst underground disasters in California history... Four bodies were retrieved, and 13 other miners were presumed dead in the tunnel. A fireman said five bodies could be accounted for by "arms and legs protruding from the rubble."

It was the third disaster to strike a section of the multibillion-dollar California Water Project, the most complex water work ever attempted, and the second explosion in the Sylmar tunnel in two days. The explosion set part of the tunnel afire and it was still burning almost 12 hours later, firemen said.

"Methane gas is one of the hazards of mining," said WAYNE PRYOR, a spokesman for Lockheed Shipbuilding and Construction Co. of Seattle, contractor for the project. Four miners were burned Wednesday in a minor gas explosion, "Apparently they hit another pocket (of gas) and one spark is all it takes," said PRYOR.

PAUL BADGLEY, 63, a miner for the past 45 years, was driving a large transporter called a "motor" in the tunnel about one mile from the blast when it occurred. BADGLEY, knocked up against a fire wall, tried four times to get to his 17 trapped fellow miners before he was driven back by smoke and heat... Asked if he had any hope for the other men, he replied: "No chance at all. If you had been in there you'd know there was no hope."

A command post was set up at the entrance of the aqueduct. The tunnel is being constructed for the Metropolitan Water District as part of a multi-billion dollar California Water Project.

List of Casualties:
FORREST ALDRIDGE, electrician.
WILLIAM I. ASHE, miner.
R. E. BALLOW, miner.
DANNY BLAYLOCK, miner.
JOSE CARRASCO, miner.
WILLIE CARTER, miner.
RONALD DEMO, miner.
JOHN DROBOT, miner.
MIKE GUTIERREZ, miner.
GARY A. NICHOLS, miner.
RUSSELL OVERSTREET, miner.
J. V. PETERS, miner.
LOUIS L. RICHARDSON, MWD Inspector.
WILLIAM J. SNODGRASS, miner.
ALVIN H. SPREEN, miner.
R. K. STOVERS, miner.
ROBERT W. WARNER, miner.

The Fresno Bee, June 24, 1971

Nick studied the names of the seventeen deceased men and spoke each name aloud. Willie Carter's name was sixth on the list, circled in faded red ink. On the margin, his mother had written in big block letters: WILLIE CARTER!

He wondered why this newspaper article was all that remained of the memory of his father. Why was it the only thing his mother had kept? What about the wives and families of the other dead men? Did his mother know any of them? Did they ever share their grief together? In his entire life, Nick couldn't remember her once mentioning any of the other unfortunate wives of the men who died in the disaster.

Nick put aside his questions about his father while he mourned his mother. He felt alone and frightened, but as he struggled to come to terms with her loss, he had a surprising insight. She had been by his side for 21 years and had nurtured and loved him. Her death was a blow, but he was grateful for the time they had shared and he had loving memories of her—memories that would last the rest of his life. He would learn to live with her loss, as every son or daughter did after the death of a parent. His father was another story. Every son needs to know his father. Nick had never had the chance to touch his father, or walk by his side, or talk to him. How was he supposed to come to terms with his father's absence when he knew nothing about him and had no memories?

Nick was determined to find out whatever he could about Willie Carter and the disaster in which he died. When he left Fresno and moved to Los Angeles, he had two objectives—to find a job with a fire department and to locate someone who could tell him about Willie Carter and the deadly explosion in the Sylmar Tunnel.

FOUR
June 22, 2014, 6:40 a.m.

A SPLASH OF GOLDEN SUNLIGHT colored the eastern sky and the heat of the previous night's passion with Cindi evaporated in the cool early morning Los Angeles air. Nick pressed hard on the accelerator of his pickup and sped down the freeway to JRIC, the Joint Regional Intelligence Center in Norwalk. He was glad he had been paged—the meeting would fill up part of what looked to be a lonely day off with nothing to do but wash his dirty laundry. He wondered about the two bomb suspects Cindi was following. She said they were as American as apple pie. Did they trigger the terrorist alert? Were they involved in something important enough to draw the scrutiny of Homeland Security, the 800-pound law enforcement gorilla?

Terrorism response had never been part of Nick's career plan. Twenty years ago, all he had wanted to do was work for a fire department—not as just a boot firefighter, but as a member of one of the elite urban search and rescue teams. Fool that he was, he thought at the time that becoming a USAR expert would honor his father. Honor his father? What a joke. He knew better now and years ago had erased that from his to-do list. He had accepted the fact that his career was the result of a falsehood, a lie, a deception that had misdirected his life, and moved on. Regardless, Nick loved his job and was addicted to the excitement and challenge. Over the years, he had become one of the go-to guys for confined space and tunnel incidents—the more dangerous, the better.

Nick arrived at JRIC at 6:45 a.m. When he drove around to the back of the building, he saw that the parking lot was filled with the plain, solid-colored Crown Victoria Fords favored by government and law enforcement agencies.

Most of the vehicles had FBI, Homeland Security or other insignia and the distinctive cluster of communications antennae sprouting from the roofs. The Joint Regional Intelligence Center was staffed 24/7, but the presence of this number of automobiles on an early Sunday morning underscored the fact that something unusual had occurred.

Nick was late, but it didn't matter; his presence wasn't critical. He was just a TLO—a temporary liaison officer—assigned by the County Fire Department to advise JRIC on possible search and rescue matters. Once before, he had attended a terror alert briefing relating to a potential threat at the Los Angeles International Airport. He sat for several hours without saying anything, listening to an endless discussion of data-points and what-ifs, and it never turned into anything real. Forty-eight hours later the alert was lifted.

He parked next to the only bright red fire department vehicle, an extra-long Suburban from County Fire's HazMat Task Force. The rear gate was open, and he saw Sam Cosgrove, a battalion chief, standing at the back. Nick took his security ID from a locked compartment under his seat, opened his door, and said, "Morning, Sam."

"Hey, Nick, how are ya?" Cosgrove said, as he pulled a laptop out of the back of his vehicle. "Looks like we've got a real one."

"Could be. My girlfriend was called out early this morning on a bomb threat." Nick thought for a second about how it would have sounded if he said his fiancée instead of girlfriend. "She works for the ATF."

Cosgrove closed the rear gate of the Suburban. "I was advised there could be a major HazMat issue."

Nick looked around the crowded parking lot. "This is a first. The fire department's the last on-scene."

The two men walked to the front of the eight-story building located in Norwalk, an industrial town on the southern edge of Los Angeles County. In a neighborhood of old warehouses and factories, it was the tallest structure around and stood out like the Washington Monument. JRIC shared the structure with several other law enforcement and intelligence agencies, each with its own special acronym: the Los Angeles Joint Drug Intelligence Group—LA DIG; the Los Angeles Regional Criminal Information Clearinghouse—LA CLEAR; the Inland Narcotics Clearing House—INCH; the Intelligence Support System—ISS; and the California State Threat Assessment System—STAS. Nick's JRIC certification had required that he learn all the abbreviations and understand the organizational structure of each entity, which were all parts of the Southern California intelligence community. It had taken him weeks to differentiate what each agency did, and he had forgotten the acronyms soon after he learned them. He had never visited any floor in the building other than the sixth, occupied by JRIC.

At the unmarked entrance, Cosgrove said, "You know, I can never remember what all these agencies do."

"Me neither," Nick said. "That's probably why we're firefighters and not cops."

The two men held their ID cards up to the reader embedded in the wall and the tinted bulletproof glass doors slid aside. They stepped into a tiny, empty lobby and each stared into a retina-scanner. A small green light on the wall flashed and the doors of the elevator opened. They stepped inside and waited.

Nick looked at the panel with eight numbered buttons, but no other markings, and chuckled.

"What?" Cosgrove said, as the doors closed.

"I was just thinking about the first time I used this elevator. I pushed the button for the sixth floor and nothing happened, so I pushed it again, and again, and finally I just jammed my thumb against it. The button didn't light up and the doors didn't close, but two security guards appeared. I don't even know where they came from, but they were wearing body armor and had drawn their pistols. One of them told me that the elevator already knew who I was and where I was going. If I would just wait a few seconds without touching anything, it would function automatically. It didn't need my help."

"You got farther than I did the first time," Cosgrove said. "I couldn't even get the retina scan to work."

"So what happens if the power goes out and we have to take the stairs?" Nick said. "Where are they?"

"And would we need special authorization?"

"What are the odds that the fire department has ever inspected the emergency exits in this building?"

Both men laughed as the elevator made a quick, silent ascent. It opened on the sixth floor entryway, a tiny enclosed space—the FBI called it a "man-trap"—lined with stainless steel to prevent anyone from firing a weapon into the JRIC operations area. When they stepped out, they saw their reflections on the highly polished metal. Cosgrove was 6 foot 2—almost 5 inches taller than Nick.

Their humor dissipated while they stood and waited again. When the elevator closed behind them, the entry doors slid aside and they entered an open work area where several men and women—intelligence analysts—sat next to each other at computer workstations. Nick felt the tension the minute they entered the space. Everyone looked weary and stressed and Nick assumed they had been on duty all night. Some of the analysts stared at their screens, while others conversed with each other or spoke into communications headsets. They were busy, intent on their work, and didn't look up to acknowledge the two newcomers. The air conditioning hadn't kicked in yet, and Nick smelled burnt coffee and nervous sweat in the warmth of the room.

When Nick was first shown through the JRIC facility, an FBI agent explained, "There's a flood of information streaming in here and we have to figure out what to do with it. It comes from Southern California police and fire departments and from federal intelligence and law enforcement agencies around the country. He waved his hand in the direction of the people at their computer consoles. "These analysts are trained to identify and evaluate random bits of data and piece together possible scenarios. With any luck, when the right situation presents itself, someone will connect enough dots to see the framework of a real terrorist threat."

The room reminded Nick of a cave and had the kind of illumination he was most comfortable with. The overhead lights were off, the ceiling was dark, and the only light came from the computer screens and several large, bright, flat-panel television and multimedia displays hung on the walls. In a glance, he saw Los Angeles area air traffic, a display of the highway system around Southern California—all roads showing green on an early Sunday morning— and muted news broadcasts with subtitles from CNN, ABC-TV, and the Arab channel Al Jazeera. In the corner of the room, a full-sized monitor cycled through pictures of wanted terrorists. The picture of a man with hard eyes, a cruel mouth, and an ugly scar across his cheek, along with his name, Mugtar Turki, flashed across the screen. The time in Los Angeles, Washington, D.C., Tel Aviv, Tehran, Kabul and Zulu—Greenwich Mean Time—lit up one wall in large red digital numerals.

To the left of the elevator, a woman with the physical build of a night-club bouncer sat at an elaborate communications console. Nick swiped his ID badge, she looked at the readout on her screen, then at Nick, and said, "Good morning, Captain Carter. The meeting's already started." She nodded toward the door on the far wall. "We've got coffee if you want it, but it's stale."

"I'm good, thanks," Nick said.

After Cosgrove checked in, they walked across the sound-absorbent carpet and opened the door to the conference room. Inside, it was another world. A blast of cold air greeted them. The room was blinding bright from the overhead glare of fluorescent lights and Nick immediately squinted as his sensitive eyes reacted to the radiance. The far wall had several large windows, but the smart glass had been activated and while it appeared dark from the outside, inside it was an opaque, white color that reflected more light. At least two dozen men and women were gathered around an enormous oval conference table. Most had been awakened from an early Sunday morning sleep and were sipping their first cups of coffee. Nick saw puffy faces, tousled hair, and sweatshirts with agency logos. Many carried pistols and each had a laptop and a thick white binder.

The FBI duty-agent, wearing blue trousers, a white shirt open at the collar and his tie at half-mast, stood at one end of the table. He nodded at Nick and Cosgrove as they entered the room and continued to address the group, "...for a briefing from Washington."

Nick took the closest seat, between a man he recognized as a captain from the Los Angeles County Sheriff's Department and an older, heavy-set woman he had never seen before. "Morning," Nick whispered.

"Howareya," the captain said.

The woman nodded and continued to scroll through the messages on her smartphone.

Nick reached for the white binder lying in front of him. As soon as he saw the cover, METROPOLITAN WATER DISTRICT–JENSEN FILTRATION PLANT, he knew Cindi was in fact involved in whatever had triggered the alert. The binder was a consequence management playbook, one of hundreds prepared by JRIC to cope with possible terrorist threats at specific Southern California locations. Each binder focused on planning a response at a particular location, and included a detailed action plan for every type of hypothetical incident—explosion, hostage-taking, biochemical dispersion, even gunfire and armed conflict. If an event actually occurred, the people sitting around the conference table wouldn't be involved in the actual tactical response, but they would be able to provide coordinated incident management information to their respective agencies.

The FBI agent continued, "Now I'll turn this briefing over to Arthur Barnes, the Homeland DIA—Director of Intelligence and Analysis—in Washington." One of the large screens on the conference room wall came alive, and Nick saw a man wearing a dark blue suit, white shirt and red tie, sitting at a large wood-paneled desk with a single file folder in the center. Nothing else was visible in the room except an American flag and the gray wall behind him, which had a large Homeland Security emblem. "Director Barnes, we're ready," the agent said.

The DIA appeared as if he were at the end of the JRIC conference table, even though he was thousands of miles away. The screen was almost life-size and the resolution so good that Nick could see the gray stubble on the man's face. The director rubbed his eyes and said, "Good morning. I'm sorry to call you together at this early Sunday hour on the West Coast, but, as we certainly know, terrorism doesn't go by the clock. To begin the briefing, let me give you some of the data points which have led to this alert. First, the Metropolitan Water District has been one of several entities on our watch-list for months after several California water utilities experienced attempts to hack into their computer systems. More recently, the NSA has tracked frequent searches on websites related to the Southern California water and power infrastructure. The precise origin of this activity has yet to be identified, but it's possible that foreign nationals are preparing to..."

Nick listened while he opened the white binder, and looked at the first document, a year-old Congressional report labeled, "Terrorism and Security Issues Facing the Water Infrastructure Sector." He turned to the next section of the binder, which included a summary of the Jensen plant facilities, and a map of Magazine Canyon and the water tunnels underneath it.

While Nick stared at the line indicating the Sylmar Tunnel, the DIA continued to address the people seated at the table: "Finally, early this morning the ATF notified us that they are searching for two male individuals in an area north of Los Angeles around Magazine Canyon, which is adjacent to the Jensen Water Filtration Plant. The ATF believes these individuals may be transporting ANFO or other explosives in a white van for use in an act of terrorism."

The word ANFO struck a familiar chord with Nick. He had attended a JRIC class that detailed various forms and methods of terrorism. A fertilizer bomb made of ANFO—ammonium nitrate and fuel oil—had been described in detail. An ANFO bomb was low-tech, easy to assemble, and packed a huge explosive force. The FBI described it as "the poor man's bomb."

The DIA stared directly into the camera and said, "Based on these and several other data points collected by our analysts, we have concluded the water infrastructure in Southern California may be at risk and are therefore issuing the following Imminent Threat Alert to all federal and Southern California law enforcement agencies." He paused, opened the file on the center of his desk, took out a single sheet of paper, and read from it: "The Department of Homeland Security has information of a credible threat to the Jensen Filtration Plant in the County of Los Angeles. Unknown extremists may be planning a physical attack on the facility. Explosives may be involved. This threat alert is issued for a 48-hour period. During this period the affected law enforcement agencies and other first responders will be under the direction and coordination of the FBI and Homeland Security." The DIA paused for a moment and said, "Concurrently, the ATF will retain primary responsibility for the pursuit of their suspects. I am advised that the ATF liaison agent is not present at your meeting, but they are informing the FBI of all developments."

Nick looked around at the body language of the people sitting at the oval table. Some were hunched forward, arms on the table, staring at the screen on the wall and listening intently. Others seemed more relaxed, leaning back in their chairs, gazing at the walls or up at the ceiling. The captain next to him shook his head, folded his arms over his ample stomach, and expelled a breath of air.

The DIA continued, "There is one particular data point of possible importance. Two days ago, the LAPD reported the theft of an empty Waste Management trash truck from a recycling collection center in Los Angeles."

The captain sitting next to Nick spoke up. "I thought you said the ATF is looking for two individuals driving a white van."

"That's right," the DIA said.

"You lost me," the captain said. "So how does the trash truck figure in?"

A woman from the LAPD, sitting at the table, spoke up. "We don't know for certain if the trash truck is involved, but we can't ignore it. It's not a run-of-the-mill vehicle theft. Who steals a trash truck? The last reported theft of that type was nine years ago in Riverside. We think it's significant and it could be used for transporting an enormous fertilizer bomb."

"The Jensen water plant is huge; it covers 125 acres," the FBI agent in the conference room said. "If you wanted to do real damage, you'd want more than a bomb in a van. Our explosives experts at Quantico tell us that a bomb in a vehicle the size of a trash truck would be much more effective." The agent played with his computer again and the second communications screen lit up to show a large man with a shaved head sitting in a small office filled with books and reference manuals. "This is Sam Akers at the Terrorist Explosive Device Analytical Center. Sam, do you have Washington on your other screen?"

"Yes, I do," Akers said.

Nick looked at Akers. The camera in Quantico was mounted above eye level, and it focused down on the upper part of Akers' skull, giving it a distorted, egg-shaped appearance.

The explosives man fiddled with his notes, looked up, and said, "Good morning, all. Here's a summary of our analysis. The stolen trash truck is a 2004 Mack rear loader. For a point of reference, it has about five times the cubic capacity of the van Tim McVeigh used in Oak City, and you know what that did to an eight-story federal building. To be conservative, let's say the trash truck is just loaded with 3,400 pounds of explosive-grade ANFO—only twice the amount McVeigh used. The force generated would be more than three times the Oak City blast. That would be one hell of a blow-up."

"Our JRIC analysts," the FBI agent in the conference room interjected, "have developed a possible scenario in which the trash truck is used in a major incident at the Jensen plant. Imagine a situation in which the trash truck is used to break through the perimeter fence." He played with the keyboard of his laptop and a Google traffic map appeared on a separate wall screen. "The facility occupies a site off the I-5 Freeway in Granada Hills," he said, and pointed at the map with a red laser. "It's one of the largest water treatment plants in the country."

Nick looked up at the map and followed the blue line of I-5 heading north. As his eyes traced the aerial view across Foothill Boulevard, he imagined the Sylmar Tunnel, and began to think about the men killed in the methane explosion. He shifted in his chair and brought his attention back to the FBI man's comments.

"We're dealing with a facility filled with huge tanks of hazardous chemicals," The agent said. He circled a building on the map with his laser. "This is a chlorine storage building. It has steel doors that roll up to allow entry of four rail tank cars. Fully loaded, each of these cars contains 14,000 gallons of liquid chlorine under high pressure. If one or more of those cars were ruptured, the gas would expand to 460 times the liquid volume. This is the Achilles heel of the Jensen facility."

The FBI agent paused and the room was silent while each person at the conference table imagined an exploding chlorine tank car. In Nick's mind, the blast became the explosion in the Sylmar Tunnel.

The agent turned off his laser-pointer, looked around the table and said, "Now, at the moment, this is just supposition—a possible scenario—but our job here is to consider all the possibilities, and this one makes a lot of sense. A chlorine tank car explosion could have devastating consequences. Sam, do you want to take it a step further?"

The explosives expert on the screen continued. "We're talking about a real widow-maker. If the trash truck were rammed into one of the steel roll-up doors and the ANFO detonated, the explosion would annihilate the truck, take out the warehouse and detonate the contents of the tank cars inside. Since the chlorine is under pressure, you would have immediate secondary blasts that would intensify the magnitude of the initial blast from the trash truck. Anything close to the metrics I've hypothesized would be disastrous and you'd be picking up parts of that storage building in San Diego." He paused and waited for the information to sink in.

"Thanks Sam," the FBI agent said. "Anything else?"

The explosives expert shook his head.

"Director Barnes?" The agent looked up to see that the Homeland Security screen showed an empty desk. The DIA had already departed. The agent tapped his computer keyboard and both the Homeland and the Quantico conference screens went dark.

"I don't buy it," the Sheriff's captain spoke up. "There's better ways to hit the water supply. A small bottle of something toxic would be a lot easier and more efficient. Why dick around with a 25-ton trash truck?"

"They may not be after the water supply per se," the FBI agent said.

"Well, what are they after?" the captain said.

The FBI agent gave him a "stop interrupting and start listening" scowl, and went on. "Let's take the analysis a step further and look at the consequences of a blast that rips open the chlorine tank cars." He sat down at the head of the conference table. "To the east, there are 1.7 million people spread throughout the San Fernando Valley. I repeat—1.7 million people. What we're talking about here is the potential of a toxic chlorine cloud threatening a large part of that population. It would be a disaster, a first-class act of terrorism." He looked around the table and said, "Gail, you want to jump in here?"

Gail Murphy, a small, middle-aged woman, took a sip from her paper coffee cup and then spoke without standing up. "For those of you who don't know me, I'm a chemist and air-quality expert for the EPA. I've worked up a quick analysis of the threat of chlorine vapor. If there is an incident that breaches the Jensen tanks, we're looking at a complete public evacuation of a large portion of the Valley. We would have to create a huge exclusion zone for the area where vapor concentration could cause irreversible health effects." She took another sip of coffee.

Chief Cosgrove from the HazMat Task Force spoke up. "That would be a nightmare from a HazMat point of view. An evac of that magnitude would have to be done well in advance of the event and it would be a massive effort. Are we talking about doing that this morning?"

"Not yet," the FBI agent said. "Right now, we're just assessing possibilities and considering the responses."

"How do you predict the movement of a cloud of chlorine vapor?" someone asked.

"Good question," Cosgrove said. "We'd have to set up our weather monitoring equipment some place where a change of wind wouldn't bring the gas in on us and then—"

"I don't buy any of this," the Sheriff's captain said. "An ANFO bomb in a trash truck? Gimme a break. Talk to me about cyber-terrorism and I'll work up a sweat."

The woman from the EPA ignored the captain's comments and said, "If the wind is blowing to the east, the vapor could affect a half-million people in the northwestern part of the Valley. Now, if you turn to Section 3 in your binder, we—"

Nick's phone vibrated. He pulled it out of his shirt pocket and saw a text message from Cindi: CALL ME ASAP. NEED YOU–C. "Excuse me," he said to the people assembled around the table, and stepped out of the conference room, still holding the consequence management binder.

FIVE
May 1993

GERALD RAINWATER—"BIG RAIN" TO THE firemen who had served under his command—was at the end of his career, ready to retire. He planned to move up to Oregon, do some fishing and ride his Harley while he still could. Many of the brothers his age were already gone—bad lungs from all the crap in the smoke, heart conditions, and on-the-job injuries. A fireman's life wasn't the easiest, and he considered himself luckier than most. After 38 years with Los Angeles City Fire Department, all he had was a bad back and worn-out knees. He hadn't put on too much weight and still had a patch of gray hair and a firefighter's mustache to match. The department thought he projected the right image and had promoted him to Battalion Chief in charge of recruiting. It was his last tour. The glory days of battling the fire dragon were behind him, but he still enjoyed putting on his uniform and coming to work. It wasn't a bad way to finish a long and dangerous career.

When a candidate named Nick Carter showed up for an interview on a spring morning in 1993, Rainwater guessed he was in his early twenties. The first thing Rainwater noticed was the color of his eyes. They were pale blue, the color of ice. The kid was intense, like a coiled spring. He sat down and answered a couple of questions, then let loose right away and announced that he wanted to be in search and rescue.

"There's a lot more to firefighting than search and rescue," Rainwater told him. "You interested in the other ninety-five percent?"

"Yessir, sure, I want to learn everything," Nick said. "I want to be a fireman and all, but I really want to get into search and rescue." He glanced at the name patch, and added, "Chief Rainwater."

They sat at a table in one of the small interview rooms on the third floor of the City Fire Department's training center, a huge old white building off the 101 Freeway in downtown Los Angeles. "Well, your timing's pretty good," Rainwater told him. "A lot of the bigger departments are starting to add more search and rescue resources. We're doing it too. There'll be more openings, but I gotta tell you, you don't just walk in. I don't know how much you know about how a fire department works, but it's based on seniority. There's a waiting list for every damn thing. Half the men in the department want one of maybe 50 or 60 spots in search and rescue. From the time you're a boot fireman until you get a permanent place on a USAR team, it could be several years, and that's if you're any good."

"I'm good," Nick said. "I know I can make it."

Rainwater thought the kid sounded very confident, maybe overconfident. "Got any idea what it takes?" he asked. "It's a long slog. At LAFD, you have to log a couple hundred hours of training on your own time before you even make it into the unit. Confined space, tunnel entry, trench collapse, canyon extraction—there's a lot of stuff to learn. We're even starting to train for swift-water rescue. Once you're in, it's just the beginning. There's hours of USAR training along with your regular shifts as a fireman." Rainwater looked at Nick, who was on the edge of his seat. He looked like he wanted to sign up then and there. "Can you handle that? It doesn't leave a lot of time for other things."

"I can handle anything," Nick said. "And I want to be in USAR."

Rainwater looked him in the eye. "You married? Got a son? A daughter? There's plenty of broken families in the fire service." That was something no one talked about, but Rainwater knew from firsthand experience. "Half the time you're away from home. If you work a wildland fire you could be away for a week or ten days—even longer on a big burn. Marriages break up over absences like that. Your kid could grow up without a father."

Nick gave Rainwater a strange look and said, "Naw, I'm all alone, I don't have a family."

"How tall are you?"

"Five-ten." Nick paused for a second. "Actually... uh... five-nine and a half."

"Well, you're on the small side for a fireman, but that's not all bad. We've got plenty of extra-extra-large guys with broad shoulders, and half of them can't get into a confined space. Why search and rescue?"

"It's something I've always wanted to do. My father died in a tunnel explosion."

"Was he a fireman?"

"No, a miner. He died in the Sylmar Tunnel disaster. Have you ever—"

"Sylmar? Your dad was killed in the Sylmar explosion?" Rainwater hadn't heard anyone mention the Sylmar disaster in years. "You've got to be kidding."

"You know about it?"

"Know about it? Hell, I responded to that incident." The kid's ice-blue eyes opened wide and he looked at Rainwater like he was God.

"You were there?"

"I'll never forget it." All of a sudden, Rainwater's memories came flooding back like it had happened yesterday: The ugly smoke pouring out of the portal; the crowd waiting for news; the miners from the other shifts; the burnt odor inside the tunnel. Worst of all, he remembered the corpses, which looked like charred logs... and the body parts, which were unspeakable. Rainwater felt a jolt of pain in his lower back and had to stand up.

"What was it like? Nick wanted to know. "Did you go into the tunnel? Did you see—"

"Nineteen-seventy-one," Rainwater said. He arched his back and stretched. "My God, that's twenty-two years ago." He paused for a moment, and wondered how the time could have passed so quickly. "We had the big earthquake in February and logged something like thirty thousand emergency calls the first day. Los Angeles was a wreck for months, damage everywhere. Then, just as things started to quiet down and the aftershocks stopped, that tunnel blew up. In the spring. April? May?"

"No, sir, it was June. June the twenty-fourth. It happened at 1:05 in the morning."

The kid had it down to the minute. "Yeah, that's right, it was June. Do you know much about the rescue effort?"

"No, sir. It all happened before I was born and my mom wouldn't talk about it. I read a few newspaper articles, but it's been hard to find any details."

"Well, at the time, I was working on a rescue ambulance at Station 91 in Sylmar." Rainwater sat down again, shifted around, and tried to get comfortable in his chair. "Back then, there was no such thing as a paramedic. We didn't know a hell of a lot, we just got a couple weeks of training in a hospital ER. Not that it would have made any difference. The night before, we responded to the tunnel for a small gas explosion and flash fire. They pulled four men out; none with serious injuries. We took one guy to the hospital and that was it. At that point, it was just another call, nothing special, and we were back at the station in a couple of hours." Rainwater was unable to find a comfortable position, and his back was going into a full spasm. The pain radiated all the way up to his neck. He grimaced, stood up again and stretched. The kid gave him a look, and Rainwater said, "Sorry, I have a bad back. It's hard to sit still, especially in these damn wooden chairs."

"So you got called back the next night?"

"Yeah. I was on a forty-eight-hour shift and when the big blast happened, we went back to a scene I'll never forget. We arrived in the middle of the night and the first person we saw was the foreman. He was waiting for us out at the tunnel entrance, frantic, with a wild look in his eyes. He told us there was a methane explosion, a big one, and they had lost contact with the men working inside. Smoke was pouring out of the portal, I mean, even in the dark you could see how thick it was. We had no idea how we were gonna get in there, and then the foreman tells us the blast occurred five miles in, where they were digging. I remember thinking at the time, 'Five miles? You've got to be fucking kidding.'"

"They were that far in? I never thought about that."

"Back then, we didn't have special USAR or HazMat response units, so we just called for every piece of emergency equipment and rescue-ambulance we could get. In the meantime, we're wondering what happened to the poor bastards trapped inside."

"One of those poor bastards was my father."

"Those men never had a chance. Some of them, the ones working the farthest from the digging face, managed to run a few hundred feet before they were asphyxiated. The gas in the tunnel burned for almost twenty four hours. It was a terrible situation." Rainwater saw that the kid's ice-blue eyes had clouded up. He paused for a minute and thought maybe this wasn't the time to be talking about the Sylmar disaster. Nick Carter had just come in for a preliminary interview, not to hear the gruesome details about how his father died. "You sure you wanna hear all this?"

"Yes. Absolutely," Nick said. "I've been waiting all my life to talk to someone about it. I want to know everything that happened."

Rainwater arched his back and then sat down again. "It's not a pretty story. The rescue attempt was a nightmare. In the first few hours, we couldn't do anything because of the smoke. The miners waiting at the portal went crazy. They were screaming that the fire department didn't know what it was doing. They had these old breathing devices. Hell, they weren't worth a damn, but the miners wanted to use them to go in and try to save their friends. The incident was what we called a 'high hazard rescue' and we wouldn't allow them in. There were actually a couple of fistfights between miners and firefighters and the LAPD had to step in and break it up." Rainwater shook his head. "You know what we had to do? We got two giant wind machines from Universal Studios to suck out the smoke. Can you imagine that? The fire department had to ask a movie studio for help. Then we waited 18 hours until the flames died down. We tried drilling some vent shafts, but that didn't work. When we finally did get into the tunnel, it was filled with carbon monoxide. We knew there wasn't much hope, but no one wanted to admit it. The conditions were just too bad—we all knew there wouldn't to be any rescue, just body recovery." Rainwater looked at Nick. "When you become a firefighter, you'll find out how fast word spreads about big disasters—somehow, everyone knows what's happened, and people just start showing up. A couple of hours after we arrived in Sylmar, the wives came with their kids. Then it was the relatives and friends. By morning we were overrun with disaster junkies and people from the press and the television crews. I'll never forget all those families waiting there at the portal as the sun came up, trying to be brave, praying for good news, but knowing from the get-go how bad it was. I remember the *L.A. Times* ran a picture of one of the wives, in tears, and the headline was, 'We're Not Going Home.' Was your mother at that vigil? Did she have to suffer through that?"

"I don't know; if she did, she never told me. My mom wouldn't talk about any of it. Every time I asked her something, she just told me my father died in the explosion."

"Some people deal with loss that way. They bottle it up, keep it inside. Not good."

"That was my mother, for sure."

"You've got a fire science degree, right?"

"From Fresno City College."

"Well, I'll tell you something they don't teach you in class. There's nothing like your first multiple fatality catastrophe. You never forget that experience. Maybe it's the shock of knowing that a bunch of people have died, and you're not reading about it or watching it on TV. You're right there. You're trying to save them, but you can't do anything about it and you feel helpless. Search and rescue isn't all glory. You don't save a life every time you get toned out. You don't always pull someone out of a collapsed trench and then go home and have a beer and celebrate. It just doesn't work that way. By the time you've put in a few years, you've collected all the mental snapshots—pictures of the stuff you never wanted to see. Guys who say it doesn't bother them are liars. The images lurk in your mind and pop up in the middle of the night or at some other time when you're not ready for them. They weigh you down. I have plenty of those memories, and some of the worst are from Sylmar." Rainwater watched the kid's reaction. He seemed unfazed by all the unpleasant details.

"Inside. What was that like when you went into the tunnel?"

"It was a full day before we organized the first entry. Chief Najarian was the incident commander. He was a fireman's fireman. If you meet one or two guys like him in your career, you're very lucky. I remember him barking orders to a dozen different people. Finally, he told us, 'It's time to try to go in, get moving. Get a locomotive, take extra air tanks and litter baskets, and all the first-aid equipment. You'll need Wheat lamps, it's gonna be dark.' I was on the first entry party, with another fireman named Cox, two miners, and an engineer from Lockheed. We loaded a couple of those small rail cars—for some reason, they called them 'man trips'—and the engine pushed us in from the East Portal. If you can believe it, we took a big drum of ice water with us."

"Ice water?"

"Yeah, at the time, that's what we had for burns. Can you imagine that? Ice water. What a joke. Like we were gonna find men alive inside and save them with cold water. Anyway, we started in, barely moving, and right away there was thick smoke and incredible heat. Ever been in a water tunnel? That Sylmar sucker was huge, maybe twenty feet across, and it was pitch black. We had those big lights, but we couldn't see two feet ahead. Parts of the tunnel were flooded. Ground water was seeping up through the floor and the sump pumps weren't working. We stood in the front car, trying to see something, anything. The guy from Lockheed kept saying, 'Go slow, go slow,' and the miner kept saying, 'Faster, go faster.'" Rainwater paused for a minute before he continued. He was back in the Sylmar Tunnel; he was still young and strong, his back didn't ache. "The heat was staggering, and I remember thinking this must be what it's like when you get to the gates of Hell. Later, they told us the temperature inside was two hundred degrees. That hell-hole was filled with carbon monoxide and unburned methane and all we had was fifty-minute breathing devices. We figured at least fifteen minutes to get in and another fifteen to come out, so that didn't give us much time for search and rescue. I don't know what we thought we could accomplish, but in we went. After about a mile, our car hit something and derailed. It turned out to be a miner's body lying across the tracks. Can you imagine that? We ran over a body. Then I tried walking in a little farther, but the groundwater was up to my knees in places, and scalding hot. I stepped into a hole and twisted my ankle, and we decided it was time to retreat. We all got on the second car with the equipment and rolled out of the tunnel just as they were about to send more men in to rescue us. Hell, we were the rescue team, and we came out with our tails between our legs. That first trip in gave me a taste of what it must have been like for those poor men, working underground every day, digging that damn Sylmar Tunnel."

Nick was quiet for a moment, then said, "It's nothing like what I imagined. I never really had any idea of the conditions, how bad it must have been. I'm trying to picture my father in all of that. I had such a simple idea of what went on. I never really understood what happened after the explosion."

"I can still remember how my eyes burned and how dry my throat was as we went in on that rail car. Every once in a while, I get a whiff of something that reminds me of the odor of that burned-out tunnel." Rainwater again thought about how much he should say to the kid, and decided, what the hell, his father died in the explosion and he wants to hear about it, so he continued. "If you're gonna be a fireman, sooner or later you're gonna see the kind of stuff we encountered when we finally got inside. The men farthest from the digging face suffocated trying to get out. Their bodies were completely charred, but at least you could see that they were human. When we reached the face of the tunnel, where they were digging, we found the diesel locomotive and several muck cars blown apart. An explosion in a small confined space like that magnifies the force, because the blast can only expand in one direction." Rainwater made a horizontal gesture with his hand. "A ball of flame and the expanding gas ripped up everything as it traveled out toward the portal. That huge machine they used to do the digging, the Mole they called it, was just a pile of twisted metal. The miners working there, or what was left of them, were mixed in with the rubble. I remember pulling an arm out of the debris. Just an arm—it wasn't attached to anything. We collected the bits and pieces of burned bodies and brought them out in buckets. In buckets! And then at the portal, we had to face the families."

Nick fidgeted around. "There's so many things I never thought about," he said. "Like, where was my dad when the blast happened? How long did he survive? Did he suffer before he died? Was he one of the men who tried to escape and suffocated, or was he torn apart by the explosion?" He paused for a second. "What if he was one of the men you brought out in a bucket? My dad's name was Willie. Willie Carter. Does that sound familiar? Do you remember if his body was found?"

"That was the coroner's job," Rainwater told him. "We never heard any names."

Nick stood up and went over to look out the window. He stood with his back to Rainwater.

Rainwater gave him a minute of silence, knowing he was hearing some pretty hard stuff about his father for the first time.

"And no survivors?" Nick said, still looking outside.

"Actually," Rainwater said, "it's hard to believe, but one miner made it. A search party almost walked over him. They heard a voice, and here was this guy lying in the debris, alive. It was a miracle. His face was near some water and the air vent had collapsed almost on top of him. Can you believe it? Water and air. Talk about fate, or luck, or whatever. This one guy was in the right place at the right time and lived through it. He survived." Nick turned away from the window and Rainwater thought he was lit up like someone standing on a downed power line.

"A survivor? One of the miners? He must have known my father. Who was he? Do you know his name? Is he still alive?"

"I don't remember. I just remember one man survived. It was over twenty years ago."

"A survivor. A survivor. If he's still around, I've got to find him."

"Yeah, well if you do, I'm sure he could tell you the things you want to know, maybe give you some… uh… closure."

"Is there anyone else you can think of that I could talk to?"

"You should have started looking a decade ago, son. Nineteen of us received the Medal of Valor for our efforts at the tunnel. Of those men, I'm the only one left"

Nick shrugged his shoulders. "A decade ago I was eleven."

"Battalion Chief Nadjarian would have been the man to talk to, but he died several years ago." Rainwater tried to remember the men who were in Sylmar with him. There had been so many brothers and so many incidents during his career, it was hard to keep everyone and everything straight. "There was Cox, the firefighter I went into the tunnel with. He's the only one I can think of, but he died years ago in south L.A. when a warehouse roof caved in."

"Do you remember if—"

"But there was one guy, the state safety engineer on the project. He got a lot of publicity and was all over the newspapers for a couple of years. I recall reading that he was so distraught about the accident that he left his job and moved up north, to Santa Rosa. My sister lives in Santa Rosa."

"What was his name?"

"It started with a Z. Zavaretto, Zavaterro, something like that. Check the old newspapers, you'll see it."

Nick pulled a pen and a scrap of paper out of his shirt pocket and wrote down the name. "I'm gonna try to find him."

Rainwater glanced at his watch. It was getting late. "Thanks for coming in," he said, and handed Nick a Preliminary Background Application form. "If you want to apply for a job with LAFD, fill this out, include a copy of your fire science degree and send everything back. If we want you, we'll call you in for a physical."

"Thank you for telling me about this." Nick reached out to shake Rainwater's hand. "It's not what I expected today."

"Good luck."

Nick started out of the room, then turned and asked, "How about pictures? Does the fire department keep photos?"

The kid wouldn't quit, and Rainwater answered without thinking. "Sure, we've got pictures." As soon as he said it, he knew he should have kept his mouth shut. Now it was too late. Rainwater had seen the photos, only once, and didn't want to look at them again. They were grisly.

"You do? Where are they? Are they here in the building?"

Rainwater nodded. "They're in our archives."

"Can I have a look at them?"

Rainwater looked at his watch again. "I can take you down there for a minute, but I'm warning you, they're hard to look at. You sure? Maybe it's better if you didn't—"

"No! I don't care how bad they are. I have to see them."

The kid wasn't going to be put off.

They took the stairs down to the second floor and walked along the long hall to the other end of the building. On the other side of the frosted glass door marked, PHOTO ARCHIVES, they entered a vast, two-story space, heavy with the smell of dust and stale air. The windows high on the wall were filthy, and Rainwater wondered why they were never washed. Outside it could be a beautiful Southern California day, but inside, in Archives, it was a perpetual cavern of gloom, a very depressing place. Rainwater had always felt he'd prefer to make first entry into a burning building rather than visit Archives. It was floor to ceiling with metal shelves loaded with pictures of disasters. There were no happy pictures of firemen at picnics, or pancake fundraisers with kids wearing plastic fire helmets; just images of fires, accidents, catastrophes, and the unfortunate people caught in them.

The old librarian—she called herself the curator—sat just inside the entrance. She was ancient, and Rainwater thought she should have been retired years ago. Maybe she was the only person willing to work in a photo morgue. It had been several years since he was last here, but when he walked in, he saw that nothing had changed. The curator was still the same—a shrunken old woman with gray hair pulled back into a tight bun, sitting at her long table covered with piles of photographs. He wondered if she lived in the Archives. Maybe she was born there and had never been outside in the light of day.

The curator looked up through thick glasses that magnified her dark, watery eyes. Without any introduction, she demanded, "What year?"

"Nineteen seventy-one," Rainwater said.

"Seventy-one," she echoed and stood up. "Follow me." They followed her at a snail's pace across the room, passing row after row of shelves. She stopped at the rack marked 1971, and in a toneless voice said, "Month?"

"June," Rainwater told her. "The 24th. We're looking for the Sylmar Tunnel incident."

Nick looked around. "How far back do these files go?" he asked.

"Long before you were born," the old woman said. She managed to kneel down on the cement floor and Rainwater figured he would have to hoist her back up. She ran her hand over the brown envelopes on the bottom shelf, pulled out a thin file and looked at it. "June 24," she said. "Sylmar Tunnel Explosion." She blew the dust away and handed the file to Rainwater, then grabbed one of the shelves and managed to pull herself up without assistance.

Rainwater handed the envelope to Nick.

The curator gave Rainwater a dirty look and said, "You know the archives are for authorized personnel only."

"He's related to someone who died in the explosion," Rainwater told her. "He just wants to take a quick look."

"Over here." she said, and led them to a small table under a single bulb, between the shelves for 1968 and 1969. "We don't make copies, so don't ask," she said to Nick. "And don't steal any of the pictures."

"Yes, ma'am," Nick said. He glanced at Rainwater and winked.

Rainwater decided he liked this kid and hoped he applied to LAFD for a job.

Nick couldn't wait. He opened the envelope before he sat down and pulled out several 4-by-6-inch black-and-white pictures. After all the years, they were dry and cracked, and had a faint yellow-brown color.

Rainwater knew what Nick was about to see. The first few photos were of 22-year-old fire engines, pickup trucks, and police cars parked around the East Portal. He remembered one picture that looked like an ad for one of the old police television shows. It showed three motorcycle cops from 1971, standing at the tunnel entrance, wearing high black boots, white bubble helmets and aviator-style sunglasses. Their holsters and black nightsticks hung from their belts and they had their hands on their hips, like they were posing for the camera.

The rest of the photos were grim, and Rainwater didn't care to see them again. Most of the shots were taken inside the tunnel, during the rescue effort, and showed firefighters and miners with desperate, shocked appearances, their fatigued faces black with smoke and soot. He remembered one picture of an older miner with a stooped posture. His body looked worn out, used up, and he stared ahead into the black tunnel, as though he expected to see his dead friends walking out toward him.

Nick sat down and spread the pictures out on the table. Rainwater couldn't resist, and looked over Nick's shoulder. He saw the photo of several firefighters and miners, standing around a body partially wrapped in a blanket. A firefighter Rainwater didn't recognize held one end of the cover aside, while everyone else looked at the burnt remains. It occurred to Rainwater that it might be a picture of Nick's father, Willie. If it was, Rainwater thought, the kid sure as hell wouldn't recognize him. It was just a charred body. It could have been anyone; it could have been a burnt log.

There were a couple of other photos that Rainwater had never forgotten. One was of a lone miner, standing deep in the tunnel, looking at a body, burnt beyond recognition, strapped to a stretcher. The other showed the men from his station, the 91s, wrapping another charred corpse in a canvas. The body was scorched, and the skin was tight, like burnt leather. The miner's arm and blackened fist were frozen above his head, as if he had died trying to protect himself from the oncoming flames. Rainwater thought this was the worst picture—it was the one that kept popping up in his mind over the years. Sometimes he even imagined the miner screaming in the seconds before the flames consumed him. There were several other pictures, shots of wrapped corpses being brought out of the tunnel on rail cars and photos of grief-stricken families as they received the bad news.

Rainwater wondered for the first time about why the pictures in the Archives had been taken and the reason for saving them. The racks held hundreds of files, and each file contained dozens of photos capturing the last images of victims. He wondered how many survivors there were like this poor kid, Nick, wondering over the years about the death of a father, a mother, or some family member who had never returned. The photos were there, but the survivors would never see them.

Rainwater had enough. He shook Nick's hand and left him sitting there, staring at the pictures. He went back to his office thinking he had made a terrible mistake. He should never have let the kid see the destruction that occurred in that tunnel, and knew that Nick would now carry those images with him forever, just as he did. It occurred to Rainwater that parts of Nick's father might still be in that god-damned tunnel, reduced to tiny particles, mixed with the other debris and soil.

Rainwater interviewed more candidates—they were all young and none of them had a clue about the life of a fireman. Maybe that was good, he thought. If they knew everything, they might think twice about signing up. He took a breather, stood up to stretch his back and went to the window. Outside, the sun was bright and hot, shining down on a group of LAFD men engaged in a training exercise. The rear end of a large school bus had been rigged up on top of a compact car and the men were practicing lifting the back of the bus with an inflatable device called a Vetter Bag.

Rainwater saw young Nick walk out of the building. The kid paused, watched the drill for a few minutes, put on his sunglasses and looked up at the sky, then disappeared into the parking lot.

"So, Nick," Rainwater whispered. "Do you still want to become a fireman?"

SIX

June 22, 2014, 7:20 a.m.

NICK'S FIRST CALL WENT TO Cindi's voicemail. He stood outside the JRIC conference room, still clutching the consequence management binder, and stared at the Al Jazeera news screen showing thousands of people demonstrating on the dusty street of a city somewhere in the Mideast. Older men wore robes and scarves wrapped across their faces. Younger men wore running shoes, jeans and T-shirts. The few women who had ventured out into the chaos wore hajibs. The crowd waved red and white flags. Troops in riot gear held shields and threw tear-gas canisters. The mob fired back with paving stones. Words in Arabic streamed across the bottom of the screen. The picture focused on a group of soldiers beating a bearded man wearing an Ohio State T-shirt. Blood streamed across his face.

Nick tried Cindi again and this time she answered on the second ring. "Hey, I got your message," he said. "Where are you?"

"We're near Magazine Canyon. Are you still at my place?"

"No, I got called down to JRIC. Do you know Homeland Security thinks someone may be planning to go after the Jensen plant? They're talking about foreign nationals."

"Foreign nationals? No way. We're tracking two guys from Sacramento in a white van."

Nick lowered his voice. "Well, all I can tell you is Homeland's gearing up for a full-fledged terrorist alert. And their analysts think a trash truck might be involved."

"Trash truck? We told them there was no trash truck."

"Well, their analysts think a trash truck carrying a fertilizer bomb might be used to blow up the chlorine storage tanks."

"Christ," she exploded. Nick heard her say something away from the phone, something he couldn't understand, and then she returned to the conversation. "Listen, I've got to try and straighten this out, but in the meantime, I need your help up here."

"Me?"

"Yeah, in case someone has to go into one of the tunnels or an access shaft."

"Cindi, no one's going into any of those spaces. The shafts up there are a couple hundred feet deep. The tunnels have water in them. And gas. There's methane—"

"That's what I'm worried about. What if these guys plant an ignition device or a bomb?"

"What if they do?" Nick paced back and forth outside the door of the conference room. "I couldn't go in after it by myself, and you couldn't help me with a flashlight and a hankie over your nose. We'd need backup, USAR and the bomb squad."

"I know that, but first we have to figure out what's going on. I've already got an explosives expert with me and Metropolitan Water's sending out an engineer, but I need you up here to advise me on the underground logistics. When we need the bomb squad or USAR, we'll call for them. We may have to change locations fast and right now we don't need a long convoy with flashing lights and sirens trailing after us."

"Have you found your suspects?"

"Not yet, but it's just a matter of time."

"Do you think they're really trying to hit Jensen?"

"I don't know—that's what we're trying to figure out. Are you coming?"

"Yes, sure." Nick looked at his watch. "It's seven twenty. I'll have to go by 103s and pick up some gear, and then it's at least an hour drive. The best I can do is be there around nine o'clock. Where should I meet you?"

"Don't worry about that. I'll see if I can get a fire department chopper to pick you up near your station."

"A fire department helicopter?"

"If I can. I'll let you know. There's not a lot of air resources available.

LAPD and the Sheriffs Department are out flying surveillance, looking for our suspects. It's a very fluid situation."

"Fluid?"

"Ha-ha."

"Hey, can you wrap this up fast so we can go body-surfing later?"

"No problem, I'll get right on it."

Nick thought of the blue engagement-ring box in the pocket of his jacket. "I've got something important to tell you."

"Well, it'll have to wait, I gotta go. Get up here, I need you."

"I'm on my... Hello?... Cindi?..." He looked at his cell phone. The screen showed "call ended." This is good, Nick thought. For once, he wouldn't have to wonder if she were safe; he would be right there by her side. His search and rescue mentality kicked in—maybe he would even have to rescue her. Yeah. He'd save her from something dangerous, and then propose. She wouldn't be able to say no. He'd have the ring with him and just pop it on her finger.

Nick turned his back to the open space of the JRIC operations area and ripped out two pages from the consequence management binder—the map of the Jensen plant and the diagram of Magazine Canyon with the water tunnels and aqueducts. He folded the sheets and stuffed them inside his shirt. When he walked to the elevator, he left the binder with the woman at the communications console.

The drive from JRIC in Norwalk to Station 103 in Pico Rivera, the city with the highest crime rate in Los Angeles County, took only a few minutes on an early Sunday morning. When Nick arrived, the men on the upcoming 8:00 a.m. C Shift had already been in the station for an hour, going through the daily activity of checking their equipment and vehicles. Before he parked, a text message came from Cindi: PICK UP IN 30 MIN WILLIAM SMITH PARK – ROSEMEAD ST SIDE –C. In the 15 minutes he had been on the road, Cindi had somehow managed to arrange for a fire helicopter to pick him up.

Nick left his truck on the parking apron near several air cargo shipping containers filled with rescue equipment and the trailer with the high-powered outboard used for swift-water incidents. He walked across the driveway, passing in front of the two-story equipment bay doors marked RESCUE TASK FORCE 103 – ALL RISK – ALL TERRAIN in red letters. The 6-foot image of their

USAR mascot—the rhino walking on his hind legs, wearing boots and a hard-hat, carrying a jackhammer and a coil of rope on his shoulder, and chewing a cigar—decorated one of the doors. Nick felt a strong sense of pride whenever he saw the rhino, and paused to glance at it.

Almost every day, some kind of technical rescue occurred somewhere in Los Angeles County, a 2,800-square-mile area that included 65 cities and parts of the Angeles National Forest. The County's USAR Task Force, designated California 2, was one of the best in the nation, maybe in the world, and Nick was part of it. The 103s, and their sister unit, the 134s on the other side of Los Angeles, responded to everything—swift-water incidents, mudslides, wildland rescues, over-the-side hoists, urban-trench collapses, machinery extrications, and even high-rise fires. If called up, they could also deploy anywhere in the U.S. or to a foreign country. A 70-man team of medical rescue specialists, emergency room physicians, structural engineers, heavy-equipment operators, hazardous-materials technicians, and communications experts could assemble in a matter of hours. Nick had labored along with his team members, sometimes for days at a time without sleep, to pull people, dead and alive, from sand, water, and debris on numerous assignments far from Los Angeles County. Two years ago, after a tsunami destroyed the eastern coast of Japan, he had flown there with the task force, crammed into cargo sling seats in the belly of an Air Force C-5A carrying tons of rescue tools, medical equipment, and even search dogs. A year earlier, in the midst of the earthquake devastation of Christchurch, New Zealand, he had held his breath and listened through earphones to a microphone dangling on a 15-foot cable under the debris of a collapsed building. Two years before New Zealand, his first foreign deployment had taken him to Haiti, where he stood in thick, stinking mud and unbearable heat to plumb the wind-strewn rubble with a search camera after a hurricane ripped across the island, destroying everything in its path.

Nick thought Haiti was one of the most miserable places he had ever visited, even without the effects of the hurricane. He felt sorry for the destitute people who had stripped the island bare seeking wood for charcoal, and who lived in some of the worst squalor he had seen. On the other hand, New Zealand was one of the most beautiful places he had ever visited. The mountains were stunning and the ocean was perfect for surfing. The whole country had only four million people, and they all seemed friendly—compared with the 11 million people in Los Angeles, who were not so friendly. After he met Cindi, he sometimes dreamed of taking off with her to New Zealand—and never returning.

In all of his searches, the reward was finding someone alive, saving a person who otherwise might have died. That was what all the USAR men worked for, and over the years he and the others had had many victories along with some defeats. For all his pride gained from being part of the team, however, and the camaraderie and adrenaline rush he experienced during a rescue effort, Nick never forgot the lie that had led him to his search and rescue career.

As he paused looking at the rhino on the equipment-bay doors, they rumbled open and he stood face-to-face with the enormous grille of the truck that carried the 60-ton heavy rescue crane. The monster's engine sprang to life with a deep diesel growl and the vibration resonated in Nick's body. He looked up through the vehicle's windshield to see Angel Jennings, an engineer on C Shift, at the wheel. Jennings gave Nick a quick nod and continued through his morning checklist. Although the truck was still connected to the overhead exhaust manifold, Jennings put the huge vehicle in gear, rolled forward a few feet and checked the air brakes. After a loud hiss of released air, he moved back and cut the engine.

Nick walked in through the bay, passing between the crane and the semi-trailer that carried much of their equipment. He saw a firefighter working underneath the rear of the trailer, lying on the cement floor with only his legs visible. "Hey, Lobrano," Nick said, and gently kicked his foot. "You've got a hole in your boot."

"Morning, Nick," Lobrano responded, without moving.

As Nick approached the door to Communications, someone hit the lights on one of the Engines and it lit up like a Christmas tree. Strobes, light bars, grille lights, running lights, and tail- and headlights all came on at once, flooding the side of the bay in intermittent, violent flashes of red and orange colors. Nick shielded his eyes and stepped into the communications room.

Inside, the shade on the one small window was drawn and the lights were low. The far wall was plastered with dozens of pictures of search and rescue teams responding to disasters and a collection of USAR patches from departments around the world. The radio alternated between high-pitched beeps and bursts of static. Tony Lawson, captain of the shift, sat on his swivel chair in the gloom, staring at his computer screen. When Nick entered, he looked up and said, "Nick, my man. What're you doing here?"

"I came to get some of my gear. I'm going out to assist the ATF." Nick saw a tense look on Lawson's face. "What's up?" he asked.

"The whole department's on 'all-call,'" Lawson said. "All-call" was the alert procedure by which fire dispatch notified every station and every firefighter on duty at once, placing them on radio stand-by to await instructions. "I'm just looking at the e-mail briefing. Homeland issued an Imminent Threat Alert early this morning."

"I know," Nick said. "I just came from JRIC and heard the long version. They're worried about the water system. They think the target may be the chlorine tanks at the Jensen plant."

"I've been told we'll probably be deployed up there within the hour," Lawson said. "Why are you going out with the ATF?"

"They're chasing two guys near Magazine Canyon. They may have explosives, and I think that's what triggered the alert. ATF needs someone who's familiar with tunnels and access shafts."

The door to Communications banged open and one of the men came in. "Morning, Nick," he said. "Cap, did we get the rechargeable batteries?"

Lawson pointed with a nod of his head. "On the floor in the john." He turned back to Nick and said, "Magazine Canyon? You talking about making a tunnel entry?"

"Not by myself."

"How'd you get involved in this?" Lawson asked. "You're not even on duty."

"My girlfriend's the case agent. She called me up there."

"Your honey?" Lawson pushed back from his desk.

"Hey, my 'honey' is about to be my fiancée. In fact, I was planning on proposing to her today. Of course that's on hold, with all that's going on."

"Well, it's about time you asked her." Lawson stood up and slapped Nick on the back. "Congratulations. She gonna say yes?"

"Hope so."

"Case agent? Does that mean she's running the show?"

"I don't know about the whole thing, but she's in charge of the search for the suspects. Get this—she called for a helicopter to pick me up. One of ours."

"Man, you are one important firefighter," Lawson said. "As soon as we get deployed, we'll coordinate with you."

"That's what I came in to tell you. After I get up there and do a size-up, I'll check in."

"You taking your gear?"

"Yeah. I don't really know what to expect, but I'm not going without it."

"Be careful; don't do anything crazy," Lawson said, and turned back to his computer screen.

Nick grabbed a radio from the recharger and went back out into the equipment bay. Most of the men of C Shift were now at their storage lockers, organizing their kit-bags, while music blared from a loudspeaker. At an ordinary station, each man would have one bag—the size of a duffel—that he used to carry his turnout gear, boots, helmet and other protective equipment needed for responding to an ordinary fire. At 103s, the men had additional duffels, or kit-bags, filled with equipment for each type of rescue. Most of the men kept at least four separate kits, and after a complete check of every piece of gear, each bag was loaded onto the truck at the beginning of the shift; the team had to be ready to respond to any situation as soon as they arrived on scene, and couldn't afford to stop to search for an important item. A missing item or malfunctioning piece of equipment in the midst of an emergency was unacceptable.

Nick was known for the painstaking arrangement of his gear. He used five kits, and every item in each bag had its particular location. Nick liked to know exactly where everything was, and had even gone to the trouble of having extra pockets sewn into hold specific pieces of hardware.

"Morning, guys," he said as he opened his locker.

"You subbing for someone?" one of the firefighters asked.

"Nah," Nick said. "I'm doing something else."

"What?" the firefighter asked.

"A search and capture," Nick said, and grinned.

"Oh yeah?" another firefighter said. "Search and capture? You chasing rats in your girlfriend's basement?"

"You got it," Nick said. He opened his locker, pulled out his tunnel entry kit and dropped it on the floor. He kneeled down, unzipped it and eyeballed his gear: helmet; type-3 body harness; knee and elbow pads; two head lamps and extra batteries; nylon ropes; tag lines; a whistle; duct tape; carabiners; and the small, razor sharp knife that he carried behind his neck in case he had to cut himself free from a tangled rope or line. He checked the headlamps to make sure they were working, and blew his whistle. Nick wondered what kind of situation Cindi might get him into and what else he might need. He went to the supply cache and took a breathing apparatus with a 60-minute air bottle. From another cabinet he grabbed a 4-gas meter, which had been calibrated earlier in the morning.

While he finished organizing his equipment, Nick asked, "Hey, does anybody know anything about the Owens Valley Water War?"

Frank Estacio, the oldest man on the task force, said, "*Chinatown*."

"*Chinatown*?" Nick repeated.

"The movie," Estacio said. "You know, with Jack Nicholson. A bunch of crooked politicians bought up all the Owens Valley water rights and sold them to Los Angeles. Then the city built an aqueduct and drained the lake out there."

"The best part," a firefighter interjected, "was when that guy stuck his knife in Nicholson's nose and sliced it open."

"The farmers retaliated and tried to sabotage the aqueduct," Estacio continued. "That's what started the water war."

Lawson joined the men and opened his locker. "Speaking of water wars," he said to Nick, "check this out, it was in this morning's paper." He handed a page of the Sunday *Los Angeles Times* to Nick. "The state's gonna dig two thirty-mile water tunnels up near Sacramento."

"Thirty-mile tunnels?" Nick said. He looked at the paper, and saw the NEW WATER WAR headline.

"How'd you like to do a search and rescue in a thirty-mile tunnel?" Lawson said.

"You'd need more than a four-hour rebreather," one of the men said. "You'd need a twenty-four-hour rebreather."

"And transportation," another firefighter said. "Maybe a motorcycle or a quad."

Nick stuffed the *Times* page into his shirt pocket, slung his SCBA over one shoulder and grabbed his tunnel kit. On his way out, he said to Lawson, "I'll contact you."

Kurt Kamm

Just as he dropped his gear in the back of his truck, Nick's cell phone vibrated and he saw another text message from Cindi: LOCATED SUSPECTS–C.

Nick drove to the far edge of William Smith Park, less than a mile from the station. The park wasn't in the best of neighborhoods and the last time he was there, several years ago, a gang had raped a 13-year-old girl in one of the restrooms. They didn't need the 60-ton rescue crane for that incident, just a female paramedic with a soft shoulder for the victim to cry on.

He parked on Rosemead Street near a playing field, and waited in his truck for several minutes. Finally, he got out and scanned the horizon. Even through his sunglasses, the bright blue emptiness of the sky reflected back into his sensitive eyes, and he held his hand up to block out the glare. The helicopter was nowhere in sight and Nick walked around to the back of the truck to check his gear again. He unzipped the bag, looked over everything he had packed inside, and thought for a moment about how far search and rescue techniques had come. Twenty years ago, when he began looking for a job, Chief Rainwater had talked about the growing interest in developing USAR resources. At that time, even the best fire departments only had basic training programs and first-generation equipment. Today, most big cities had teams of men like the 103s, highly trained in multiple disciplines and supported by some amazing equipment. The sensitive, multi-gas meters and the underground video and listening devices didn't even exist two decades ago. The new 4-hour, recirculating breathing device—the rebreather—was the most incredible device of all. It was twice the physical size of the regular SCBA, which used a 60-minute air bottle that would be useless for any extended period underground. The rebreather weighed 33 pounds and resembled a backpack an astronaut would wear. It captured exhaled air, filtered it, added new oxygen and fed it back into the mouthpiece. It even required an ice pack, because the filtration process was exothermic, giving off heat. Nick had often wondered whether some of the miners might have been saved from asphyxiation if the rebreather had existed in 1971, at the time of the Sylmar explosion.

Nick took off his jacket to stow it in his bag and realized the box containing Cindi's ring was still in one of the pockets. He knew he should have left the ring at Cindi's apartment, hidden somewhere where she wouldn't find it, but it was too late to do that. He couldn't leave it in his truck, didn't want to carry it around all day in his pants pocket, and decided it would be safest in his bag. It would be hard to misplace a large, heavy USAR equipment bag and no one was likely to walk off with it. It was the safest place for the ring.

Nick tucked the ring box into an empty pocket, zipped the kit, and walked partway out onto the dirt field to scan the empty morning sky again. He listened for the telltale sound of the chopper and wondered what could be taking so long. The only noise he heard was from a group of men playing soccer on the nearby grass, screaming at each other in a language he couldn't understand. He watched them until the team with the blue shirts scored a goal, and then went back to his truck.

He sat, waited, and pulled out the page of the *Times* that Lawson had given him. The NEW WATER WAR article described a looming battle between the farmers of the Sacramento-San Joaquin River Delta and the state water authorities who were proposing to divert more of the runoff from the Sierra Nevada snowpack, which collected in the Delta. The state planned to dig two huge 30-mile tunnels to move Delta water underground to pumping plants that would send it on to Southern California. A sophisticated, specially constructed boring machine would be used to chew through the rock and dirt, using a rotating cutting head studded with steel teeth and spinning disks. Nick thought of the Mole with the hydraulic bucket-scoop used in the Sylmar Tunnel. Today it would be a puny joke, an old junkyard relic.

The *Times* article went on to describe the Delta landowners and environmentalists as "weaklings" in the battle against water agencies like the MWD and the thirsty Southern California cities. Cindi was from Sacramento and Nick recalled her description of the Delta as a fresh-water marsh where the land owners drew water to irrigate their vegetable fields, fruit orchards and lush vineyards.

Nick thought he heard the faint sound of an approaching helicopter. He laid the newspaper on the seat and listened. Yes! There it was. He locked his truck, grabbed his gear, and walked out onto the dirt field. While he waited, he thought of the last time he had been near a vineyard. It was almost 20 years ago, when he had visited Wally Zavattero.

SEVEN
August 1994

"**L**OCKHEED IGNORED MY ORDERS. AFTER the flash fire the night before, I wrote out specific instructions and told them they had to improve the ventilation in the tunnel and do continual testing for gas. They were supposed to get everyone out whenever the concentration reached two percent. You think they listened to me? Hell no! Lockheed was footage happy—they kept right on digging. They were in a hurry. Everyone was gonna get an Accutron watch and a bonus for early completion. Early completion, my ass! A person has a right to go to work in the morning and expect to come home at night. Not that night. They cut right into the earthquake fault and released a huge pocket of gas. Seventeen miners died and Lockheed said it was an act of God. I called it an act of greed. Today that job would be shut down in a minute." Wally Zavattero took a long drink of his iced tea, put his feet up on the porch railing, and felt his anger rising. Years had passed, but all he needed to hear was the words "Sylmar Tunnel," and it was like waving a red flag in front of a bull. All the damn memories came back and the thought of what happened enraged him all over again. "My phone rang at two forty-five in the morning." Zavattero went on. "I knew what had happened before I even answered. My wife got up and made coffee for me while I got dressed. I didn't come home for three days. It was the worst time of my life."

After a seven hour drive, it felt good to sit in the shade on Zavattero's porch in Santa Rosa, on a warm, lazy summer afternoon. His place wasn't much, but it was right in the middle of the Sonoma wine country, an hour north of the Golden Gate Bridge and a half hour from the Pacific Ocean. The sun cast a glow over the hills covered with late-season growth on the grapevines. He wiped the condensation from his iced-tea glass on his pant leg.

"It sure is peaceful out here," Nick said.

"That's why I moved up here. I had to get away from Los Angeles. You should have been here the other night—it wasn't so quiet." Zavattero pointed to the other side of his chain-link fence. "I had a couple of mountain lions out in that field and they were making a helluva noise. I think they caught some kind of small animal." He drained his iced-tea and said, "Sorry I popped off on the phone, but for years I got calls from reporters. They wouldn't leave me alone, and every one of them asked the same damn questions. It's been a while since anyone called, but I just assumed you were one of them."

"No offense taken. I'm glad I could come up and talk to you."

"You know, that disaster changed my life. It ruined my health. They say stress and anger is bad for you, and I believe it. Every time I look at myself in the mirror and see an overweight old guy with thinning white hair, bags under his eyes, and a tired face full of earthquake faults, I wonder if that's me, Wally Zavattero, the guy who took on Lockheed. I can't believe I look like that. Where did the time go? On the inside it's even worse—I've got a bad case of ulcers and still suffer from hypertension. I'm not even supposed to drink tea, but what the hell...." He ran his hand over his ample stomach.

"Sorry, I didn't mean to—"

"How'd you find me?"

"Last year I interviewed for a job with the L.A. City Fire Department. I met Battalion Chief Rainwater. Does his name sound familiar? He responded to the tunnel explosion. He remembered your name and said you had moved to Santa Rosa."

"Rainwater? No, that's not a name I recall."

"He told me about finding the bodies."

"You mean, what was left of them." Zavattero shook his head. "The Coroner reported that half the men died of 'traumatic injury.' Know what that means?"

"Uh... not exactly."

"Well, I'll tell you. I served in Korea, in the Army, and I saw dead men on the battlefield, but it was nothing like what I saw in that tunnel. I went in when the body recovery began. The explosion was like what happens in a gun barrel—incredible force expanding in one direction. Some of the miners were in one piece, just burnt beyond recognition. But at the digging face, the fire department was collecting pieces of those men; incinerated arms and legs sticking out of the rubble. Severed body parts—that's what the coroner calls traumatic injury. I remember watching one firefighter collecting what was left of a body and putting it in a bucket. A goddamn bucket! I'll never forget that. It was a big, oversized, galvanized steel bucket, and it had parts of a man's body in it. I stood there looking at it and I couldn't move. I was the state safety inspector. My job was to protect those men and now the fire department was taking them out in buckets." A look of despair spread across Zavattero's face. The emotions returned, still fresh and raw after all the years. He rubbed his eyes with his fists, as if to blot out the memories. "You know," he said, "one body was never found. Not even any parts of that poor miner. He was just, 'poof,' gone. He was in the middle of a divorce and some people said he walked out of the tunnel and disappeared. I never believed that; it wasn't possible. I think he was pulverized."

The images from the archive photos returned to Nick with perfect clarity. "I saw some of the fire department's pictures—they were pretty grim."

"Lockheed tried to twist the facts, but I swore there'd be justice for those men. There was an investigation and a criminal trial that took forever. The jury found gross negligence, but under the law at the time it was a misdemeanor. Seventeen miners died and it was a goddamn misdemeanor? Then two Lockheed executives were convicted on violations of the safety code and they were supposed to get jail time. So what happened? Their sentences were reduced to probation, and one of them committed suicide. After the criminal trial, there was a civil suit. Lockheed tried every trick in the book again, and the appeals lasted almost six years. It just dragged on and on, and I kept appearing in court and testifying. That's what really ruined my health, but I couldn't let go until it was over. One good thing did come out of that disaster. California enacted the strongest tunnel safety rules in the nation. That was my contribution—in the end those men didn't die for nothing." Zavattero gazed out over the empty field with a vacant look in his eyes. "Something good did come out of it," he repeated. "You want some more tea?"

"Yeah, thanks." Nick held out his glass.

"So what exactly d'you want to know?"

"I'm trying to find out anything I can about my father. He died in the explosion, and it happened before I was born. His name was Willie Carter. Does it sound familiar?"

"Willie Carter?" Zavattero shook his head. "No, but I didn't know any of the miners personally. I had only been on the Sylmar job a couple of months. I worked for what was called the Division of Industrial Safety and spent most of my time with the supervisors, the men from MWD and Lockheed."

"I don't know anything about the kind of a life my father had; what it was like to be a miner working in that tunnel. I wanted to know...."

Zavattero looked at Nick and wondered how he could have these questions. "How's that possible? You can't grow up in a mining family and not know every detail about the life." Zavattero knew that tradition ran generations deep in those families. Grandfathers, fathers, brothers, uncles, cousins and sons worked their entire lives underground. Mining was all they knew, all they ever talked about, all they ever lived. "Where's your family from? Kentucky? Virginia? They all come from somewhere in the coal mining country."

"My mother grew up in California, and I don't know where my dad came from. They were only married for a couple of years."

"What did your mother tell you?"

"Nothing. She wouldn't talk to me about my father or the accident."

"Yeah, I've met plenty of widows who wouldn't ever mention the husbands they'd lost underground. Too painful. Mining's a hard life. People live in denial of the danger and then when something happens, they just try to shut it out. I remember the Sylmar crews did a lot of drinking and carousing. That's how miners relieve the stress from working underground. They'd knock each other silly in a bar fight, and then be the best of friends on their next shift. A tough bunch."

"I'm looking for anyone who knew my father. Chief Rainwater mentioned—"

"Ralph Brissette, that's the person you want to talk to. He's the one man who survived the explosion."

"Yes," Nick exclaimed. "That was one of the reasons I wanted to talk to you. Chief Rainwater told me one of the miners made it, but he didn't have the name."

"Brissette was the eighteenth miner on the graveyard shift. They found him in the debris on the floor of the tunnel. If he's still alive and you can locate him, he's the man to see."

"How do you spell Brissette?"

"Just like it sounds. B-R-I-S-S-E-T-T-E."

"Do you have any idea where I should look for him?"

"I dunno. Last I heard, he had a bait shop in Inglewood. That's not even on the water; it's near the Los Angeles airport. But that was a long time ago. Ten, fifteen years." Zavattero poured himself another glass of iced tea and held up the pitcher.

Nick shook his head. "If he is still around, I'll find him."

"Have you been out to Sylmar? Seen the spot where the East Portal was?"

"Where the end of the tunnel's sealed off? Yes. I went out there about a year ago, right after I graduated from the Fire Academy. Not much to see—just the bulkhead sticking out of the ground and the pile of old cement tunnel liners. You'd think there would be a memorial, or something."

"Some people don't want to remember it, and everyone else has forgotten about it."

"Did they ever finish it?"

"The tunnel? Sure. It was supposed to be the first of four to move water to the eastern part of Los Angeles County. A billion gallons a year. The other three never happened, but Sylmar was finally completed. Twenty-nine thousand fifty-five feet long. Most of the time, it's empty, but during drought periods, the MWD does send water through it. It comes out in Sylmar, runs through some underground valves, and empties into a storm drain. Eventually it ends up as part of the Burbank water supply."

"You know, until I learned about the Sylmar Tunnel, I'd never even heard of the MWD."

"Most folks have no idea how big and powerful it is. It controls the water distribution to most of the cities in Southern California. That means aqueducts, tunnels, reservoirs and some huge filtration plants."

"Who thinks about where the water comes from? You just turn on the faucet and it runs out."

"There's a lot of history and politics behind the water in Southern California. Los Angeles shouldn't even exist. It's in the middle of a desert, and all those millions of people living there need their precious H-2-O." Zavattero got up and walked to the end of his porch. "You know what happens when you pour a glass of water into the desert sand?" He turned the empty ice tea pitcher upside down.

"What?"

"Nothing. It disappears into the ground and it's like it was never there. Then you need more, and you need it every day and every night. So you depend on the MWD, even if you've never heard of it."

"Now I know."

"I'm sorry I can't tell you anything about your father, but come out to the garage. I've got something that may help."

They walked around to the other side of the house. An old '82 Chevy pickup with four flat tires and riddled with rust, sat in the middle of the gravel driveway. Zavattero's garage looked like it hadn't been painted in decades, and in places the bare wood was starting to rot. Enormous spider webs hung across the doors, which groaned on un-oiled hinges when he struggled to push them open.

Zavattero knew he was a dilapidated man living in a dilapidated house. "I keep my memories in here," he said. "I try not to let them see the light of day, but they have a way of getting out." Inside, he switched on the overhead fluorescent fixture but only one of the two bulbs came to life.

Nick followed him in and looked around. The place was a mess. More spider webs hung from the inner wood plank walls, and rat droppings littered the cement floor.

Zavattero felt embarrassed about the disarray in the garage and wondered what the young guy with the pale blue eyes thought. "This is what's left of my life as a safety engineer," he said. The floor was covered with coiled nylon ropes, an open box of dusty blue and white helmets, a pile of half-used rolls of yellow tape marked DANGER in black letters, and a dozen shovels and hand tools, still caked with dried mud. Old aluminum suitcase-style containers of different sizes, some plain, others marked AIR or GAS MASK, were lined up along one wall. A large white NO ENTRY–DANGER sign leaned against a 4-foot-tall plastic Christmas tree. Zavattero still remembered the day he threw that sign in the back of his truck after he had reopened a small pipeline project in Riverside County. Somehow it had remained on the truck bed, and years later ended up in his garage. A thick layer of dust covered everything in the garage and gave the appearance of powdered snow on the plastic Christmas tree branches.

Nick stood in the gloom and sneezed a couple of times. "Dusty," he said.

Zavattero went to the back of the garage, where a stack of cardboard boxes reached almost to the ceiling. One box, resting on the floor, was open. He blew the filth away, reached inside, pulled out a book, and handed it to Nick. "Here," he said. "Take this. It tells the whole story of the explosion."

Nick looked at the gray cover of *The Sylmar Tunnel Disaster*, by Janette Zavattero. "Did your wife write this?"

"No, Janette was my sister. She's dead. My wife's name is Mercedes—I call her Mercy."

Nick read aloud from the cover flap, " '… an accident… seventeen men dead… and one angry man's lonely fight against the system…' Is that you?" he asked. "The one angry man?"

"It was me.… Yeah, I guess it is me. I'm the angry one."

Nick opened the book and saw the 1978 copyright date. "Hah. This was written when I was seven years old."

"Check the dedication on the following page," Zavattero said.

"To Those Who Died," Nick read aloud. His eyes traced the list of the 17 miners and saw Willie Carter's name. "Hey, here's my dad's name," Nick said, and ran his fingers over the print, as though he was touching his father's flesh.

"The book wasn't a big seller. After Janette passed, the publisher sent me the unsold copies. I guess when I die, they'll dump them into my grave. Sylmar's an old disaster; no one cares about it anymore."

"I do. It's not old to me."

"C'mon, let's go outside. I hate this garage, it's depressing."

Nick walked past a series of boxes stuffed with files, spread out on the cement floor. "What's all this?"

"Oh, I was putting together a history of the water resources in the Sacramento River Delta, but I kinda lost interest. Haven't worked on it for a couple of years."

"I grew up in Fresno. I do know our water comes from the Delta."

"That's where almost everyone's water comes from." Zavattero stopped and looked at the open boxes collecting dust. He nudged one with the tip of his shoe. "Half of California's runoff, everything that comes out of the Sierra, drains into the Delta. The problem is, a lot of people want it. Most of it gets diverted to Southern California, or to the Ag farms in the San Joaquin Valley. There's also a lot of folks farming rich land in the Delta that needs irrigation. Then there's the endangered fish swimming around in the Delta waters. All in all, it's a hell of a stew. The diversion pumps are chewing up the fish, the local farmers are afraid of losing their water supply, and everyone in Central and Southern California is trying to get a bigger share."

"Is there a shortage?" Nick asked.

"Not yet, but there will be soon, and then I predict a bitter struggle. But at least it's a dispute within the state of California. The rest of our water comes from the Colorado River, and if you think the water politics of the Delta is complicated, try satisfying half a dozen different states as well as Mexico."

"I'll stick to firefighting," Nick said. "No one's going to cut off water to fight fires." He followed Zavattero out into the sunlight, squinted, and waited while he closed the doors.

They walked back around to Nick's pickup, and Zavattero asked, "So which fire department do you work for?"

"Los Angeles County. I started six months ago. Eventually I want to be in search and rescue."

"You like being underground?"

Nick nodded. "I always have."

"Well, maybe you are from a miner's family." Zavattero reached out to shake his hand. "I hope you find out more about your dad," and added without much enthusiasm, "if I can help, you let me know."

"Thanks; I'm gonna start looking for Ralph Brissette as soon as I get back to Los Angeles."

Zavattero started back to his house. He paused, turned to Nick, and said, "Hey, I have to ask you something."

"Sure."

"What did your mama do with the money? It was enough to be a life-changer, but most of the families just squandered it. They went through it real fast."

"The money?" Nick stared at Zavaretto. "What money?"

"The compensation, the money from Lockheed."

Nick gave Zavattero a blank look.

"Each family got about half a million bucks in damages," Zavattero continued. "Except Brissette. He got less, because he survived. That's funny isn't it? They paid him less because he lived through their goddamn disaster."

"Lockheed paid the families?" Nick looked at Zavattero to see whether he was playing some sort of joke.

"You bet they did."

"We never got any money—at least, none that I know of."

"That's what the civil suit was all about. They called it recompense. That's why I kept testifying. It took six years, but we finally nailed them. You can read all the details in the book." Zavattero started back to his house, turned once again, and asked Nick, "How could you not know your mother got a half-million dollars?"

EIGHT
June 22, 2014, 8:05 a.m.

T HE FIRE HELICOPTER CAME IN from the east. Nick heard the rhythm of the engines, but for a moment the aircraft was lost in the glare of the morning sun. When it did appear, he saw it was a Bell 412 instead of one of the bigger, more powerful Blackhawks. In a search and rescue situation, he preferred to have the larger craft hovering overhead—it had more room inside, which made it easier to load a stretcher or stokes basket when a bruised or broken body had to be airlifted to a hospital. For a 20-minute flight up to Magazine Canyon, it didn't matter.

Nick grabbed his equipment and the SCBA, and walked out onto the dirt field. When the men playing soccer on the grass heard the noise, they stopped their game long enough to watch the approach of the silver bird with yellow and black stripes, the rectangular aluminum water tank mounted under its belly, and the flashing red lights on its tail. Through the cloud of dust from the downdraft, Nick saw the pilot in the right-hand seat, looking down at him through the copter's plastic chin bubble. He wondered if his friend Herc Drakos was behind the helmet with the sun shield. The County Fire Department employed several helicopter pilots, all with years of military or commercial experience, and they enjoyed an elite status among the firefighters because of their flying ability and the fact that if someone had to be lifted to safety, either a civilian or a firefighter, they made it happen. They were no-nonsense men who tended to keep to themselves. Nick knew a few of them by sight and had flown several times with Hercules "Herc" Drakos. Drakos was a senior pilot who usually flew one of the Blackhawks and was known for his ability to make pinpoint water drops. He once told Nick that even one of the twin engines on a Blackhawk was powerful enough to allow it to hover fully loaded. "On the 412," he said, "one engine won't do much more than get you to a forced landing spot."

The blades continued spinning after the 412 touched down. Davis, a paramedic wearing the standard blue flight suit and white flight helmet, slid the side door open and waved Nick aboard. Expecting to see someone in uniform, he shouted over the sound of the engine, "Captain Carter?" Nick nodded, passed his equipment bag and SCBA up to Davis' outstretched hands, then hoisted himself aboard. The minute he was inside, and before Davis could slide the door shut, the sound of the engines grew louder, the vibration in the cabin increased, and Nick felt the helicopter get light-on-the-skids as the craft lifted off. Through the cabin window, Nick watched William Smith Park and the soccer players drop away as the 412 gained altitude.

The second paramedic, Alvarez, grabbed Nick's gear and secured it to metal rings set in the gray steel floor. "We don't want your stuff bouncing around in here," he said.

Nick sat down on one of the forward-facing jump seats in the center of the cabin. A large blue Mobil Medic bag and a Zoll defibrillator were harnessed to the two seats facing him and a compact medical stretcher was secured to the floor of the cabin on the left side. Looking forward between the two seats in front of him, Nick saw the flight controls and the multitude of gauges, switches and buttons that covered the instrument panel. The pilot had both hands on the sticks.

Alvarez passed him a flight helmet plugged into a communications jack. Nick hated these helmets—unlike the lightweight ones used for search and rescue, these were clumsy and heavy, with thick padding inside to muffle the sound of the engines. He eased it over his head and as he adjusted the chinstrap, he heard the pilot say: "Welcome aboard your private air taxi, Captain Carter. It'll be a short flight, so we won't be serving refreshments." It was Drakos, and his voice was crystal-clear coming through the speakers inside the helmet. "Sorry we're late. We were on a trauma run. Took a little girl to Children's Hospital."

"Hey, Herc," Nick said. He clipped into the seat harness and inhaled the faint smell of hydraulic fluid inside the cabin.

"Pull anyone out of a 1,000-foot hole lately?" Drakos asked.

"Not this week."

"You know the safety drill, right?"

"You're the one who taught me." Nick definitely knew the drill and went through it in his mind's eye: secure anything you bring into the cabin; if the craft makes an emergency landing, wait for the rotors to stop before exiting; if there's a fire onboard, don't wait for the rotors to stop; if possible, get out on the downhill side of the craft and move away at a right angle. The last item on the protocol, the part about an emergency landing on water, was the only part that had always seemed problematic to Nick. Drakos had explained that the copter would roll over as soon as it hit the water. The procedure was to stay calm, wait until the cabin was fully flooded, kick out a window, and then "swim toward the light." At the time, Nick had wondered how far down the copter would sink before he could break loose and swim upward. As the years passed and Nick made more flights, he concluded that flying in one of the Department's birds was actually much safer than making entry into an unknown, dark tunnel. He gave Drakos the thumbs-up sign and leaned back against the jump seat.

The copter banked and headed northwest. "I have a lat-long for a dirt access road that runs into Magazine Canyon," Drakos said. "I'm supposed to drop you near some Caltrans construction equipment. We're looking for a black SUV."

"I'll recognize it," Nick said.

"It's all business on the radio this morning. You know about the Homeland alert, right?"

"That's why you're flying me up to Jensen." Nick thought about Cindi and wondered what kind of danger she was facing. He understood that drug dealers, madmen with bombs, and lunatics with semi-automatic guns were all part of her daily life—and he tried not to let it bother him—but somehow the word "terrorist" implied a higher level of danger. He pushed the thought from his mind and looked out the window. After growing up on the vast, empty farmland around Fresno, Nick never ceased to be amazed at the aerial view of Los Angeles. Today the view was spectacular. The early morning haze had burned away and on the right, he saw the blue-gray San Gabriel Mountains and the southern part of the Angeles National Forest. The city stretched in every direction as far as the eye could see, as if someone had carelessly poured it from a huge bucket and let it spread across the ground until the ocean, the mountains, and the desert sands stopped the flow. The colors below were green and blue. Trees, vegetation and grass covered the landscape. Lawns, golf courses, parks, and even center dividers on the streets were lush. Aqua-blue swimming pools sparkled from thousands of backyards, from the courtyards of apartment buildings, and on the rooftops of hotels. Nick remembered the comment Wally Zavattero had made about pouring water into the desert sand and watching it disappear. On this sparkling morning, the desert known as Los Angeles seemed to have as much water as it needed.

The copter flew on, over a vast piggyback-trailer rail yard, and Nick saw thousands of containers—rust-colored, red, blue, and gray—lined up precisely, creating a vast herringbone pattern on the ground. Continuing northwest, they soared over Dodger Stadium and he looked in vain for the Los Angeles City Fire Department training center where Chief Rainwater had interviewed him long ago. Finally, the 412 banked again and headed toward the Jensen Filtration Plant.

"Be there in ten," Drakos announced, and Nick heard him request the ATF tactical frequency from Air Ops.

Nick pulled the two JRIC binder sheets from his shirt and studied the first one, which included a diagram of the water tunnel intersection under Magazine Canyon. Branching off this junction was the short Balboa Tunnel, which carried the water west, under the I-5 freeway into the Jensen Plant. Branching off to the east was the 5 ½-mile Sylmar Tunnel, marked "sealed." Several rectangles appeared near the tunnel junction. They weren't identified, but Nick knew these were the pyrotechnic magazines and he wondered again what idiot had authorized the storage of tons of explosives near a main intersection of the Los Angeles water system and directly across the freeway from the state's largest water treatment plant.

The 412 approached a large electric substation and a jungle of 100-foot-high power transmission towers reached up toward them. "Not a nice place to go down," Drakos said through the earphones. They passed over the gray steel pylons and continued on until the filtration plant came into full view, resting on a plateau in the foothills of the Santa Susana Mountains. "They're keeping the airspace over Jensen clear," he said, as the 412 began a wide arc around the facility.

Nick gazed down at the filtration plant and compared it with the JRIC map. He had driven by the plant on I-5 many times and had never bothered to give it a second look; he had no idea the water treatment process was so complicated and took up so much space. Dozens of rectangular settling basins, each half the size of a football field, flashed reflections of blue sky back at him. On the south side, Nick saw the chlorine storage shed with roll-up doors and tracks running into it, just as it was described at the JRIC meeting.

The 412 slowed, crossed above the I-5 freeway, and began to descend as it approached Magazine Canyon. A chain-link security fence topped with a spiral of razor wire ran around the floor of the canyon and disappeared up the side of the mountain. The access gate on the dirt road was open and a sign with red letters lay face-up on the ground, warning DO NOT FIGHT AN EXPLOSIVES FIRE. Inside the fenced area, Nick saw the round vault-like cement structure that covered the entrance to the access shaft leading to the underground water tunnel junction. Farther into the canyon he saw the explosives magazines. Most were simply extra-long shipping containers, like the ones they had flown over in the piggyback rail yard, but there were also several larger, old brick storage buildings with metal roofs.

"This is it," Drakos said. The helicopter made a tight circle.

Nick saw a cluster of orange Caltrans dumptrucks, backhoes, and a road grader parked by the access road. "I don't see the SUV," he said to Drakos.

"Wires!" Drakos yelled out to no one in particular. "What the hell are they thinking? Between the power lines and the hills, where are we supposed to land?" Nick listened as Drakos called dispatch and said, "This is Copter 11. We're over Magazine Canyon. I need a connection to the ATF, pronto."

"Get hold of Agent Burns." Nick said.

"This is fucked up," Drakos said. "We may have to drop you down on the cable."

"Do you see anyone down there?" Nick asked. He loosened his seat harness and knelt by the window to get a better view. The area was deserted.

"Screw it," Drakos said. "The com channels are jammed. I'm just gonna try to find a place to set you down."

"Drop me in the canyon and I'll walk out," Nick said.

Drakos nodded, and said to Davis through the helmet mike, "Get out on the strut and make sure we're clear. I'm gonna set it down on the other side of the fence near that storage building."

The 412 crept into the canyon and dropped to 100 feet above the ground.

Davis attached the cinch strap on his safety harness to an anchor ring on the wall and slid the door back. As soon as he opened it, the wind whipped through the cabin and the sound from the engines intensified. He stepped carefully out onto the strut, holding on to an outside grip with one hand as the wind buffeted him. He scanned the ground and told Drakos, "You're clear."

"See anyone?" Nick said into the helmet mike. "A black SUV from the ATF?"

Davis leaned out over the strut and looked again. He shook his head.

"How about a van?" Nick asked. "They're searching for a white Ford van."

Davis shook his head again.

The helicopter circled in the canyon, flying tight orbits and Nick moved again to the open door and looked down. All he saw was the shadow of the helicopter moving across the ground. Cindi and her crew were nowhere in sight.

Davis eased his way in off the strut, detached his cinch from the wall anchor, and secured himself in a jump seat. Just as Davis sat down, Nick heard a metallic voice in his helmet: "THIS IS AIR OPS. COPTER 11, ABORT! MOVE OUT OF MAGAZINE CANYON. REPEAT, WAVE OFF! MOVE AWAY IMMEDIATELY!" Before Nick could react, the sound of the engines increased, the vibration in the craft intensified, and the nose of the helicopter dropped as Drakos tried to draw more air toward the rotor to gain forward airspeed. The sudden shift threw Nick off balance. He stumbled back from the open door, and lunged for the nearest jump seat. Before he could get a secure grip, the canyon below erupted. Nick thought he heard two detonations—a smaller one, followed by a much larger, ear-shattering explosion, as one of the brick storage buildings directly below the helicopter disintegrated in a concussion of sound, orange flame and black smoke.

A massive shock wave hit the helicopter. The 412 rocked violently in the turbulence as it was thrust upward by the powerful cloud of expanding gas. A ball of fire surged up around the helicopter with a brilliant, almost other-world intensity, followed by smoke and dirt mixed with stone and metal fragments from the brick storage building. The 412's engines sucked in the debris-filled air and faltered. Nick listened to the roar turn to a whine as the engines spooled down, and finally there was an eerie silence as they seized up. Drakos struggled to autorotate the heavy ship down, but they were too low and the four-ton helicopter made an uncontrolled descent to the canyon floor. Nick lost his grip on the seat and was thrown across the cabin. As he crashed against the wall, he heard Drakos cursing. Through the open door, Nick saw the ground coming up to meet them. A cold flush of adrenaline shot through his body, and a nauseating, weightless feeling started in his stomach and ended in his throat. Nick stuck out his arm to cushion his fall as he slammed onto the steel deck. He felt a surge of pain in his wrist and tried to grasp one of the large floor-bolts with his other hand.

The craft hit belly first. The water tank compressed, the landing skids crumpled, and the 412 crashed onto the hard floor of the canyon. The impact was a bone-cruncher—Nick felt pain everywhere in his body. In the split second after his head bounced against the steel floor and before he lost consciousness, flashes of light danced before his eyes. His final thought was, this was the day he was going to propose to Cindi.

When he opened his eyes, Nick was lying face up in what was left of the 412's cabin. Through a gaping hole in the side, he saw smoke and fire. He smelled the overpowering odor of cordite from the powder explosions, as if someone had fired a gun under his nose. Flames were already spreading through the brush surrounding the broken body of the helicopter. Every nerve ending in his body registered the shock of the crash. He swam through a sea of pain. His thoughts were slow and confused. What should he do? What were the safety procedures? His head throbbed, it pounded.

Someone floated over him. Nick struggled to focus his eyes. Alvarez' lips were moving. "What?" Nick mumbled.

"We've got to get out," Alvarez said.

"I—" Nick said, and closed his eyes.

NINE
September 1996

MORE THAN TWO YEARS PASSED between the time Nick visited Wally Zavaterro in Santa Rosa and the day he located Ralph Brissette. In the interim, Nick read *The Sylmar Tunnel Disaster* so many times that the spine cracked and some of the pages fell out. The book provided him with his first real understanding of the disaster and the subsequent rescue attempts, and if pushed, Nick could quote whole paragraphs of the text. Now he was more determined than ever to find the man who had worked with his father in the tunnel and survived the explosion.

Nick began by searching the phone book and made a list of bait shops from the Yellow Pages. On days when he wasn't on duty or practicing search and rescue drills, he began to visit bait and tackle shops around Los Angeles, asking about the miner turned fisherman. It took time—a lot of time. He started in Inglewood, the city Zavattero mentioned, but no one there had heard of Ralph Brissette. Nick moved on to Marina del Rey, then to Redondo Beach and finally, with little hope left, he visited the Santa Monica Pier.

"Ralph Brissette?" a man in the Pier Tackle Shop said. "Yeah, sure. The guy who got all that dough from Lockheed?"

"That's the one."

"He bought a bait shop on Pacific Coast Highway, out toward Malibu, named it Ralph's. But that was years ago. I ain't heard anything about him in a long time."

"Finally," Nick said aloud, as he descended the steep stairs leading from the pier down to the parking lot.

Nick drove out Pacific Coast Highway toward Malibu, watching both sides of the road. The morning marine layer had lifted and the sky was a glorious blue. A hot, dry Santa Ana wind blew in through the window of his pickup. It was early September, the nicest time of the year at the beach in Southern California, and surfers had come from everywhere to ride the waves. Nick watched them paddling out to meet the waves on their boards and wanted to join them. He had begun surfing at Redondo Beach a year earlier and discovered he loved it. Everyone said the dude from landlocked Fresno was a natural.

When he reached Topanga Beach, he almost missed Ralph's Bait Shop. It was just a shack, set back from the road, almost lost between the Topanga Ranch Motel and a restaurant that featured Thai food. The motel was a series of dilapidated white stucco cottages with red roofs. The paint was peeling, plywood covered broken windows, and a sign nailed to the office door said: SORRY WE'RE CLOSED. The Thai restaurant, in a blue wooden building as decrepit as the motel, was still open for business. It was mid-afternoon and the place looked deserted.

Nick parked behind the bait shop on a patch of gravel surrounded by black 55-gallon drums connected with a heavy marine rope. A few half-dead palm trees struggled to survive at the edge of the asphalt. His heart pounded in his chest and nervous sweat soaked his T-shirt. After years of searching, he was about to speak with someone who knew his father, someone who had heard Willie Carter's voice, someone who had shaken his hand. Every search and rescue game Nick had played as a child, all the times he tried to imagine his father, all the people he talked to—everything had led him to this bait shop on Pacific Coast Highway to meet the miner who was in the tunnel the night the explosion ended his father's life. All that was left for Nick to do was walk inside, introduce himself, and hear the stories. He got out of his truck and started across the gravel, feeling a mixture of excitement and anxiety.

When he entered the bait shop, an electric eye set off a shrill whistle and Nick paused inside the door next to a whiteboard that listed the local tides. The place was crowded with fishing gear and supplies. Pictures of men holding fish they had caught were tacked to the walls.

Someone emerged from the back—an older man, but still strong and vital looking, 6 foot 1 at least, with thick arms and huge hands. He paused behind the counter, looked at Nick and said, "Yessir, you after some fresh bait?"

"Mr. Brissette?"

"Yes?"

"Ralph Brissette?" Nick imagined this man, 20 years younger, with sweat and grime on his face, his clothes damp and mud streaked, working next to Willie Carter in the Sylmar Tunnel.

"Who're you?"

"My name is Nick Carter." Nick took a couple of steps inside the shop and hesitated. "I've been looking for you for two years. I'm Willie Carter's son."

Brissette stared at Nick for a moment before he came around the counter and paused next to an upright white freezer. His deep brown eyes seemed to cloud up. He opened the freezer door, which released a cold mist, and said, "You want squid strips, anchovies, some shrimp? How about worms? We got night crawlers, lug worms, whatever you need."

"No, I—" Nick began. He felt the draft of cool air from the freezer.

Brissette closed the door and came across the wooden floor. He stood directly in front of Nick. His hands hung at his sides and he clenched them into fists. "Who the hell you say you are?"

Nick looked up at Brissette, who was several inches taller. "Willie Carter's son. The miner." He tried to steady his voice. "The man you worked with in the Sylmar Tunnel. He was my father."

Brissette gave Nick a cold stare. Traffic whined outside on the Coast Highway. An automobile honked. A truck's diesel air horn responded. The compressor in the freezer kicked in and filled the room with a humming sound. Over everything, Nick heard his pulse pounding in his ears. For the first time, he noticed the faint marine odor in the shop, a mixture of stale fish and saltwater air.

Brissette shook his head and said, "I don't know who you are, but you sure as hell aren't Willie Carter's son. No way."

"I am," Nick protested. "My name's Nick Carter. I'm Willie Carter's son."

"You're not." Brissette took another step toward Nick. Now they were a foot apart. "Willie was a black man, like me. And he never had a son. He had two little girls. Girls, not boys."

Brissette might as well have hit him in the stomach with his fist. Nick's mind turned itself inside out; his gaze bounced around the store, landing on fishing nets hanging from the walls, a glass case with fishing reels, shelves full of lures, a rack of surf-casting rods, and the carved coconut heads dangling from the ceiling. Nick felt unsteady, as if the floor was falling away. He backed up and collided with a small refrigerator. He opened his mouth to speak, but no words came out.

"Willie Carter's son, my ass."

"Mister Brissette, I…"

"Look at the color of your eyes, man. They're pale blue. No black man has eyes that color." Brissette glared at Nick for a moment, then his face softened. "What's your first name again?"

"Nick."

"Well, Nick, you don't look so good," he said, and opened the small refrigerator. "You want a beer?"

"No… no thanks." It was all Nick could say. He was still trying to get his mind around what Brissette had just said to him. He felt deflated, as though his body had shrunk. When he'd entered the bait shop a few minutes earlier, he was a grown man, a firefighter. Now he felt like a child again—a small child, still searching for answers to the same old questions about his father.

Brissette took a beer for himself and opened it. "C'mon outside, let's get some fresh air."

Nick followed Brissette through the storage room, out the back door of the bait shop, and onto the gravel parking area surrounded by the black barrels. Pickups, open jeeps and retro vans painted in psychedelic colors filled the neighboring motel parking lot. Surfers stood around in groups, talking, waxing their surfboards, and pulling on their wet suits. Nick watched several of them as they dodged the traffic and walked across the highway to the beach.

Brissette paced around on the gravel and looked at Nick's T-shirt. "So you work for the County Fire Department?"

Nick nodded.

"I was a fireman in the Navy. The biggest blaze I ever fought was when an oil depot ignited. A lot of thick black smoke."

"Oil burns like that," Nick said. "We're called firefighters now."

"Yeah, right, firefighters. So, you want to start at the beginning?"

"The beginning?" Nick kicked at the gravel, sending a spray of stones toward the surfers. "I'm not sure I know where the beginning is. I grew up in Fresno. I was born a few weeks after the Sylmar tunnel disaster, and when my mother thought I was old enough to understand, she told me how my father,

Willie Carter, died in the explosion. Now I'm trying to find out whatever I can about him, and I thought you were the one person who could help me."

"And your mother told you he died in the tunnel?"

"That's right."

Brissette took a swig of his beer. "I don't know what's goin' on here, but you need to go and talk to your mother again."

"Can't do it. She died four years ago."

"Well, I'm sorry to hear that, but she lied to you."

"Lied to me? From the time I was a little kid, it was the only story she told me. She said my father was a miner, working on the construction of the Sylmar Tunnel, and that he died underground when they hit a methane gas pocket and it exploded."

"Part of that is true. There was a gas explosion, and men were killed, but I'm telling you here and now that your father wasn't one of them. You're having tunnel visions."

"I saw an article from the Fresno paper. And even read a book about what happened. My father, Willie Carter, was listed among the dead."

"There was a Willie Carter who died in the Sylmar Tunnel, but like I said, he was a black man. I knew him, he was my best friend."

"Why would my mother lie to me? There's no reason—"

"How'd you find me?"

"The safety engineer, Wally Zavattero told me about how you survived. I've been looking for you." Nick was distracted for a moment by a girl in a tiny bright-blue bikini, who climbed out of a nearby car.

"Zavattero? The guy who testified in the court case?"

"Yes," Nick said, and wondered if this man Brissette could have suffered a head injury, or some other trauma in the accident. Maybe he was still impaired after all these years and didn't remember clearly. "Are you sure about Willie Carter? It was a long time ago. More than twenty years."

Brissette laughed. "Twenty years? So what? I still think about it almost every day and it seems like it happened yesterday. I knew every man on my shift. We worked together six days a week. We were the best of the best, the elite crew that made twice the footage in half the time. We drank together. We went hunting and fishing. Sometimes we even fought with each other. There's no mistake."

Nick remembered Zavattero's words, "Those men were a tough lot."

"Willie Carter was in the tunnel with me the night of the explosion," Brissette went on. "And I can tell you, there's no doubt, no mistake, no forgetting. The Willie Carter who died in that tunnel was not your father." Brissette drank from his beer bottle. "People's skin don't change color."

Nick pressed his hands against his forehead. "I can't believe I'm hearing this."

"I was working on the muck train that night. The blast flattened me. I was face down in that tunnel. I couldn't get up, and I heard some of the men screaming. The next thing, I woke up in the hospital and they told me I was the only survivor. That was two days later. I had burns, a broken arm, and several cracked ribs. There's still a spot here that isn't quite right." Brissette touched his rib cage through his shirt. "My whole body hurt; it ached for months. After I was up and around, I went to see all the families of my fallen brothers. There were thirty-four children. A total of thirty-four kids, who had to grow up without their fathers, but you weren't one of them. I sat in Willie's living room in Riverside, and watched his wife and daughters bawl their eyes out. Believe me, there was no son crying in that room."

Nick thought of his mother's words at the kitchen table. There was no doubt about what she had told him: "There was an accident, Nicky, a tragedy. Your father died underground in a methane gas explosion." Nick wished Brissette could hear her say that. How could his mother have been lying?

Brissette went on. "The worst of it was, every time I talked to someone, I knew what they were thinking—why did this guy survive? Why did he live, and my husband, or my father, or my son die? And you know what? I don't know." A tear leaked from his eye, and he brushed it away. "It's been more than twenty years, and I still have nightmares. I have bad days when I feel guilty, and sometimes when I have a good day, I feel guilty about not feeling bad. I've asked myself thousands of times, why did I survive when everyone else died?" Brissette glanced up at the empty blue sky. "I've tried to make my survival stand for something; I'm trying to live a good life and help people. I'm a caregiver at the hospital." He dabbed at his eyes.

Nick thought Brissette was about to break down. Both men were silent for a moment, then Nick said, "The money from Lockheed…"

"What about it?"

"Did every family receive a payment?"

Brissette nodded. "Every family. That's how I bought this bait shop. But we had to wait years while they fought it out in court. First I went back to work at the tunnel. That lasted a day—I couldn't do it. Then I tried driving a truck, but I couldn't even stand to be inside the cab. So I worked as a pile driver for four, five years on the Guy Atkinson barge, in the Los Angeles Harbor. Ever heard of it?"

"No."

"You know, when we were working on the tunnel, Lockheed promised us some kind of new electronic watch when we finished. We never got them. Lockheed never gave us anything. Without Zavattero we never would have collected a cent. He's a good man."

"He told me about the Lockheed payments. After I heard that, I started to wonder if my mother ever received a half million dollars. It bothered me, because I think I would have known about it. She worked and struggled every day of her life. We never had that kind of money; we never had any money at all. I don't think we ever got a payment from Lockheed."

"There you go," Brissette said. "Your father was someone else. Another person. A different Willie Carter."

"I don't understand why my mother would leave me an article about the disaster from the Fresno paper. She even circled his name in red ink."

"Maybe she wanted you to think that miner was your father."

"Maybe, but why? I don't know what to think now." Nick picked up a piece of gravel and threw it against one of the steel drums. "I grew up not knowing who my father was. Twenty-five years later, I still don't know. Now I find out my mother lied to me until the day she died."

Brissette shrugged his shoulders.

"Ever since I was a kid, I've imagined how my father died in a tunnel explosion. I dreamed about it. I invented the details. We went underground together. That's been my whole life, and it was a fucking lie."

Brissette shrugged his shoulders again. "Sorry, I don't know what to tell you."

Nick tried to smile. He stood in the parking lot of a bait shop on Pacific Coast Highway in Malibu, California—and had no idea who he was.

"You know, miners like to drink—a lot. They had beer waiting for us at the end of the shift in the dry house, even at eight in the morning. Can you imagine that happening today?" Brissette drained the last of his beer, tossed the container into a trash can, and turned to Nick. "You sure your mother's married name was Carter?"

"It's my last name."

"Ever seen your birth certificate?"

"No. Why?"

"It would have your father's name on it. Maybe his name wasn't Willie Carter. Maybe he was really... uh... John Doe."

"What if it does say Willie Carter? What if the name is Willie Carter?" Nick said, his voice rising. "What if my father's name really is Willie Carter?" he shouted. "Then what? What am I supposed to do? Track down every Willie Carter in the state? Will I ever know?" Nick paused, and realized that some of the surfers across the way were staring at him. Embarrassed, he turned away.

Brissette laid a hand on Nick's shoulder. "I don't know. Sorry I had to be the one to give you all this bad news."

Nick tried to regain his composure. After a moment of silence, he said, "Well, thanks for talking to me." He extended his hand. "I was sure I would walk away from here today with a different feeling."

Brissette shook his hand. "Let me know how it turns out, OK?"

"Yeah, I'll keep in touch."

"You want to take some ghost shrimp? I got a special goin' on ghost shrimp."

"Ghost shrimp? What do I want with ghost shrimp? I don't even know what they are. Are you supposed to eat them?"

"No, they're good for bait. This is a bait shop, remember?" Brissette pointed at his sign. "I'll give 'em to ya, free."

"Do people actually fish around here? All I see are surfers."

"Sure. They surf-cast for perch on the beach. People go out in inflatables and rowboats and bring in cabazon and bass. There's even halibut around the rocks. I don't make big bucks here, but there is a steady demand. It's my life now, and I enjoy it. Every day I remind myself how lucky I am—luckier than at least seventeen other men." Brissette turned and walked back into the bait shop. At the door he said, "Bye, Nick—you take care."

A feeling of gloom descended on Nick as he drove back toward Los Angeles. He turned off Pacific Coast Highway and parked in one of the beach parking lots. In the late afternoon, a volleyball tournament was underway on the sand. A crowd of women in bikinis and men in bright-colored shorts played at a dozen nets stretched between poles anchored in the white sand.

Nick got out of his pickup, walked past them toward the water, and stopped where the Pacific Ocean surf crashed onto the beach. He thought about what Brissette had told him. Could there be a reason for him to lie? Nick walked along the shoreline and watched the shorebirds advance and retreat with the waves, probing with their long, pointed beaks for food in the wet sand each time the surf receded. No, he decided, Brissette wasn't lying—he was too genuine, too sincere. Nick was certain he had heard the truth from him. The Willie Carter who died in the Sylmar Tunnel disaster was not his father.

TEN
June 22, 2014, 9:20 a.m.

NICK LAY ON HIS BACK. He opened his eyes and saw the familiar gray vinyl interior of a Lifeline ambulance. Was it moving? He felt no vibration, no motion. Nick tried to turn his head. He couldn't. He struggled to think clearly. What had happened? He remembered a vague feeling of plunging toward the ground. He saw fuzzy, blurred images. Nick tried to move his head again. He couldn't. He was paralyzed.

A paramedic leaned over him, his face only inches away.

"Hey," Nick said.

"Hey," the paramedic said. "Open wide, I want to look at your eyes." He shined a small light into Nick's right eye.

Nick squinted.

"Follow my finger," the paramedic said, as he moved it past Nick's nose. "OK." He did the same with Nick's other eye. "Your pupils look normal."

"Am I...?" Nick said. He checked his extremities; he tried to move his legs—they responded. He moved his right arm and flexed his fingers—a sharp, stabbing pain shot all the way up to his shoulder. "Ahhh," Nick groaned. "That really hurts." He reached for his head with his left hand, touched Velcro, and realized a C-Spine collar was wrapped tight around his neck. "I thought I was paralyzed."

"Paralyzed?" the medic said. "No, but you must have hit your head pretty hard. Even with a flight helmet, you can catch a pretty wicked blow in a crash like that."

"Crash?"

"You went down in a helicopter. Do you remember that?"

Nick searched his memory. "No. My wrist is killing me, is it broken?"

"I don't know," the paramedic said, and reached for Nick's arm.

"Ahh, don't touch my wrist."

"It's swollen. Could be a fracture, or just a bad sprain. You'll need an MRI."

Nick tried to sit up. He heard noise outside the ambulance. People. Vehicles. Barking—the deep sound of a large dog, a German shepherd.

"Lie still a minute," the paramedic said. "How do you feel?"

"I think I'm OK. My ears are ringing."

"Do you know your name?"

"Carter, Nick Carter."

"What day is it?"

"Sunday?"

"Is that a question?"

"No, I'm sure. I think." Nick's brain rebooted. "Yes, today's Sunday. I was going to ask my girlfriend to—"

"Do you know where you are?"

"No, where am I?" The ambulance had to be parked somewhere near a highway. Nick recognized the deep diesel sound of trucks. "What's going on out there?" He sat up and pulled at the C collar with his left hand. "Can you take this damn thing off? There's nothing wrong with my neck."

"Sure." The paramedic removed the collar. "I'm going to immobilize your wrist with a temporary splint."

Nick turned his head left, then right. Now he felt pain seeping into his upper body, muted at first, then growing more pronounced. It joined the pain radiating up his arm from his wrist. "The helicopter went down?" He looked at the paramedic for confirmation. "That's what happened?"

The paramedic nodded, and closed the splint around Nick's wrist.

Nick winced at the pain. "What happened to the aircrew? Are they alright?"

"They're banged up, but nothing too serious. The pilot fractured his collar bone. They should be at Olive View by now." The paramedic began to fill out a form attached to his clipboard. "When we got to you, you were lying on the ground. One of the flight crew said he dragged you out. He said you weren't strapped in when you hit."

"I don't remember the crash. How long was I unconscious?"

The paramedic checked his watch. "In the last twenty minutes, you've been in and out. That means you've got a concussion. Do you remember the ride over here? You were babbling about a black SUV."

"Where's here?" Nick heard more voices, and static from radios. He thought he heard the sound of a helicopter passing overhead. "What the hell is going on out there?"

"There's a county-wide deployment for a terrorist alert. We're parked at the staging area near the reservoir on the south side of the Jensen water plant."

The morning resurfaced in Nick's memory—the early phone call to Cindi, the JRIC meeting, the 103s. The last thing he remembered was Drakos heading into Magazine Canyon.

"You know," the paramedic said, as he looked into Nick's eyes again, "I've never seen a human with such pale blue eyes. I had a Husky with eyes that color. He got run over by a truck."

"What brought the helicopter down?"

"We were told that one of the explosives magazines in the canyon was detonated. When we went in to pull everyone out, there was a black hole in the ground, a lot of debris, and the beginning of a nasty brush fire. Quite a sight. The copter was all broken up. It must have been one helluva blast to bring it down."

Nick tried to remember the crash. His mind was blank.

"They said the water tank absorbed part of the shock. Lucky for you."

"What about my USAR gear?"

"What about it?" The paramedic shrugged. "Probably still in the wreckage. We went in behind a couple of Engines and pulled everyone out of there before anything else blew. The fire was spreading and no one was thinking salvage. We had to get in and out as fast as we could."

"I had all my equipment; and my cell phone, where's my cell phone...?" Nick patted his pockets. He felt his radio, still clipped to his belt, but his cell phone was gone. "Awww," he exclaimed.

"What?" The paramedic leaned toward him. "Wrist hurting?"

"I just remembered. I stashed my girlfriend's engagement ring in my equipment bag. I was planning to propose today. I can't believe it. I thought it would be safe."

"Well, you're alive. That's all she'll care about."

"It's probably still there."

"Could be, but you can't go back right now and look for it, if that's what you're thinking. The whole place is in flames."

Nick touched a sore spot on the side of his head and felt the swelling. "I think I need some aspirin."

"Does your head hurt?"

"Yeah, and my wrist." Nick was sure the pain in his head would fade and the swelling would go down in a day or two. His wrist was something else.

"Tylenol, no aspirin if you have a concussion," the medic said, and opened his meds kit. "As soon as I-5 reopens, we're gonna run you over to Olive View for some scans."

Nick thought about Cindi. He had to get to her. Where was she? "I can't go to the hospital right now. I've got something important to take care of with the ATF."

"Look, brother, a whack on the head is nothing to mess around with. And you may have a broken wrist. You're a firefighter, you know the drill. You've got to have a doctor take a look at you."

"Not now, I—"

"And then you go home, stay in bed for a day, and have someone check on you every two or three hours. You can't do any vigorous activity for—"

"I said, I'm not going to the hospital." Nick was getting impatient. "Not right now."

The paramedic shrugged his shoulders. "Fine, it's your decision. I can't make you go, but you're making a mistake. If you're going to do something stupid, you'll have to sign a release."

"I'm alright," Nick insisted. "Just give me something for the pain." He felt claustrophobic in the back of the ambulance. He wanted to stand up and move around. "What I need is some fresh air."

The paramedic pulled a page from his clipboard and marked it with an X in three places. "Sign."

Nick did a bad job of scribbling his name with his left hand. Now he heard sirens outside, getting closer.

The paramedic gave him two extra-strength Tylenol and a bottle of water. "You shouldn't be doing this," he said. "My partner's taking a leak. Wait for him to come back, and we'll get you to the hospital."

Nick swallowed the pills, drained the bottle, got up, and opened the back doors of the ambulance. "Thanks, I appreciate your help. Sorry about your dog."

Nick stepped out onto the broad expanse of hard-packed dirt and reached for his sunglasses, still in his shirt pocket. He felt so clumsy, using his left hand as he slipped them on. When he looked around, he thought he was hallucinating and had walked into the middle of some kind of first responder video game. At second glance, he realized everything he saw was real and it appeared as if an invasion of the water plant was about to begin. One of the JRIC contingency scenarios was playing out before his eyes. The staging area was filled with law enforcement vehicles and fire equipment. Red, orange, and blue lights flashed everywhere. Idling diesel engines rumbled and spewed clouds of exhaust. Bursts of static and the echoes of voices from emergency radio communications filled the air. Police officers, sheriff's deputies and federal agents were gathered in groups. SWAT teams in tactical gear, wearing Kevlar vests and carrying assault rifles, stood next to their armored vehicles. Men from the K-9 units tended to their dogs. A Sheriff's Department mobile communications van—a huge, square, olive-green vehicle—rumbled past and stopped in the center of the activity.

Along with the law enforcement army, fire paramedics and LifeLine ambulance EMTs waited around their vehicles. Nick saw most of the County Fire Department's HazMat task force, several Engines from 129s in Lancaster, as well as trucks from 123s and 126s in Santa Clarita. He didn't see Chief Cosgrove, but two other fire battalion chiefs stood near their extra-long SUVs, conferring with the police brass.

As Nick watched the scene in the staging area, the pain in his body faded as a sudden surge of elation swept through him. He felt euphoric. He had just survived a near-death experience! He had walked away—well, almost—from a helicopter crash. He was alive. He was invincible. He was all-powerful. Now he had to find Cindi. He wanted to embrace her. He wanted to kiss her. It didn't matter about the ring. He wanted to propose to her, ask her to be his wife, right away, even in front of all the cops, federal agents and firefighters.

Nick wondered how to reach Cindi without his cell phone. He looked around for his own USAR team, but they were nowhere in sight. He remembered his radio, pulled it from his belt, held it in his left hand and stared at it. What frequency should he use to reach the 103s? He switched to the tactical channel for local communications, and said, "This is Captain Carter, is USAR 103 in the area?" The frequency was jammed with dozens of conversations. He waited, repeated himself twice, and got no response. He switched to the command channel, but it was filled with overlapping conversations between battalion chiefs and Command and Control. It was the typical problem during any major incident—clogged radio communications at every level. Finally, Nick switched to Blue-4 and reached County Fire Department dispatch. "This is USAR Captain Carter," he said. "I'm at the deployment site near the Jensen water plant. Can you locate Task Force 103?" Nick sensed he was talking too fast.

"Just a minute," came the reply. "We're jammed here."

Nick took a couple of deep breaths, felt a surge of pain in his ribcage, and wondered exactly what had happened to him when the helicopter hit the ground. While he waited, he looked across the freeway toward Magazine Canyon, and saw flames from the brushfire and clouds of black smoke rising into the morning sky. From where he stood, he could also see all five lanes of northbound traffic on I-5 backed up behind a barricade of California Highway Patrol cars. Nick wondered if the closure was a result of the explosion in Magazine Canyon or the threat at the filtration plant. The southbound lanes were deserted as well, and he assumed they had been shut down farther north. I-5, the Golden State Freeway, a ribbon of asphalt running from the Mexican border to the Canadian line was the backbone of California. Now it was closed right where it intersected several other busy Los Angeles freeways. In an hour, even on a Sunday, traffic would be backed up for miles in both directions and most of Southern California would be in gridlock.

"Captain Carter," the dispatcher radioed back. "I've located Engine 103 and the rest of the USAR task force. They're caught in the northbound traffic backup on I-5 and are attempting to exit and take local streets. Estimated time of arrival at the staging area is over an hour."

"Thank you," Nick said. "Alert them to contact me by radio when they arrive." He rubbed his eyes and felt a throbbing in his head. The Tylenol wasn't making any difference yet, and he thought he ought to drink some more water. The euphoria he had felt just a few minutes ago was beginning to fade. He was slowing down and pain was creeping into his body.

Nick walked over to one of the HazMat trucks, the "Box," which carried protective gear, gas meters and other equipment. "I'm Captain Carter, from 103s," he said.

"Morning, Captain." The firefighter sitting at the wheel stared at Nick. "Looks like you've already had a rough day. Were you in an accident?"

"Do I look that bad?" Nick said. "Have you got an extra bottle of water?"

"Sure." The firefighter glanced at Nick's bandaged wrist. He opened a bottle and handed it out through the open window.

"Thanks. I'm gonna get up on the back of the Box to look around for a minute. I'm trying to find someone."

"Be my guest."

Nick hoisted himself up onto the back platform of the Box, felt the pain ripple through his body again, and then climbed up to stand on the top, where he was high enough to get a view over most of the vehicles parked on the dirt. He steadied himself against the satellite dish, strained to focus his eyes, and searched the area. After a moment he saw a truck marked ATF and a black SUV, both parked on the far edge of the field, away from the rest of the activity. He thought he recognized Cindi's trim figure. Nick climbed down and headed through the maze of men and equipment toward the spot where he had seen her.

It took him several minutes to reach the edge of the staging area. As he approached, he saw two men standing near the ATF truck. One wore tan Army camouflage, a green bullet-proof vest marked "ATF–EXPLOSIVES" in gold letters on the back, and a pistol strapped to his thigh. He was talking to another man, much smaller, wearing blue work clothes. Cindi was several yards away, standing by the open rear door of the SUV, leaning in and talking to someone inside.

Nick called out, "Cindi."

She looked up, shouted, "Nicky," and came running toward him. "Are you OK? I tried to call you. I couldn't find out what happened after the helicopter went down." She grabbed him in a bear hug. "I'm glad you—"

"I lost my phone in the crash," he said, and held her in a tight embrace, grimacing at the pain in his ribs. He felt her taught, muscular body and her breasts pressed against his chest. Her lips brushed his cheek. It felt so good to hold her. He thought of their night together. It already seemed long ago.

Cindi pulled away to look at him and wiped away a tear running down her cheek. "I was so worried about you. I didn't know what to do. It was chaos. Are you alright?" She looked at his wrist.

"I'm fine. I banged my head pretty hard and hurt my wrist." Nick looked at her face. She had scratches and blood oozing across her forehead and on one cheek. "What happened to you?"

"I had a run-in with one of the twins in the brush."

"The twins?"

"The brothers, remember? Duane and Dwight. He's cuffed in the SUV and I was just about to swab his hands for residue." She hugged him again, said, "I'm so glad you're safe," and turned back to her prisoner.

The ATF man in the bullet-proof vest approached Nick. "Captain Carter?" The man had a voice like gravel.

"Call me Nick."

"Daniels, ATF Explosives." He extended his hand, then noticed Nick's wrist splint.

Nick saw that Daniels had played with one too many explosive devices. His right hand only had three fingers and a thumb; his pinkie finger was gone. His skin had scars running up to his elbow, and the right side of his cheek showed a series of small pockmarks that two days' growth of beard couldn't hide. Daniels looked like he might be 40, old enough to have handled a lot of bombs. He was tall, his muscles had muscles, and he had the high and tight haircut Nick associated with the military. Daniels could have stepped right out of a Special Forces movie—one that featured bad-ass warrior types who did nothing but bench-press 400 pounds in their spare time. He dwarfed the smaller man standing next to him.

"This is Gene Morris," Daniels said. "He's a field engineer from the MWD."

Nick shook Morris's hand. The engineer had all his fingers and the skin on his hand was soft and pale. He was in his early 50s, thin, nearly bald, and wore wire-rim glasses. If Daniels was the anti-hero in a movie, Morris looked like the accountant who supervised the film's budget. In fact, the film was probably way over budget, because Morris didn't look happy. He had a worried look on his face and creases across his brow.

"Glad to see you're still in one piece," Daniels said to Nick. "I've seen my share of copters shot down, but I've never even heard of one that crashed because it sucked in debris from an explosion. Your pilot must have done a helluva job."

"Debris?" Nick said.

"One of the black powder magazines, a brick storage building, blew. Once our explosives team gets in there, we'll know what the setup was. The preliminary report is that there's no indication of the remains of a vehicle, so that would rule out an ANFO bomb." Daniels glanced toward the SUV. "My bet is that one of our twins managed to get hold of a sheet of C4 and detonated it next to the storage unit."

"You were on the helicopter they brought down?" Morris said.

Nick nodded.

"Was anyone hurt?" Morris asked.

"Some broken bones," Nick said. "And a multimillion-dollar aircraft was destroyed. The County Fire Department isn't gonna be happy about that."

"It was like the Fourth of July—shock and awe," Daniels said. "Flash powder produces a great effect. That's why they call it 'movie magic.' When it's mixed with perchlorates and aluminum dust, it gives off more energy than TNT. But you're only supposed to use a small amount, not a whole fucking bunker full. Part of the tin roof from the first explosion landed on I-5. That's almost a quarter of a mile away."

"The first explosion?" Nick said.

"The second went off about 15 minutes later," Daniels said. "That one was a just a piggy-back trailer."

"I don't remember that," Nick said. He glanced toward Cindi standing at the open rear door of the SUV. "So you got the bomber? How'd you catch him?"

"He came running out the access road to the canyon," Daniels said, "just as we were going in to look for him. Maybe his brother was supposed to pick him up after he left the explosives. He saw us and took off and we chased him through some god-awful brush. Cindi got to him first and brought him down. She's a tough one, I gotta tell you."

"Just one of the things I love about her," Nick said. The image of the lost diamond ring flashed through his mind.

"After the takedown," Daniels continued, "we tried to warn the helicopter, but we were too late. You were already circling over the magazines and then the bomb went off. You must have some extra lives, because you used one today."

Nick looked over at Cindi and the man in the SUV again. "So that's it? It's over?"

"Not exactly," Daniels said. "The other brother's still on the loose, and Cindi's trying to find out where he is. Hell, they're twins. We can't even figure out whether we caught Dwight or Duane. We'll have to fingerprint him to find out."

"Even identicals have different prints?" Nick asked.

"That's right," Daniels said. "Similar patterns, but different details."

"What do you know about these guys?" Morris said.

"They've been involved in protests about water rights up north," Daniels said. "The family owns a farm on the Sacramento River Delta and the father died recently at a demonstration. Things got violent and in the middle of it all, he had a heart attack."

"So what are the brothers after?" Nick asked. "Are they trying to blow up the water plant?"

"Who knows?" Daniels said. "Jensen's enormous and the perimeter security isn't great. One of them could have gone over the fence in the middle of the night and left a bomb. Or maybe he's driving around right now with a pile of ANFO or some other kind of bomb in the back of his van. Maybe they just want to get their name in the paper."

"What about the trash truck?" Nick said. "Did they find it?"

"What trash truck?" Morris said.

"I don't think a trash truck was ever involved," Daniels said. "JRIC's problem is TMI—too much information, and too much imagination. This isn't Al Qaeda filling up a Waste Management front-loader with fertilizer and going on a jihad. We're dealing with two homegrowns driving an old white van. Cindi thinks this is all tied in to the water dispute up north. They've just taken it to another level."

"I never thought two farm boys could cause so much trouble," Morris said. "They've brought everything to a standstill. We had to shut down the whole Jensen water system and evacuate everyone but the emergency crew. That explosion was—"

Nick looked at Morris. "Don't I know you?"

Morris stared back at Nick.

"Didn't you speak at one of the County USAR drills a few years ago?" Nick said. "About tunnel safety and gas risks?"

"Yes," Morris said. "For a while, I was doing it twice a year."

"What's your involvement with this?" Nick asked him.

"I was on call for emergency response at Jensen today," Morris said.

A blast of sirens from the freeway interrupted their conversation. Nick looked over to see a convoy of vehicles with flashing lights heading up the empty part of I-5 toward the filtration plant. Black trucks marked LAPD BOMB SQUAD led the way, followed by other vehicles, some armor plated, from the ATF and Sheriff's Department. Nick recognized the big black and silver semi-trailer, carrying the round bomb containment vessel. It looked like a cement-mixer.

"Explosives teams and bomb-sniffing dogs," Daniels said. "Been there and done that. If there's any possibility one of our twins planted a bomb somewhere inside Jensen, they're gonna have to search the entire plant. A painstaking job; it'll take forever."

They heard Cindi curse. "Dammit, keep quiet for a minute and listen to me."

The three men edged closer to the SUV to listen to Cindi question her prisoner, whose hands were cuffed to a metal ring mounted inside the rear doorpost. Nick got a good look at the man sitting on the rear seat. He was young; Nick guessed he hadn't hit 30, and he had wild black hair and a beard to match. He wore jeans, a sweatshirt, and the high-top desert boots that American troops wear. His tanned skin said he spent most of his time outdoors. His hands were rough looking and he had dirty fingernails. Nick watched him squirm around. He pulled at his cuffs, and blood dripped through the broken skin on his wrists. He was agitated, full of energy, and couldn't sit still. His left foot tapped out a staccato beat against the floor of the SUV and Nick wondered if he might be high on something.

"You want to tell me your name," Cindi said. "Which one are you? Duane? Dwight?"

The twin replied with a hateful glare.

"You're from Bethel Island, right?" Cindi softened her tone as she spoke. "I know where that is. It's near the State Recreation Area in the Delta, right? I'm from Sacramento. It's a beautiful place."

"Beautiful?" he said. "It won't be when they drain away our water." His foot continued its beat.

"I understand how you feel, but—"

"Fuck you. You don't understand anything. You're a cop."

"Actually, I'm a federal agent. ATF."

"Big fucking difference." He looked up at Nick and stared at him with hatred in his eyes. "Who's this asshole? Is he another—?"

"Hey!" Cindi interrupted him. "Stop running your damn mouth and listen to me."

He glared at Cindi again. "You can't arrest me, I'm just standing up for my rights. People are stealing our water. The water belongs to the farmers who live on the Delta, not to fucking Los Angeles."

Nick saw Cindi's face tighten. She clenched her jaw and he could see she was getting pissed.

She narrowed her eyes, bent down, and looked into her prisoner's face. "You just set off a bomb. That's terrorism. It's against the law. Now you're under arrest and you're in federal custody. Do you understand that?"

"We're just developing our demolition techniques," the twin said, "In case they decide to dig the new water tunnels."

Cindi glanced quickly at Nick and Daniels, and then said, "You can't start blowing things up just because you're upset about the water supply. Where's your twin brother?"

"None of your damn business. Federal custody? Think either one of us is afraid of fucking federal custody?"

Morris paced around next to the SUV. He glanced at the fire in the canyon. He stared at I-5. He gazed up at the sky. The only thing he didn't look at was the man cuffed inside the SUV. Morris' brow was furrowed and Nick heard him mumbling to himself.

"What?" Nick said.

"History repeats itself," Morris said.

"What does that mean?" Nick said.

"It's Owens Valley a hundred years later," Morris said. "People in one place taking water from people living somewhere else."

"Lemme go, bitch. Take off the cuffs."

Cindy took a deep breath and exhaled. "The cuffs aren't coming off. Now, we can do this the easy way, or the hard way. You're in big trouble. We need some cooperation. It's your choice. Do yourself a favor. Tell me where your brother is. Is there anyone else helping you?"

"Fuck you, bitch. My brother and I lived through a suicide bombing in Afghanistan. You think you can scare me?"

"Looks like it's gonna be the hard way," Daniels said. "I'll probably have to cut off a couple of his fingers."

"What?" Morris looked at Daniels. He stopped pacing around, took off his wire rim glasses and began to clean them.

Daniels gave Morris a serious look, then laughed, and said, "Just kidding. We don't do that anymore; it's way too messy. We'll just take him somewhere and water-board him."

Morris put his glasses back on.

Nick thought this might be the most exciting day of Morris' dull life, and he didn't seem to be handling it very well. He looked very unhappy.

"I can understand why this guy is upset," Morris said. "The pumping station up in the Delta is destroying the ecosystem. Now they want to dig two 30-mile tunnels to divert more water down here."

Nick remembered something else from the haze of the early morning—the *Times* article Lawson had given him before he left the station. "How do you dig a thirty-mile tunnel?" he asked Morris.

"They've developed some awesome tunnel boring equipment," Morris said. "The machines are the size of locomotives. They can run twenty-four-seven with just a couple of operators."

"Last chance," Cindi said to her prisoner. "You're headed for some serious time in prison. Do you understand that? Help us out here."

Nick thought Cindi was doing a great job of controlling her frustration. Knowing her, he was certain she was ready to strangle the guy.

"I got nothing to tell you," the twin said. "You want me to say something? Call the press. I'll talk to a TV station. Call Channel Seven. Get the pretty blonde. The one with the tits. I'll tell her what's going on up in the Delta." He drummed his left foot on the floor of the SUV.

"He'll be singing a different tune," Daniels said, "when he finds out how many years he's facing."

"Last chance," Cindi said. "Otherwise we're finished."

"Let me loose, bitch," he snarled. He twisted on the seat and tried to kick Cindi, but was held secure by the cuffs.

She stepped back.

"That's one nasty farmer," Nick said.

"They were in the Army for a short time," Daniels said. "They barely escaped being killed by a suicide bomber and were discharged for combat stress. Of course, since they're twins, they both have PTSD issues."

"When was that?" Nick asked.

"I think about a year ago. You know, by the time they come home, most of the troops have learned how to make EODs—explosive ordinance devices. I'm thinking the twins used a battery and a washing machine timer for ignition in Magazine Canyon."

Cindi turned to the three men and shook her head. "I'm done. I'm not getting anything out of this asshole. I don't even know which one he is." She came closer to Nick. "How are you feeling?" She looked into his eyes. "Are you sure you're alright?"

"I'm fine, really, I just have a headache." The manic, hyper feeling he had felt earlier was completely gone now. In its place, Nick was beginning to feel drained. His body hurt and he felt a pressure inside his head. It throbbed.

"Thank God you're alive," Cindi said. "You could have been killed."

"What are you… uh… going to do with him?" Morris asked Cindi.

"I already told you," Daniels said. With both hands, he poured an imaginary bucket of water.

Cindi gave Daniels a puzzled look and said, "As soon as I can get some transport, he's headed to a holding cell in our Glendale field office. He'll probably call a lawyer, and then the pros can question him. In the meantime, we've got to figure out where his twin is and if there's anyone else involved."

They moved away from the SUV and Nick said, "Maybe it's all over. Maybe the other one got spooked and took off for Montana."

"And maybe pigs can fly," Cindi said, "My bet is they have another target. The explosion in the canyon didn't do much but stop traffic. They're not making a statement about water problems by detonating a magazine full of movie explosives. It was something to keep us busy while they go after their real target. The question is, what is it?"

"Go after something else?" Morris said. "Like what?" He fiddled with his glasses.

"I don't know," Cindi said. "All we know is that our informant told us they were planning a bombing. I assume it's water related."

"Informant?" Morris said. "You have an informant? Who's your informant?"

"That's not something I can share that with you," Cindi said. The emergency tone on her cell phone rang.

Nick looked at his watch. It was 10:45 a.m. So much had happened in the six hours since that same tone had awakened them in her bedroom. He rubbed the side of his head again.

"Agent Burns." Cindi held the phone to her ear. "Oh, no... you bet I'll tell him. Thanks for the update." She put her cell phone in her pocket. "Well, the twins are in more trouble. There's been an accident on I-5. A car rear-ended a big rig and two people were killed. That's a felony-murder." She turned to the SUV. "Hear that twin brother? Now you're in it up to your eyeballs. You just committed murder."

"Nooo," Morris said.

"Yes," Cindi said.

"I'll bet this is the biggest thing that's happened to the MWD since the methane explosion in the Sylmar Tunnel," Nick said.

"Explosion in the Tunnel?" Morris said.

"Yeah," Nick said. "In seventy-one."

Morris stood with his mouth open. "Methane," he repeated. The furrow on his brow became the Grand Canyon. "Oh my God!" he said and looked toward the canyon. "I just thought of something."

"What?" Daniels said.

"Do you think it's safe to go up into the canyon?" Morris asked.

"No, it's not," Nick said. "Not with the fire and all the explosives."

"There's a shaft that vents gas from the Sylmar Tunnel," Morris said. "I've got to get a look at it."

"What about it?" Nick asked.

Morris ignored his question. "I need high-powered binoculars. There's a back road. If I can get part way up, I may be able to look down into the canyon."

"I've got a scope on my rifle," Daniels said. "Think you could use that?"

"Sure," Morris said.

"There's a brush fire burning up there," Nick said. "Can't this wait?"

"No," Morris said, "It can't."

"You could get trapped in the fire," Nick said. "You might get in there and have the whole hillside explode in flames." Nick thought of his friend Tony Santa Cruz who was burned in a brush fire. He was on the side of a mountain, the wind reversed direction, and he was caught in a burnover. Morris wasn't even a firefighter and Nick didn't have time to teach him about wildland fire. He simply said, "That brush probably hasn't burned in twenty-five years, be careful."

Morris didn't hear him. He had Daniels' rifle scope in his hand and was already walking to his truck.

ELEVEN
December 1998

A HARD, COLD DECEMBER RAIN blew against the windows of Station 125 in Calabasas when C Shift sat down for the morning briefing. Captain Dave Sarrano had just dumped three scrambled eggs onto his plate when Nick burst in and announced, "I got the call. I'm going to USAR."

"Right this minute?" Tony Santa Cruz said. "Not even gonna finish your shift?"

"Not today, asshole," Nick said. "The Department notified me they're beginning a build-up of the USAR Task Force. There's several openings, and my name's near the top of the waiting list. Sometime next fall."

"Well, that's great, Nick," Santa Cruz said. "You deserve it." The other men around the table chimed in with their congratulations.

Santa Cruz considered Nick one of his closest friends. They graduated together from the County Fire Academy, Class of 1993. From day one at the Academy, Santa Cruz remembered Nick's intense, single-minded desire to be on one of the search and rescue teams. When most of the other cadets were just worried about getting through the Academy—surviving the physical challenges and learning the basic firefighter's skills—Nick was already planning for his future in USAR. His strength, relatively small size, and experience in underground spaces made him a natural for the tunnel and confined space drills.

Santa Cruz' own career path at the fire department hadn't been so simple. Ten months after graduation, he was caught in a burnover while battling a brush fire in the Angeles National Forest. On a hellish day when the Santa Ana winds were blowing and thousands of acres had burned, he was part of a wildland crew cutting line on a mountainside. When a wall of angry flames roared up toward them, Santa Cruz was the farthest down the side of the mountain and was trapped. He suffered deep-tissue burns to his face, arms, and upper body. Much of the cartilage in his ears melted, his nose needed reconstruction and his face was badly scarred. Months of painful skin grafts and rehabilitation followed.

Nick visited regularly, telling him, "Tony, I'm here for you. You can get through this," and Santa Cruz credited Nick with getting him through the most difficult period of his life. He eventually emerged from his ordeal with a patched face and misshapen ears, but was able to return to his career as a firefighter. Now he was sharing the C Shift at 125s with his old buddy.

"Yup," Nick said, and leaned back in his chair. "I'm on my way." After all the years, his goal of joining the USAR team was almost within his grasp. When the call came the previous day, he decided it marked the beginning of a new part of his life. His future was starting to take shape. After the conversation with Ralph Brissette led to a dead end, Nick decided to concentrate on building his own life and shake off his preoccupation with his father's identity. This morning, in spite of the wet winter weather, he still felt the optimism and thought about his sunny future as part of a USAR team.

In the early evening, C Shift was gathered around the conference table, eating dinner. When the station telephone rang, one of the men jumped up to answer it. "Engineer Foster, Station 125," he said. "Firefighter Carter? Nick Carter? Sure, hold on please." Foster looked at Nick and held out the receiver.

Nick took the telephone and went to the other end of the room, stretching the long cord. "This is firefighter Carter." No one had ever called him on the station phone.

"I have a collect call from Pleasant Valley Prison," the operator said. "Will you accept the charges?"

"What? Pleasant Valley Prison?"

"Yes, in Coalinga, California. Will you accept the charges?"

"I don't know anyone at Pleasant Valley Prison. Who's calling?"

"Just a moment," the operator said. She was back on the line in just a few seconds. "It's a collect call from Willie Carter. He says he's your father."

"Who?" The strength drained from Nick's body; his legs were rubber. He leaned against the wall for support.

"Willie Carter is calling."

"Willie Carter?" Nick gasped. This wasn't possible. He clutched the receiver and said, "Uh… operator… ma'am… you're calling a County fire station, I can't accept a collect call."

The line again went silent for a moment before the operator returned. "The calling party wants to know if there is another number where you can be reached."

Nick stretched the long cord of the receiver to its limit and turned his back to the men at the other end of the room. "Reached? My number?" Nick knew he sounded like an idiot. "My number…is…uh…" Now he couldn't even remember his own number. "It's…uh… 818-745- 4347…no, 4743."

"818-745-4743?" the operator repeated.

"Yes, that's it." Nick's voice was almost a whisper.

"Thank you," she said. The line went dead. Nick stood motionless, stupefied, holding the receiver and listening to the empty line.

"Nick," Captain Serrano asked, "What's up? You alright?"

Nick hung up the receiver and returned to the table. "No. No, I'm not." He sat down and held his head in his hands.

"What?" Serrano asked.

"Someone who says he's my father just called me… from Pleasant Valley Prison."

There was a loud silence at the table. Finally, one of the men said, "I thought your father died in some kind of a tunnel explosion."

"Yeah, he did," Nick said.

"Where's Pleasant Valley Prison?" another firefighter asked. "I never heard of it."

"The operator said Coalinga." Nick pulled out his cell phone and held it in his shaking hand. He looked at it as though he expected it to ring at any second, but it remained silent, and he put it away. The other men at the table concentrated on eating their dinner while Nick pushed the food around his dinner plate with his fork until he decided he wasn't hungry. He got up from the table and said, "Guys, I think I'll skip dinner."

Nick retreated down the hall to one of the small, windowless rooms at the back of the station. He lay down on his bed with his back propped against the wall, listened to the rain pound against the roof, and tried to comprehend what had just happened. Pleasant Valley Prison, he thought. My father is at Pleasant Valley Prison in Coalinga?

His thoughts were interrupted by the tones: *Station 125. Engine 125 and Squad 5125 respond to car over the side off Las Virgenes Canyon Road. Two miles west of Piuma. Sheriff on scene.*

Nick jumped up and ran out to the locker room. He was thankful—a dangerous, high-angle extraction in a dark, muddy, rain-soaked canyon was better than lying in the dry warmth of his room and thinking about his father. He grabbed his yellows and ran into the equipment bay along with the other men.

The minute the doors opened and the Engine rolled out, the rain drummed against the roof of the cab. The paramedic squad followed right behind them as they headed to a spot three miles into a steep canyon. The 88s in Malibu would also be called out, but they were at the other end of the canyon, a dozen miles away. The USAR squad from 103s—Nick's future home, he hoped—would also respond, but they were more than an hour away in this weather.

The Engine entered the canyon and Nick slipped his headphones off for a moment to listen to the water pounding against the windshield and the slapping of the big wipers.

Pleasant Valley Prison?

After a full day of rain, gushers fell onto the road from the steep hillsides. The Engine slowed and swerved several times to skirt mudslides and bowling-ball-sized rocks lying in the treacherous pavement.

"Can we get some light on this?" the deputy sheriff said, his eyes reflecting the red glare of the highway flares he had placed on the road. "I can't even see a vehicle down there."

Nick looked at the spot where a vehicle had hit the guardrail and snapped off two of the thick wooden support posts. A piece of the galvanized steel railing hung out over the cliff.

Captain Serrano walked to the edge and pointed his light down into the canyon. It disappeared in the rain. "No way," he said. "It's too dark, and too steep for us to do an extraction in this weather. We're gonna need air support. Let's get someone down there to find out if anyone survived."

The paramedics had already moved the squad to the edge of the dirt, front bumper facing the abyss, and put blocks under the wheels. They turned on the spotlights mounted on the front of the truck and secured a rappelling line to the front bumper. One of the men buckled on his harness and slipped a medical kit over his shoulder. "Nice night to go off a cliff," he said to no one in particular.

Serrano called dispatch. "It's gonna have to be a helo extraction. Tell air ops we need a copter with a big light, and a three-hundred-foot hoist cable."

The rain cascaded off Nick's helmet and down the front of his Nomex jacket as he stood by the Engine gazing out into the darkness.

Pleasant Valley Prison?

A second sheriff's car arrived. The deputy joined the group clustered at the edge of the canyon and asked, "Do we know what kind of vehicle it is?"

"Negative," someone answered.

"How many people inside?"

"Undetermined."

"Fatalities?"

"We have a paramedic on the way down."

Engine 88 and another paramedic squad arrived from Malibu. A minute later, a LifeLine ambulance appeared. Behind the ambulance, a battalion chief rolled up, parked on the dirt, stepped out into the pouring rain, and took charge. The crowd of first responders stood at the edge of the canyon, waiting for a report from the paramedic who had rappelled down. In the headlights, the reflective tape on their gear created a maze of glowing white and yellow lines.

Several minutes later, the paramedic appeared out of the dark abyss. "It's an ugly wreck," he said, and climbed back up onto the road. "Two males, both deceased. It's a compact car, I don't know how many times it rolled, but it's upside down. The roof compressed and they're crushed in their seats. We're gonna need the Jaws, and it'll be a bitch to cut them out. The vehicle's on a steep slope and it's unstable. We're gonna have to crib it." He disconnected his line and took off his vest, then reached into the medical bag slung over his shoulder and handed two wallets to one of the deputies. "I got these."

The deputy opened the first one and shined his light on a driver's license. "Nelson Powers, 48." He looked inside the second wallet. "Brian Powers, 19." He paused for a moment. "Both from the same address in Malibu. Probably a father and son."

"Who knows," the paramedic said.

"Sad," the deputy said.

Nick agreed, it was sad, but at least the son knew his father, and they spent their last moments together. That counted for something, Nick thought, but didn't utter a word. No one would understand.

The 103s finally arrived with the USAR semitrailer, and the heavy rescue crane arrived moments later. The battalion chief briefed them. "No survivors," he said. "Nothing to do tonight; too dangerous in the dark."

The USAR captain agreed. "We'll come back in the daylight," he said.

"I'll cancel the bird," the battalion chief said.

Through the rain Nick looked at the USAR mascot—the rhino in a hard-hat—painted on the side of the trailer. Before the evening phone call from Pleasant Valley, it would have thrilled him just to see it. Tonight he was numb.

Nick lay on his bed at the station again and looked at the glowing numerals of his watch. It was 2:40 a.m. They had returned four hours ago and he was still wide awake. In his mind, he replayed the operator's words: *"Willie Carter. He says he's your father."* Nick thought of all his childhood fantasies about the man with the indistinct face and the pale blue eyes, the man who had died in a tunnel explosion. Wally Zavattero had asked him, "What did your mama do with the money?" Ralph Brissette had told him, "Your mother's lying." Nick realized he had spent the last few years in denial, floating along, not wanting to face the fact that his father didn't die in the Sylmar Tunnel. Now his father had called him from prison. Nick couldn't hide any longer.

He knew it would be a night without sleep. "Aw, screw it," he muttered, got out of bed, pulled on his jeans and a T-shirt, and went into the kitchen. In the faint glow of a single bulb, Nick took some juice from the refrigerator, sat down and put his bare feet up on the conference table.

"Nick." Santa Cruz emerged from the darkness and joined him at the table.

"What're you doing up at this hour?" Nick said.

"Can't sleep. I kept imagining the poor guys in the car at the bottom of the canyon. Trapped out there in the darkness and rain; waiting to be brought in. You?"

"Just thinking."

"About the call? Was that really your father ? I mean…"

"I don't know, Tony, I guess it was."

"I don't get it."

Nick took his feet off the table and sat up in his chair. "There's stuff I never told you. I found out years ago that the families of the men killed in the Sylmar Tunnel got compensation, like almost a half million dollars each. I'm sure we never got any money."

"Maybe your mother—"

"No, not possible. We were poor. If she ever had that kind of money, I would have known about it. When she died, she left me four grand. That's all. Four thousand dollars, and who knows what she gave up to save it."

"So your father's in prison?"

The rain outside stopped, the hammering on the roof ended, and the station grew silent. Nick lowered his voice. "There's something else. I talked to the one miner who survived the explosion. You know what he told me? He said the Willie Carter who died in the tunnel was black. A black man. That couldn't have been my father."

"This is really fucked up."

"Years ago, I ordered a copy of my birth certificate. I had to call the Hall of Records in Fresno County. I wanted to see whose name was on it. I thought maybe my father might have some other name."

"What? Like Jimmy Carter?" Santa Cruz gave Nick a weak smile.

Nick emptied his glass of juice and was silent for a moment. "The name was Willie Carter. That's my dad's name for sure. But apparently not the Willie Carter who died in the tunnel explosion."

"So why don't you talk to this guy who called, and find out what's what?" Santa Cruz grinned. "Maybe he stole a million bucks and he wants to tell you where it's buried."

"Uh huh, and I'm the King of England. If my father's really in prison, do I want to know about it?"

"What choice do you have?"

"I suppose you're right." Nick got up and paced around, barefoot, in the semi-darkness of the meeting room. "But I think I like the original story, the one where he died in a tunnel explosion, even if it's not true. At least that Willie Carter was a decent guy. I even imagined him as some kind of a hero. I don't want to have a father who's in prison."

"Listen Nick, when I had my accident, I thought my life was over. You're the one who kept me going, you're the one who convinced me I had a future."

"What's that got to do with anything?"

"You can't let this thing with your father take up your whole life. You're you. You have your own future. A good one. I mean, you're going to USAR, that's what you've always wanted to do. It doesn't matter who your father is. That was then, this is now. Understand? He doesn't matter."

"No, he does matter. He matters a lot." Nick turned to look at his friend. "It took me a long time to understand myself, and you know why I want to be in USAR? The real reason?"

"No, why?"

"Because I always thought somehow I could make things right. You know? I was going to save other people because my father died with a bunch of miners in a tunnel disaster where there was no rescue possible. Isn't that crazy?"

Santa Cruz nodded. "Yeah, like I said, this is really fucked up."

Nick stood up and started back to his room. "Who knows why he's in prison anyway? I don't want to find out my father's been sitting in a jail cell all these years for doing something terrible. What if he's a sex offender? What if he molested children?"

"What if he ran over a grandmother in a DUI?" Santa Cruz said.

The clock showed 3:55 a.m. The rain was coming down hard again. Nick was back in bed, his eyes open, staring up into the darkness. Scenes from his childhood passed before his eyes, and the sound of the rain prompted the recollection of a lost memory—the rainy day in Fresno when visitors came to the small apartment where he lived with his mother. When the doorbell rang, she looked out through the peephole and became agitated. No, she wasn't agitated, she was frantic. "Go to your room," she ordered Nick. "Now. And close the door." Before he even got down the hall, Nick heard her at the door, shouting, "Go away. I talked to you once, that's enough. Leave me alone. Don't bother us." Nick went into his bedroom and stood at the window while the rain beat against the glass. He watched three strangers trudge back out to the street. Their blue van had a large sun painted on the side, and underneath it said THE BAKERSFIELD CALIFORNIAN. Nick thought of what the woman at his mother's funeral told him—" We were friends, twenty years ago, in Bakersfield."

Nick rolled over on his bed and realized that sooner or later he would have to make a trip to Pleasant Valley Prison in Coalinga.

TWELVE
June 22, 2014, 11:55 a.m.

NICK GAZED UP AT THE hills above Magazine Canyon and thought they should never have let Morris go up there alone. After a dry spring and an early summer of single-digit humidity, the chaparral and manzanita on the hillsides was bone dry and waiting for an excuse to burn. The fire started by the explosions in the canyon had climbed higher and it was now burning just below the ridgeline. As the burn worked its way up, it moved beyond the mild breeze drifting through the canyon and into the strong onshore wind raking the tops of the mountains. Black smoke, a sign of incomplete combustion from a fast moving brushfire, billowed into the air. The wind was blowing eastward, just as the woman from Health Services at the JRIC meeting had predicted, but instead of carrying a toxic cloud of chlorine gas into the San Fernando Valley, it was pushing a tide of fire through the 10-foot-high brush. The first populated area in the path of the flames was Sylmar, four miles away.

Nick tried to get a report on the fire, but couldn't get through all the emergency traffic on his radio. He walked back across the hard-packed dirt to the HazMat Box.

The same firefighter was still there, sitting behind the wheel. He nodded to Nick. "How you doin'?" he asked.

"Not bad," Nick said, although his head was pounding and the Tylenol the paramedic had given him hadn't helped." Carrying any Tylenol?"

"No, but I got some aspirin, if you want it."

"No thanks. I'm not supposed to take aspirin." As Nick spoke, a shock wave of sound thundered through the air. The pressure of the concussion hit his eardrums and a surge of pain shot through his head.

"Mother!" the firefighter exclaimed.

Nick turned to see an expanding ball of flame and smoke billowing up from Magazine Canyon.

"What a bitch," the firefighter said. "More explosives?"

"Every one of those magazines is probably going to blow when the flames get to them."

"How many are there?"

"That's a good question." Nick reached into his shirt. The two pages from the JRIC binder were still there, plastered against his chest. He pulled them out and looked at the diagram of Magazine Canyon. "Looks like a total of eight," he said. "Three down and five to go." Nick folded the pages and stuffed them back into his shirt pocket.

"After the bomb squad gets organized in the water plant," the firefighter said, "we're supposed to get the call to set up our air monitoring equipment on the perimeter. That means we're gonna be right across the highway from all those explosions." Static and conversation erupted from the radio in his truck and interrupted him. He turned the speaker down.

"What's the size up on the brush fire?" Nick asked.

"Forty-two acres, spreading fast, and headed east. They're trying to knock it down before the wind pushes it into Sylmar. Dispatch deployed an augmented wildland response."

An augmented wildland response was usually reserved for extreme fires during Santa Ana wind conditions, when flames could quickly get out of control. At least 200 firefighting personnel, and helicopters and fixed-wing water tankers would be involved in such a call. Nick thought again about Morris and wondered where he was and if he had been anywhere near the last explosion. With any luck, he had given up trying to get up near the ridge.

"But there's a logistical problem," the firefighter continued. "Nothing's flying because of the alert, and less than half the equipment is on scene because the freeways are all backed up. They're calling for mutual aid to come in from the Ventura County side."

As the firefighter spoke, Nick saw Morris' pickup turn off the road and churn up a cloud of dust as it bumped across the dirt. The white vehicle was covered with ash from the fire.

"Thanks for the info," Nick said, and walked back to hear what Morris had to report. He looked at his watch. It was almost noon.

By the time Nick reached them, Morris was already out of his truck, holding the rifle scope in one hand while he spoke to Cindi and Daniels. "I've never even been close to a brush fire before," he said. "The flames were huge, and the heat... I'll take my chances in a gassy tunnel any day."

"You're lucky you weren't there when that last magazine went off," Nick said.

"What did you find out?" Cindi asked Morris. "We've spent an hour here waiting for you."

"This is a disaster, a real disaster," Morris said.

"What?" Cindi said.

Nick watched as she drummed her fingers on the hood of the SUV. It was something she did when she was impatient, which was most of the time.

"I think I know what they have planned," Morris said. "Where is that guy, the twin? Can I talk to him?"

"He's on his way to our field office," Cindi said. "They're probably stuck somewhere in the traffic."

"What did you see up there?" Daniels said.

"This is terrible," Morris said.

"What, dammit," Cindi said.

"They could be planning to blow up the Sylmar Tunnel," Morris said.

"Blow up the Sylmar Tunnel?" Cindi said. "That's their target?"

"You're kidding," Nick said.

"The what?" Daniels asked.

"It's an empty water tunnel," Nick said. "It starts up there in the canyon and runs east to Sylmar."

"How would they do that?" Cindi asked.

"Methane?" Nick said.

"That's right," Morris said.

"Great explosive," Daniels said. "As long as you've got enough of it."

"They've managed to block the gas vent," Morris said. He paced around. "I can't believe it. They're trying to ignite the methane in the tunnel."

"A vent?" Nick said. "How big is it?"

"About three feet across," Morris said. "And it sticks up about four feet."

"The explosions haven't flattened it?" Cindi said.

"No," Morris said. "It's sheltered by the cement structure that houses the access shaft. There's a metal grate over the top that lets the gas disperse. It's supposed to be secure, but they must have opened it and covered the vent."

"And you know this because…?" Daniels asked.

"I used your scope. Very impressive. You could probably shoot an ant off a tree limb a mile away using this thing." Morris handed it back to him. "I managed to get a look at the vent from the road running up to the ridge. It looks like these farmers attached something to the underside of the grate. They've sealed it off so the gas can't get out."

"Do you think they did it last night?" Cindi said. "There was about a four-hour window when our surveillance team lost them."

"No," Morris said. "That wouldn't be enough time for the methane to build up. They'd have to have done it months ago."

"How often does the MWD inspect the vent?" Nick asked.

"Maybe once a year," Morris said. "If we do it on schedule."

"*Once a year?*" Cindi said.

"It's not like that's all we have to do," Morris said. "The MWD ships water to eleven million people every day. You're talking about a gas vent on an empty tunnel. It's not high priority."

"Well, it is now," Cindy said. She pulled out her phone and hit the speed dial. "Get me one of the analysts.…Who is this? Davis?…This is Cindi Burns. I need whatever information you can get on the Sylmar Tunnel. It runs from Magazine Canyon through part of Sylmar. Find out the exact route. I need it ASAP, call me back."

"So if they blocked the vent months ago…" Nick said. He took a step backward, and leaned against the SUV as a wave of dizziness engulfed him.

"Enough gas could collect in the tunnel to trigger a huge explosion, maybe as big as the one 40 years ago," Morris said, finishing Nick's sentence.

Nick concentrated on keeping his balance as a feeling of nausea passed through him. He thought he might vomit.

"Nick," Cindi said, "what's the matter?"

"Just feeling a little woozy," Nick said. He didn't mention that his wrist was throbbing and radiating pain up through his arm, and he was beginning to think it was worse than just a sprain.

Cindi turned to Morris and asked, "Can't we just open the vent and let the gas clear out?"

"It's not safe to go into the canyon," Nick said.

"What if we… uh… no, I guess we couldn't," Daniels said.

"What?" Cindi said.

"I was thinking we could put a small shell into the vent and blast it open," Daniels said.

"You could," Morris said. "And you could set off an explosion that could ignite the entire tunnel."

"And there's no other vent?" Cindy asked.

"No, just this one at the high end of the tunnel," Morris said. "Methane is lighter than air; it rises. That's the only place to vent it."

"Do you really think enough gas could accumulate for an explosion?" Nick asked. The nausea had passed, but his wrist still ached and he continued to lean against the SUV.

"You bet," Morris said. "Part of the tunnel was dug through an old gas field, and there are all kinds of VOCs—volatile organic compounds—in the soil. Some of those vapors seep in through cracks in the cement lining. What's worse, an explosion in the tunnel could ignite a secondary blast of the VOCs. Then you're looking at above-ground destruction." Morris removed his glasses and polished the lenses furiously. "This is serious. These guys are crazy. I can't believe that's what they're planning to do."

"How do two farm boys get all this information?" Daniels said. "How many people even know about the Sylmar Tunnel?"

"It's available on the Internet," Morris said. "If you know what you're looking for."

"How far below ground is it?" Daniels asked.

"Close to two hundred feet," Nick said.

"No, not everywhere," Morris said. "At the East Portal, where they started digging, it begins at ground level and runs shallow, only thirty or forty feet below the surface, for almost a quarter of a mile. That's where the greatest risk of surface damage from an explosion is."

"The East Portal?" Cindi said. "Where's that?"

"It's in the middle of a Sylmar neighborhood," Nick said. "I went to see it once, twenty years ago, just after I graduated the Fire Academy."

"How would they trigger this?" Cindi asked Daniels. "Do you think they left a detonator inside the vent?"

"It's possible," Daniels said. "If they did, they could set it off anytime with a cell phone."

"Another good reason to stay out of the canyon," Nick said.

"But a blast at the top of the vent might not travel far enough down to ignite the gas in the tunnel," Daniels said, "To get a really effective explosion, you'd want your ignition device down in the horizontal part, on the floor of the tunnel. A phone signal wouldn't reach that far inside. You'd need to place a timer down there—and then get the hell out."

"There's a bulkhead that seals off the East Portal; it sticks right out of the hillside at ground level," Nick said. "What if they just detonated their van next to it?"

"That would definitely work," Daniels said.

"I think we need to get over there," Cindi said, "instead of standing here with our thumbs up our asses."

"Cindi," Daniels said, "you have such a charming way of expressing yourself."

"Morris," Cindi said, "do you have any kind of a street map, or a map of the tunnel?"

"Not with me, no," Morris said.

"Where is the East Portal?" Cindi asked. "I have to alert my SAC."

"Your sack?" Morris said.

"Special Agent in Charge," Cindi said. "My boss."

"Fenton Avenue and Maclay Street, in Sylmar," Morris said. "And I've got to notify the MWD that the tunnel could be the target. I'm sure they'll order a partial evacuation of the East Portal neighborhood." Morris looked at the fire burning in the canyon, and said, "I can't believe this is happening."

Cindi hit her speed dial. "Hello, J.J.? Did they deliver the twin yet?... No, we have no idea which one he is.... Listen, the engineer from the MWD thinks the second twin could be at the other end of the Sylmar Tunnel, possibly with a bomb.... Uh huh, it's an abandoned water tunnel. It looks like they plugged an air vent and now it's filled with methane. The engineer says there's also gas in the ground around the tunnel, so the end game here may be a big blast.... Yes.... He expects the MWD to order an evacuation of the neighborhood. It looks like Jensen may not be the target after all.... Yes.... Yes, we're headed over there right now. Can you get any resources to meet us? How about a Special Response Team?... Yeah, it's at Fenton and McCoy Streets in Sylmar."

"Maclay," Morris said. "Fenton and Maclay."

"Fenton and Maclay," Cindi repeated. "Just a minute, J.J...." She turned to Morris. "How far away are we? How long will it take to get there?"

"It's about five miles, one exit east on the 210," Morris said. He looked out at the traffic at a standstill on I-5. "I'm not sure how long it'll take."

"Did you hear that, J.J.?" Cindi said. "What's going on at Jensen?... Are they sweeping the facility? My bet is they don't find anything. Are you talking to the FBI?... Let them know and see if we can get some help at the East Portal."

"Let me say something," Nick said, and pulled her phone away with his left hand. "Hello, sir, this is Fire Captain Carter. Warn your people that there should be absolutely no gunfire. If the methane vents somehow, it could set off an explosion." He handed the cell phone back to Cindi.

"J.J., I'll check in with you when we get over there," Cindi said, and disconnected.

"What's happening?" Daniels asked.

"What do you think?" Cindi said. "The FBI's doing their own thing and not listening. They've got all their resources focused on the Jensen plant."

"Same old same old," Daniels said.

"Let's get going," Cindi said, "before I have a methane explosion on my performance record." She asked Morris, "Do you want to ride with us?"

"No, I'll take my truck," Morris said. "I need my gas meters and monitoring equipment."

Nick watched Morris begin to rummage around in the back of his pickup. He looked at all the gear: a white hardhat with the MWD logo; rolls of yellow plastic emergency tape; a laptop; and several meters and other measuring devices. Nick remembered the items that Zavaterro had stored in his garage. If Zavaterro were alive today, would he know Morris? Would they be friends? They were both tunnel safety men, but had such different temperaments. Zavattero was an intense, outspoken, take-charge guy. Morris was quiet, he seemed to be a brooder, a worrier.

Morris pulled a Draeger multi-gas detection meter from a metal case and began to calibrate it.

"Morris," Cindi said. "What are you doing? Can that wait?"

"Sure." He placed the meter back in its case. "What's the plan?" he asked Cindi.

"The plan?" Cindi said. "The plan is we follow you over to the East Portal ASAP, and find out if the twin is parked at that end of the tunnel with a bomb. If he is, we stop him. If he's not there, we'll figure out what to do next."

"Who would have thought of them planning a methane explosion?" Morris said. "Did you know, on Titan there are thousands of methane lakes?"

"Titan?" Nick said.

"It's one of the moons of Saturn," Morris said.

"Jesus," Cindi said, "Can we just get going? We haven't got time for an astronomy lesson."

THIRTEEN
May 2000

In 1994, WILLIE CARTER WAS one of hundreds of prisoners moved from Folsom Prison—like everyone else, he called it River City—down to Pleasant Valley, the new detention facility in Coalinga, a town in Central California. Willie was certain the name was meant to be a nasty joke. "The inmates thought they was goin' somewhere special," he told anyone who would listen. "Hell, it shoulda been called Flatland Fucking Nowhere Prison. They built it in Coalinga. That's nowhere for sure, just a piss-ant little town about a hundred miles from Bakersfield where I grew up."

Willie Carter had been in Folsom for more than 20 years before he was transferred. For most of that time, he lived on Unit 1, the most populous cell-block in the United States, sharing a 6-by-12 cell with another Aryan Brotherhood inmate. "We had everything we needed—two bunks, a toilet, a sink, and a hot tub," Willie would say. "Well, we didn't really don't have no hot tub, but we had runnin' water—the faucet in that stainless steel sink was drippin' before I got there." By the time Willie was transferred, he was sleeping in the old Folsom license plate factory, where about 250 beds had been set up in rows, divided by gang membership. "One thing ya didn't do, Willie said, "ya didn't go into another gang's neighborhood, even if ya was sleepwalking. Ya stayed with the men who wore yer brand. That's how ya survived."

"My kid's finally comin' to see his old man." Willie told his cellie at Pleasant Valley one morning. "Imagine that. After all the years I spent tryin' to locate him. While I was at River City, I only talked to his bitch of a mother once, and that was when she came to tell me she was divorcin' me. She goes on a rant and tells me her father was right, she never shoulda married me, and I was never gonna see my son Nick. That's all I knew about him, his first name. Finally I decided I was gonna find him. I had my whole life and nothin' else to do. And man, it did take forever to check out every Nick Carter in the state of California. If he'd moved away, I never woulda located him. It's not like I could hire a private detective, you know? So after all the years of searchin', it turns out he works at a fire station in Los Angeles. I call and then the little fucker doesn't accept the collect charges. I tried a coupla more times on his cell phone, and each time he don't accept. So I give up. I thought, what the hell, I got along all these years without him; I don't really need to see the little shit. Except, after all, he is my son, my own flesh and blood, and that's important. I'm his father and he owes me. If he don't wanna talk to me or see me, he can still send me a few bills. Right? He has a job. Firemen get paid good. A couple a hundred dollars would go a long way. Five hundred dollars would make me, like, a king in the A Yard. But then I don't hear from him, and finally I give up and think, fuck him, FUCK HIM. Then, six months later, surprise. He's comin'! He's comin' to visit his old man. I always say, families gotta stick together. I'm gonna see my kid!"

From the time his father called Nick at Station 125, a year and a half passed before he gathered the courage to visit Pleasant Valley. He changed his mind a half-dozen times, looked for any excuse not to make the trip, and finally decided he might as well get it over with.

"They had a riot and a stabbing last month," the woman at Visitor Processing told Nick on the telephone. "B Yard and D Yard are on lockdown for the foreseeable future. Do you know which yard the prisoner is in?"

"No, how do I find that out?" Nick asked.

"Go to the Department of Corrections and Rehabilitation website and use the Inmate Locator. If he's not on lockdown, you can visit on any Saturday or Sunday between 8:30 a.m. and 3:00 in the afternoon."

By the time Nick set out to see his father in May 2000, Willie Carter had been in prison for almost 30 years, the last six at Pleasant Valley. Built to house 2,300 inmates, the population had grown to 5,000, and they were living on top of each other, just as they had at Folsom. The only difference was, at Pleasant Valley the walls were cleaner and the sinks didn't drip.

Nick made the 200-mile trip from Los Angeles to Coalinga, following I-5
north. For much of the trip through the San Joaquin Valley, the California
Aqueduct ran parallel to the Interstate. He watched it from the right side window
of his truck, a concrete highway transporting water by gravity, hundreds of
miles under a blazing sun from the Sacramento River Delta to Southern
California.

Nick arrived in Coalinga on a late Friday afternoon and found a cheap
motel. He had always known one useless bit of information about the town—it
got its name a century earlier when it was Coaling Station A for the Southern
Pacific Railroad. After he received the telephone call from his father, he knew
something else about Coalinga—his father, Willie Carter, was doing time there.
Nick settled into a room carpeted with a dirty, stinking, brown shag rug and
watched a flickering television screen as the Los Angeles Lakers defeated the
Indiana Pacers, 4-2, to win the 2000 NBA Championship. Although Nick had
become an avid Lakers fan after he moved to Los Angeles, he was too anxious
about the impending visit with his father to care much about their victory.
When the game ended, Nick spent a restless night, dreaming of caves, tunnels,
and the man he was about to meet in the morning.

The sun was a white-hot sphere in the sky. Even with his sunglasses, the harsh
light bothered his eyes. Nick felt the heat radiating up from the pavement while
he stood with 100 other people, baking on a strip of asphalt outside the 640-
acre prison. He looked at the few men standing in the crowd in shorts, soiled
T-shirts, and flip-flops, and regretted wearing his fire department blues. Women
with babies and small children made up the majority of the group. Most were
Latinas, but several blacks, some whites, and a few Asians were also among the
crowd. Without trying, he overheard bits of their conversation.

"I sent my son a Bible, from Amazon…"

"Don't use the vending machines. The chips are stale and I lost my money
twice…."

"There's a free bus, comes up here from diff'rent cities…."

"We got married and then he went to prison. I ain't seen him since…."

The kids standing in the heat with their mothers were restless, and the
youngest ones were starting to cry. Thirty minutes earlier, Nick had listened
to the woman behind him tell her child, "Be patient, honey, it won't be long."

Now, when the little boy began to wail, she slapped him and snapped, "Be quiet, dammit." He wondered how many of these children hadn't seen their fathers in months, and how many had never seen their fathers at all. He stood among them, a 29-year-old child, waiting to see his own father for the first time.

Nick had arrived at the prison early and was near the front of the line. Standing in the middle of this crowd of strangers, each related somehow to a convict, his resolve was draining away and he wondered if he had made the right decision. Maybe the visit was a big mistake. Perhaps he should just walk to his truck and head back to Los Angeles. It would be so easy. He repeated the lies he had told himself since the first call from his father: it was impossible, he couldn't be related to anyone in Pleasant Valley Prison; there was a mistake, the Willie Carter who had called wasn't his father; his father was a miner who died in a tunnel explosion in 1971.

Theresa, a correctional officer on the far side of 200 pounds, came out, distributed forms and announced that the visitors would enter in groups of 15 after clearing security. Nick felt trapped—it was too late to flee. Theresa waited patiently, shading her eyes from the glare, while the sorry crowd of visitors completed their questionnaires. After collecting them, she escorted Nick and the rest of the first group into a small brick building housing the metal detectors. Shoes, belts, sunglasses, keys, wallets and purses, and everything for the children, including diaper bags and milk, went into plastic bins for a journey through the scanner. A handwritten sign taped to the metal detector said, "IF YOU CANT PASS A SECOND TIME, YOU WILL BE DENIED ADMISSION." A woman in front of Nick pushed two little girls through the portal and, after she set off the metal detector three times, a female guard pulled her aside for a physical search before passing her through.

On the other side of the scanner, Nick showed his photo ID, and along with the others was ushered through another door into an outdoor cage created by a 12-foot-high fence with chain link laid across the top. An electric gate closed behind them, another slid open, and Nick found himself in the maximum-security area, behind two parallel fences decorated on top with vicious coils of razor wire. A third fence, between the other two, was marked with signs of a lightning bolt and the warning, ELECTRIFIED FENCE – DANGER. Guard towers manned by armed officers were spaced out along the perimeter and surveillance cameras were mounted everywhere on poles. Two hours after arriving in the vast prison parking lot, Nick was now officially inside the Pleasant Valley California State Prison. It was not a comfortable feeling.

A guard accompanied Nick into the visitor's area and guided him to a seat in front of a three-foot-square window marked 27. Polished aluminum partitions jutted out from the wall between each space to give visitors a false sense of privacy. Nick moved as if in a dream. His mouth was dry and he felt lightheaded. He was barely aware of the white cinderblock walls, the countertop of blue Formica, or the matching blue plastic chairs. Voices and sounds—women sobbing, children whining—drifted through the room. In the adjoining stall, a little boy, 4 or 5 years old, sat cross-legged on the counter, face and hands pressed against the window, looking at a man on the other side. "Daddy, daddy," he cried.

Nick sat down as if he was lowering himself onto a pile of broken glass. He rested his arms on the counter top, clenched his fists, fixed his gaze on the window and waited. The overhead lights cast a bright blue-white light that hurt his eyes.

Willie Carter was looking forward to seeing his son Nick for the first time. He imagined him sitting on the other side of the glass in the visitor's area, waiting for him, holding a fat wad of 20-dollar bills. There were sodium vapor overhead lights everywhere in Pleasant Valley, and they bothered Willie's eyes. If someone came to see you, you had to sit there in the glare of that bright blue-white fucking light. And it smelled just like every other part of Pleasant Valley—stale and thick with the institutional stink of body odor and disinfectant. Willie had been on the free side a few times to clean the floors. He had watched some of the visiting women sink their fat asses onto the chairs, lean forward on the countertop and try to kiss their mn through the three-foot-square glass windows. There were polished aluminum partitions between each space, but there was no privacy, and the corrections guards stood there, watching and listening to everything. All a visitor could do was look through the glass and talk on the telephone. That's all. No one was gonna pass anything like drugs or a shank to an inmate. And if someone brought money? They would have to deposit it in the inmate's account.

It was hot in the visitor's room, and the air was so thick with body odor and disinfectant that Nick thought he might suffocate. A minute passed, but it seemed like a lifetime before a door opened into the room on the far side of the glass window. Nick saw a short man walking slowly toward him. After all the years, the vague, indistinct face that had accompanied Nick throughout his life came into focus and a slight shiver passed through his body. The man's pale blue eyes had no depth, they were hard and cold and they gave nothing away, but they told Nick everything he didn't want to know—the convict on the other side of the glass was his father.

Nick stared at the man who sat down. His skin was white and pasty, the unhealthy color of someone who had spent most of his life, 23 hours a day, inside a prison cell. Tattoos on the creased skin of his neck peeked out over the collar of an orange prison uniform. Gray stubble covered his jaw. His mouth was a tight, thin line turned down at the corners. His broken nose was slightly off-center and Nick saw the faint dilation of his nostrils as he breathed. Two deep, vertical creases in his forehead separated thick, wild eyebrows. A scar, most likely from a knife fight, began on the left side of his forehead and drifted off toward his ear. His long gray hair, parted in the middle, hung almost to his shoulders.

When Willie looked through that glass window, he knew it was his son for sure. He was wearing some kind of dark blue uniform from the fire department. He was short, just like Willie. Maybe 5 foot 8 or 9. And he had the pale blue eyes, just like Willie's, whose prison name was "ice-eyes." He was squinting in the bright overhead lights, just as Willie was squinting. Like father, like son, Willie thought. He thought his son must spend a lot of time outside, because he had a tan. He seemed like a clean kid, he didn't have any tats, at least none Willie could see. He looked like he was in good shape, no fat, strong. How old was he? Willie counted on his fingers. Twenty-nine? Hell, Willie thought, I'm gonna be sixty in a coupla months; I'm twice his age but I bet I could trash him. Willie had had plenty of time to work out. All of his life, in fact. He lifted weights every day at the iron pile. That's what he did—he spent hours, days, years working out in prison.

The kid looked back at Willie through the glass. He wasn't smiling, and he wasn't waving a wad of twenty-dollar bills. Willie reached for the receiver hanging on the wall. The Corrections Department had it all figured out. The chain around his waist and wrists was just long enough so he could hold the receiver to his ear. He waited for his son to pick up at his end, but he just sat there. For a minute, Willie's kid was giving him a look like an Aryan Brother would give an EME piece of crap if they met up in an alley.

Willie said, "Pick up." The kid couldn't hear him, but he could read Willie's lips. Finally, his son reached for the telephone.

Nick watched Willie Carter stare back at him. When he reached to take the telephone receiver from the wall, Nick saw the chain around his waist that secured his wrists. Willie Carter must have spent most of his years in prison working out. His arms were huge and his biceps were the size of softballs. They stared at each other until his father put the phone to his ear and mouthed the words, "Pick up." Nick knew he should take hold of the receiver on his side, but felt incapable of movement. He sat frozen for a few more seconds, looking through the thick glass at the man gazing back at him. Finally, Nick reached for the telephone, pressed it to his ear, nodded at the man on the other side of the glass, but said nothing.

The first thing he heard from Willie Carter was, "Welcome to Flatland Fucking Nowhere Prison. It's heaven on earth. How come ya never accepted my calls?"

"What do you want?"

"I been looking for ya forever."

"So now you've found me."

"Ain't ya happy to see yer old man?"

"Thrilled." Nick glared through the glass.

"How's yer mother?"

Nick couldn't believe his mother could have ever been married to this prison rat. "She died eight years ago."

"Well, that's too bad. Ya know, we were married for less than two years before she divorced me, kicked me to the curb, deserted me. She said I'd never see ya. She swore ya would never know me, never know who I was." Willie Carter flashed Nick a lopsided smile. "But here we are. Father and son. Finally together after all this time."

"Is that it? You wanted to see me?"

"Sure, we should know each other, don't ya think? Who knows how long I got to live? Somebody could shank me tonight."

"You're not coming out?" It was the first good thing Nick had heard since he arrived.

"Doin' all day and a night. Know what that means? It means life without parole. When I come out, it'll be in a box."

Nick continued to glare through the glass. "What're you in for? What did you do? It must be bad if you got a life sentence."

"Ya don't know? I killed a cop." Willie Carter smiled again, like he was proud of his accomplishment.

"A cop?... You killed a police officer?"

"Yeah. Bakersfield Police Captain Robert Hope. Except they pronounced it HO-PAY. Like he was somethin' special. He wasn't. He was just a cop."

Nick pushed back from the window.

"It wasn't my fault," Willie said.

"Not your fault?"

"No. The dumb fuck pulled up to a convenience store about the time I was cleanin out the cash register. He just showed up, maybe he was gonna buy some bread, or milk, or I don't know what. He could've gone on, not stopped, then he'd still be alive, and I wouldn't be in this joint. But no, I come out, and there he is, gettin' outta his car. Listen, Nick, I could use some help."

The sound of this man using Nick's first name was repulsive. "Some help?"

"Financial help. Ya got any money for yer dad?"

"What?"

"Didn't they tell ya? Ya coulda brought me some cash or rolls of quarters. Or stamps."

"You want a roll of quarters? That's why you called me? For a goddamn roll of quarters?"

"Hey, hey, justa minute. Don't get pissed off here. No, I don't want no roll of quarters or stamps. What I really need is for ya to deposit some serious money into my account. Help out yer old man. Since I knew ya was comin', I been thinking a lot about it. Maybe five hundred dollars. Five hundred would last forever. Make my life easier. Don't ya wanna help yer old man?" Willie Carter leaned right up against the glass. "Ya know what? Ya look just like me. Like father, like son. Same color eyes. Ain't that something? We're a family."

"No." Nick shouted into the phone. "No. I'm not your son. I don't even know you. You're not my father. My father died in the Sylmar Tunnel explosion."

People in the visitor's area turned to look toward Nick's cubicle.

"Huh? The what?" Willie Carter said. "What the fuck ya talking about? I am yer father. We got the same eyes. That proves it."

A cold feeling seeped into Nick's body—it was the realization, the understanding of what his mother had done. The coincidence of time. The convenience of an identical name. The story of a miner named Willie Carter, lifted from a half-page news article in the *Fresno Bee*. The vague evasions. The flawed explanations. The absence of any trace of his father. Now it all made sense. Nick took a deep breath. "Oh, Mom," he whispered, and wondered how he could have been so stupid, so gullible. Nick felt anger and hatred for the man on the other side of the glass, but tears welled up in his eyes. He tried to hold them back, but they came anyway. He felt them roll down his cheeks, over his lips. He tasted the salt on his tongue. Nick stood up and knocked over the blue plastic chair. He dropped the receiver and left it swinging at the end of the spiral metal cord. As he turned from the window and started to walk away, a wave of nausea rolled through him. Nick's stomach churned. It convulsed, and he couldn't suppress the surge of bitter liquid which rose up into the back of his throat. He bent over and vomited. His breakfast spewed out of his mouth onto the floor. The stench filled the room.

"Oh," a woman said.

"I'm sorry. Excuse me. I'm sorry," Nick said to no one in particular. He looked down and saw that he had thrown up on his boots. He wiped his mouth with the sleeve of his blue uniform shirt and without looking back, walked toward the guard standing at the exit.

Once outside, the sun and heat pressed down on Nick as he walked across the asphalt to the parking lot. He stopped to spit several times, trying to rid his mouth of the rancid taste. He picked up a drifting piece of newspaper and tried to wipe the vomit slime from his boots.

"Father?" Nick shouted in the deserted parking lot. He looked back at the prison buildings and screamed, "You're not my fucking father." For a few minutes, Nick walked aimlessly among the parked vehicles, talking to himself.

"A father loves his son. A father nurtures his son. A father is there to help his son grow up. You're not my goddamn father." Nick attracted the attention of two off-duty correctional officers who were walking to their cars, and he saw them stop to watch him. Nick quieted down and looked for his truck.

The inside of the pickup was an inferno from sitting in the sun. He opened both doors and rolled down the window. He sat in the heat inside the cab, smelled the residue of puke on his shoes, and waited for the overheated air to dissipate.

For a moment, it was raining, hard, and Nick stood at his bedroom window watching the unknown visitors walk away from his front door. Now he remembered one of them had carried a video camera on his shoulder. Their blue van had a large sun painted on the side, and THE BAKERSFIELD CALIFORNIAN in silver letters. Nick understood what he had seen. A newspaper crew had come to interview Willie Carter's family.

FOURTEEN

June 22, 2014, 12:15 p.m.

"So they blew up the magazine as a diversion—to keep us focused on the Canyon, and the Jensen plant while they went after the East Portal," Cindi said to Nick. "And the FBI bought it, hook, line and sinker." She followed Morris' pickup as he tried to merge from the on-ramp into the stream of traffic on the eastbound 210. Behind them, Daniels hugged her bumper in his truck. Across the way, on the westbound side, three lanes of traffic headed toward the I-5 closure were at a complete standstill, backed up as far as the eye could see. A shallow gully separated the eastbound lanes from those headed west, and vehicles were making U-turns, cutting across the dirt, trying to get onto the eastbound side. The result was more congestion, and the traffic headed east was at a crawl.

Cindi slammed her palm against the steering wheel. "We should never have tried to get on the freeway. What was Morris thinking? This'll take forever. Do you know where we're going?"

"You just have to get to the next exit and you're on Foothill," Nick said. "I think the first street is Fenton and it's two or three blocks to a dead end."

"The East Portal isn't open is it? There's no way to get into the tunnel from that end?"

"I think it's completely sealed off with a bulkhead."

"But our twin could get his van right next to it? There's no wall or anything around it?"

"Unless things have changed, all he'd have to do is drive down a shallow embankment."

"Then he wouldn't need an ignition device. He can just park, let loose with a bomb, blow up the bulkhead, and ignite the gas in the tunnel."

"All this to make a statement about diverting their water? What happened to marches and protests?"

"The water disputes here in California have gone way beyond that. Over time, these people have become more aggressive because there's more at stake, and no one will listen to them. When they start messing around with explosives, that's when the ATF gets involved. The twins are all the more unusual because you have combat stress added to the mix."

"After all that's happened today, I'm afraid to see their main event."

"Sometimes these people start something and just don't think about the collateral damage. They plan one bad act, screw it up, and end up causing all kinds of other shit to happen."

Nick closed his eyes for a moment and massaged the side of his head. "There's something else about the tunnel, something I'm trying to remember—"

"What?"

"That's the problem. I don't know, but I think it's important. I'm having trouble concentrating."

"Nick, I'm worried about you. You must have really cracked your head."

"The paramedic said I might have a concussion, and now I'm beginning to think he was right. Also, my wrist is killing me. When this is over, maybe you can take me to the ER at Olive View. I think maybe I ought to see a doctor."

"You should be there right now."

"A couple of hours won't make any difference."

"I'm not so sure." Cindi looked at Nick.

"I'm not dying."

"I mean, this might take more than a couple of hours."

"I'll make it."

Cindi watched a few cars turn off the blacktop of the freeway and continue east, driving over the unpaved ground. "Hold on," she said. "Let's see if we can go off-road as far as the next exit." She followed the other vehicles onto the field strewn with rocks and covered with weeds and low scrub brush.

Nick looked back to see Daniels bouncing along behind them. Morris wasn't following; he was trapped in the traffic on the freeway entrance.

"Where are your USAR guys?" Cindi said. "What if there is an explosion?

How fast could they get here if we need them?"

"They were stuck on the I-5 and were supposed to radio me when they got to the staging area." Nick looked at his watch. The numbers squirmed around like small insects. He squinted until they stopped. "It's been over two hours." He reached for his radio, but it was no longer clipped to his belt. "Where's my damn radio?" he cursed. "Did I drop it back at the staging area?" He pressed his hand against his head. "How could I do that? Firefighters aren't supposed to lose their radios." A thought tugged at Nick's memory. What else had he lost? Something valuable. He couldn't remember what it was. "Let me use your cell phone, maybe I can get hold of them."

Cindi handed him her phone. Nick held it in his left hand and tried to remember who was on duty at 103s when he went in to get his equipment in the early morning. Was it A Shift or C Shift? He couldn't remember a single name or face. His own phone had the direct cell numbers for every man in the USAR Task Force, but it was somewhere in the rubble of the downed helicopter. "I can't remember anyone's number."

Nick had barely finished his sentence when Cindi's emergency tone rang and she took the phone from his hand. "Agent Burns," she said, and listened for a moment before she lost her temper. "No, dammit, we already know there was a methane explosion there forty years ago. I said, find a map. I need to know the route of the tunnel through Sylmar, and anything you can get about the East Portal. Find out if there's any other way into it. Contact MWD if you have to, OK?... Yeah, we do have one of their engineers with us, but I want another opinion. Call me as soon as you find out something we don't already know." She drove over a large rock hidden in the weeds and the SUV rocked from side to side. "Dammit," she exclaimed.

Nick did remember something—he had lost the engagement ring. He imagined the wreckage of the downed helicopter, burning in the brushfire. In the midst of the debris, his equipment bag was probably now a pile of ashes. The ring was gone. "We were supposed to spend today together," he said. "I had something special planned."

"Well, we are together, aren't we?" Cindi gripped the wheel with both hands as the front of the SUV dipped into a depression in the ground.

"Along with half the first responders in L.A. County."

"That's what happens when someone spooks Homeland and the FBI."

"I was hoping for something more intimate."

"Date a cop, live the life." Her cell phone interrupted again. Cindi answered and said, "Agent Burns... hi J.J.... That's right, I asked Davis to get me some info on the tunnel.... No, the traffic's a disaster in both directions. Right now, we're driving across a field. If I don't break an axle, we should be there in a few minutes. Where's the response team?... How long?... Yeah, that's what I was afraid of. Thanks." She turned to Nick and said, "Surprise, our backup is caught in the traffic jam. Dammit, if the ATF had its own helicopters, this wouldn't be a problem."

After a 10-minute bone-jarring ride over the ground along the side of the freeway, Cindi followed the other vehicles over a curb and bounced onto Foothill Boulevard. Morris was nowhere in sight.

"That's Fenton," Nick said, and pointed. "Take a left."

Cindy waited a moment for Daniels to come up behind the SUV, then made the turn and drove three blocks to a dead end in a rundown Sylmar neighborhood.

Nick pointed to the other side of the street. "The portal's over the side of that embankment."

Cindi parked and was out of the SUV with her Glock drawn before Nick could even release his seat belt. Daniels made a U-turn and left his truck facing out of the cul-de-sac. He jumped out wearing a Kevlar vest and grabbed his helmet and assault rifle. "The tunnel?" he said.

Nick pointed, and paused next to the SUV as another wave of dizziness overcame him.

Daniels was the first to approach, his rifle raised. Cindi began to follow him, holding her Glock in both hands, but Daniels motioned for her be quiet and to stay back. He got down on his stomach and crawled to the edge of the embankment, cradling the gun in his arms. He peered over the side into the shallow ravine and then shook his head. "Nothing," he said, and stood up. "It's deserted."

Nick and Cindi joined him, and they stood looking down at the dirt wall and the huge bulge where the East Portal of the Sylmar Tunnel had been sealed off and sprayed with Gunnite.

"The last time I crept up to a ravine holding my rifle was in Afghanistan,"

Daniels said. "I was doing demolition with a Special Forces unit in Paktia Province. We caught some Taliban hunkered down; they were eating. It was like shooting fish in a barrel."

Nick gazed down into the shallow ravine. Forty years ago, bulldozers had created a small mountain from the soil taken out of the 5-mile tunnel. Now it was covered with thick vegetation and trees. Nearby, dozens of the seven-thousand-pound semicircular concrete pieces used to line the tunnel's interior, each a dirty gray color and streaked with water stains after decades in the sun and rain, lay in a jumble, like a giant's toys. Nothing had changed since Nick had last visited the spot except the chain link fence was gone and the brush had grown thicker. He stood silent for a moment and imagined the scene in June 1971 on the night of the explosion. He saw the spotlights creating a pool of light in the darkness surrounding the portal. He heard the diesel engine of the muck train and saw it emerge from the tunnel, pushing two cars filled with exhausted miners coming off the swing shift. He watched them jump down from the cars and plod to the dry house to change out of their filthy clothes. As they headed in, they mingled with another group of more energetic men, walking toward the portal. Willie Carter and Ralph Brissette were somewhere in the crowd of miners coming to work on that fateful graveyard shift. That night, Ralph Brissette would experience a life-altering event, something he would remember forever. For Willie Carter, forever would only be a matter of hours; he wouldn't live to see the daylight.

Cindi stood next to Nick, also looking into the ravine. He knew she had no visions of the past—her law-enforcement focus was strictly in the present. "No van, no bomb," she said. "Not even tire tracks. It doesn't look like anyone has been here since the Ice Age. Twin brother, where the hell are you?"

Morris walked into the cul-de-sac, carrying his gas meter.

"Where's your truck?" Cindi said. "Did you walk from the freeway?"

"No, I parked down the block," he said. "In case there was an explosion."

"Not likely," Daniels said. "The place is deserted."

"I checked in with the MWD," Morris said. "They're not taking any chances. They've called for a mandatory evacuation for the area over the shallowest part of the tunnel." He looked around like a frightened child. "It's the first three blocks here along Fenton."

"Who's going to do that?" Nick asked.

"The LAPD," Morris said. "An evacuation squad is on the way. They're supposed to be here any minute."

"Our guys are tied up in traffic," Cindi said, "and the LAPD says they're gonna get here on a moment's notice? Dream on."

Nick looked at the poor, blue-collar neighborhood. Almost every driveway had an ancient camper or a rusted automobile hidden under a torn blue tarp. None of the homes had been painted in a decade and many had damaged roofs and missing shingles. A particularly run-down house in the middle of the block had two plaster lions on either side of the front door. One lion had been painted red, and the head of the other had been broken off. A child's rusted swing sat in the yard. The adjacent house was surrounded by a 5-foot chain link fence. The yard was nothing but dirt and foot-high weeds. A huge dog that looked like a vicious mix of shepherd and wolf bared its teeth, snarled, and looked as if it was about to chew through the wire. Across the street, a pit bull, smaller but equally mean looking, paced back and forth behind its own fence and growled in response. "Nice neighborhood," Nick said under his breath.

"Has this tunnel ever had water in it?" Cindi asked Morris.

"A couple of times a year, during the dry season, they send water through to Burbank."

"They send water to Burbank?" Cindi said. "I thought it was sealed with a bulkhead. How does that happen?"

"It moves through an underground conduit at this end," Morris said. "There's something called a flapper-valve that opens one way and feeds the water into a storm drain hidden in the brush down there. The water eventually drains into Burbank."

"Could someone get into the tunnel through the... uh... flapper valve?" Cindi asked.

"No way," Morris said.

"How about the storm drain?" Daniels asked. "Is it above ground? Can you get into that?"

"Sure," Morris said, "but it's just a regular storm drain."

Cindi and Daniels exchanged looks. "It should be checked out," Cindi said. "Morris, you wanna show me where it is?"

Another wave of pain washed through Nick's head and he closed his eyes for a moment. When he heard the wail of a siren, he opened them and saw a black-and-white from the LAPD roll into the cul-de-sac. At least I'm not hearing things, Nick thought.

A sergeant and an officer emerged from the patrol car.

"This is an evacuation team?" Morris said. "Two men?"

"It's the best we can do at the moment," the sergeant said. "We're trying to get some more resources over here, but it'll take some time. We've got patrols out everywhere responding to the terrorist alert, and on top of that, there's a god-awful traffic tie-up. Nothing's moving in the Valley. So right now, we're the evac team. You are…?"

"Gene Morris. I'm a field engineer at the Metropolitan Water District. This is Fire Captain Nick… uh…"

"Carter," Nick said. "I'm from the County Fire USAR Task Force."

Daniels and Cindi joined the discussion. "Rick Daniels, ATF Explosives," Daniels said, "and this is Special Agent Burns."

"So do you know what we're dealing with here?" Cindi said.

"Not really," the sergeant said. "Just what we got from the FBI terror alert briefing."

"Well, here's our version," Cindi said. "We were tracking two suspects early this morning. They're twin brothers. We took one into custody after they detonated some explosives in Magazine Canyon. We're still looking for the other one."

"They blocked an air vent, and there's methane trapped in the tunnel," Daniels said. "We think he may be trying to ignite it."

"The tunnel?" The sergeant looked around. "What tunnel?"

"The Sylmar Tunnel," Nick said. "It's a water tunnel. You're standing on top of it."

"We're standing on it?" the officer said. He looked down at the ground.

"How do you blow up a tunnel full of water?" the sergeant said.

"It's empty," Nick said.

"It terminates down there in the ravine," Morris said.

"We figured he would be here with a bomb, maybe a van full of ANFO," Daniels said.

"Maybe he's stuck in traffic," the officer said.

The sergeant gave him a dirty look.

"One of our Special Response Teams was supposed to meet us here," Cindi said. "But it doesn't much matter now."

"I wouldn't count on them arriving anytime soon," the sergeant said. "We made it here because we were close by and we came on local streets."

"How long is this tunnel?" the officer asked.

"Five and a half miles," Nick said.

"And how much of an evacuation zone are we talking about?" the sergeant asked.

"Right now, we're just concerned with clearing the first three blocks of Fenton," Morris said. "The tunnel runs very shallow along here."

"We'll do what we can," the sergeant said. "People don't always cooperate, and there's only two of us."

"But it's a mandatory evacuation, right?" Morris said. "So there's no problem."

"Technically, there's no such thing as 'mandatory,'" the sergeant said. "We can make an announcement, but we can't force anyone to leave their home. If we had the manpower—which we don't—we'd go door-to-door and ask them to sign a release if they refuse to leave. We might even ask for names of their next of kin, just to frighten them, but if they wanna stay, there's nothing we can do." He turned to Cindi, and asked, "How much time do we have?"

Cindi shrugged her shoulders and said, "We don't know. There's no sign of our suspect at the moment, but he could have already planted some kind of ignition device with a timer somewhere. It could go off anytime. I say get everyone out as soon as possible, just to be safe."

"Sounds good to me," the officer said. "I don't wanna be standing here when it blows up."

"If it does," Cindi said, "I'll recommend you for a medal for bravery." Her cell phone rang. She listened for a moment and said, "So it's Duane.... Is he talking?... Did you learn anything?... OK, at least we know which twin we're looking for."

"They got an ID on the twin?" Daniels asked.

"Yeah," Cindi said. "It was Duane. We're after Dwight."

"Duane. It *was* Duane," Morris mumbled.

"What?" Daniels said.

"Uh…" Morris was startled. "She said it was Duane. The one you arrested was Duane. Right?" His eyes darted from Daniels to Cindi and back to Daniels.

"We're gonna get started with an announcement from the street," The sergeant said. "Then we can try knocking on the doors where no one comes out." He pointed to the home with the large wolf-dog growling behind the fence. "That's one place where we're not going to the door."

"I want to take a look at the storm drain," Cindi said. "Morris, can you lead the way?"

"Sure," Morris said.

The sergeant turned to Daniels and Nick. "We could use some help with the evacuation," he said. "Can you do that?"

"We can help until Agent Burns gets back," Daniels said.

"This is one screwed up day," Nick said.

"That's an understatement," the sergeant said, as he got into the patrol car.

FIFTEEN
January 2001

Nick pulled off the highway onto a tiny patch of blacktop marked with a SCENIC OVERLOOK sign. The turnout was at the top of the Grapevine Grade, before a steep, 6 ½-mile descent. It was near the end of the stretch of I-5 that climbed 4,100 feet from the Los Angeles Basin, traversed a rugged ridge of mountains, cut through the Tejon Pass, and then descended to the lush farmland of the San Joaquin Valley.

When he got out of his truck to stretch his legs, Nick shivered in the cold morning air and shoved his bare hands deep into the pockets of his windbreaker. His breath came out in a white cloud—it was below freezing. A few flakes of snow still swirled in the air, left by an early season high-pressure cold front that had started in the Gulf of Alaska, moved south over the Pacific Ocean, and then made a right hand turn, bringing snow, rain, and wind to Central California. The gray, cloudy sky suited Nick's mood. He walked a few steps to the guard-rail, grasped the ice-cold metal and leaned against it. Most of the year the weather was hot and dry, and the sky was deep blue over the San Joaquin Valley, but on the day Nick had chosen to drive up from Los Angeles to Bakersfield, there was no visibility and no scenic view. Somewhere below him lay some of the richest farm land in the world—acre after acre of citrus groves, almond trees, cotton fields and vegetable farms—but today it was hidden under mist and low-lying clouds.

Since his visit to Coalinga in May, the face of Willie Carter, California Department of Corrections and Rehabilitation inmate number AF7562 at Pleasant Valley State Prison, had haunted Nick. His father's image appeared in his dreams, passed before his eyes when he let his mind wander at work and, worst of all, stared back at him every morning when he looked into the bathroom mirror. Nick saw the tattoos on the white, pasty skin. He saw the thin, cruel mouth. Most of all, he saw the eyes—the ice-blue eyes, like his own, that looked so hard and cold. Nick wondered what kind of man this was, at once so familiar and yet such a stranger, who had told him: "You don't know? I killed a cop.... Bakersfield Police Captain Robert Hope, pronounced HOPAY... It wasn't my fault."

Nick returned to his pickup, revved the engine to blow heat on his chilled body, drove back onto the highway, and began the descent into the San Joaquin Valley. He had forgotten how steep the Grapevine was, and in minutes the pickup was moving too fast. Nick tapped his brakes, downshifted and drove more carefully down the wet, winding four-lane highway to the bottom, where he turned off onto Highway 99 for the final dozen miles into Bakersfield. If he had continued north on I-5, in another hour he could be in Coalinga again, visiting his father. In less than two hours he could be in Fresno, looking at the apartment where he grew up and reliving the fantasies of his childhood. Today, however, Nick needed reality, not make-believe. He was headed to the newspaper archives of *The Bakersfield Californian* to try to find out what his mother had said when the paper interviewed her.

Nick stood at the entrance and gazed at a bronze plaque indicating that the newspaper's building was listed in the National Register of Historic Places. Another plaque announced that *The Bakersfield Californian* was a proud, family-owned newspaper that traced its roots back to August 1886, when its predecessor began publication during the Gold Rush.

Inside, at the information desk, Nick was directed to the Reference Department, where he found Harold Taylor, an old man wearing a little name badge. Harold was born in 1930 and had spent his entire life in Bakersfield, a city in the center of some of the largest heavy-oil deposits in the world. He was too young to serve in World War II, and had never been outside the State of California. He had traveled as far as Los Angeles several times, and once had gone all the way to San Diego, but Harold was happiest remaining in the city where he was born. When he began working for the paper in 1946, the price of a barrel of domestic crude oil was $1.63. When he hit his stride as a City Desk reporter in 1962, crude cost $2.85 a barrel. His current job, which he took very seriously, was to help people search for news articles and information in back issues of the newspaper. It wasn't a demanding job and he wasn't paid much, but he had been an employee longer than anyone else, and the editor was committed to allow Harold to spend whatever time he had left remaining at work. On this morning in January 2001, while Harold sat at his desk, the price of a barrel of domestic crude oil had risen to $23.00.

"We've got back issues and microfilm copies," Harold told Nick.

Nick looked at the man with the skinny, wrinkled neck sticking out of a Western-style shirt. He wore a black bolo tie, adorned with silver tips and a turquoise slide clasp. Nick wondered where you would buy a tie like it. Did they even make them anymore? He thought the guy was an old geezer, as antique as the tie he was wearing.

"But I need to know the date," Harold said.

That was the question Nick dreaded. He wasn't even sure what headline he was looking for, let alone the day, month or even the year it might have appeared. Nick had calculated that he was no older than 8 when he listened to his mother tell the news crew she wouldn't talk to them again. That meant they must have interviewed her sometime before 1979. His father went to prison in 1971, which meant an eight-year span. Now, standing in the newspaper's office, Nick had his doubts. What if the interview was never published? What if it appeared as part of some other article? What if it wasn't an interview at all? What if? Nick sensed the search was a crazy idea and that he was wasting his time, but now that he had driven all the way up from Los Angeles, he decided he might as well give it a try.

"We have everything after 1944 on microfilm," Harold continued, staring at Nick through thick bifocals. "Between 1907 and 1943 you'll have to search through our newspaper morgue and that's in a different building. From 1907 back to 1891, we were the *Daily Californian*, and we don't have those editions. Before 1891, we were the *Kern County*—"

"No," Nick interrupted. "I don't need anything that far back. I'm thinking 1971, or a couple of years later. Is there some kind of index, if I'm looking for a name or a type of story?"

"Nope. Everything works off the date. If you don't have a specific date, you just have to start searching and hope you find what you're looking for. Ever use a microfilm reader, young man?"

"Uh-uh," Nick said.

"Come along." Harold stood up and motioned for Nick to follow. "How about the WWW? Ever use that?"

"The what?"

"The world wide web. The Internet. Most people your age are familiar with it."

"I know a little about it, but not much," Nick said.

"Well you better learn. Pretty soon everything you young people want to know will be available on the Internet and you'll be using a search engine to find it. In a few years, microfilm will be a thing of the past. Until then, we're stuck with it."

"Uh huh," Nick said, and wondered what a search engine was. It sounded like something a USAR team would use.

Harold was stiff and creaky, and was slow in descending the flight of stairs to the basement. Nick waited for him at the bottom and they walked to a door at the end of a dimly lit hall. Harold unlocked it, turned on overhead lights, and led Nick into what looked like a storage room. One wall was covered with shelves holding reels of microfilm, organized by date.

Nick thought of the huge Los Angeles Fire Department archive he had visited with Chief Rainwater. That had been only eight years ago, but now it seemed like another lifetime, so much had happened.

"Each roll of film has a month's worth of newspapers. Each page of every edition is copied in order." Harold pointed to one of three machines on a table. "You said 1971?" He took a roll of microfilm marked January–1971 from the shelf. "This is the reader. You put the roll on this spindle, like this, then run the film between these plates of glass, and attach the end to this empty spool." He flicked a switch on the side of the device and a bright light shined up from under the glass plates. "Crank this handle and it winds the film across the glass. Wherever you stop, that page is magnified and displayed on this screen. It's pretty simple. Do you need help?"

Nick looked at the display screen and saw the front page of the January 1, 1971, New Year's Day edition of *The Bakersfield Californian*. "Thank you, I think I can work it."

"I meant do you need help with your search? What are you after? What's the topic? Got a name?"

"I'm good," Nick said. He was anxious to get started and wanted to be left alone.

"When you're done, you have to rewind the film back onto the original reel. Got it?"

"Will do," Nick said.

"A lot of folks just walk out of here without rewinding. It's very inconsiderate." Harold stared at Nick, his eyes magnified behind his thick glasses. "You must rewind."

"Rewind. Sure, I'll do it. Thank you." And now please leave me alone, Nick thought.

"Good luck," Harold said. He walked out and closed the door behind him, leaving Nick alone in a tomb with 45 years of newspapers on microfilm.

Nick rubbed his eyes and checked his watch. It was 2:20 p.m. He had spent almost five hours scrolling through newspaper pages. He had covered seven years of *The Bakersfield Californian*, and had found nothing. At first, not knowing what he was looking for, Nick had worked slowly, reading the headline of each article on every page. He quickly figured out he could skip several parts of the paper, including the sports reports, the entertainment section, classified ads, and the pages devoted to "high desert lifestyles." Even with those eliminations, there were dozens of pages in each edition to examine. As the hours passed, he read less carefully, cranked the film more quickly and finally realized he was moving the pages along without even seeing them. He was hungry and tired. The low light and lack of windows was no longer bearable; the air in the room was stifling and he felt as if the walls were closing in on him. Twice he had heard faint noises and guessed that mice, or rats, lived behind the shelves that held the microfilm.

The old man returned four times to ask, "Find what you're looking for?" Each time Nick had told him, "Not yet," and suspected the old man's real purpose was to make sure Nick hadn't created a pile of reels he hadn't rewound. When Harold Taylor returned for the fifth time, Nick decided it was time to quit. "I think I'm done," Nick announced, rewound the last spool—December 1979—under the old man's watchful gaze, and put it back on the shelf.

"What exactly are you after?"

Nick considered for a moment how much he wanted to share. "I think my mother talked to your paper about a Bakersfield police officer who was killed. I wanted to get the details."

Harold tugged at the ends of his string tie. "But you don't know the date?"

"I had a range of time, a few years, but I didn't find anything, and I'm done looking."

"Was it an accident?"

"An accident?"

"Was the officer involved in an accident?"

"No, he was killed. Someone shot him."

"A BPD officer? What was the officer's name? Was it Robert Hope?"

He pronounced the last name HO-PAY, the same way his father had. "Yes. Yes it was. That was his name." Nick was astonished that the old man had pulled this information out of thin air.

"I knew it had to be Robert." The old man became animated. He went to the shelves and removed one of the microfilm reels. "That would have been reported in our City Section. Let me see if I can find it."

"Thank you," Nick said. He was so tired, he couldn't even see straight. Could this old man actually remember something that happened 30 years ago?

"I think it was 1971," Harold said, and threaded the film through the reader. He put a hand on each crank, moved the film forward rapidly, stopped, rolled it backward, then forward again, stopping to glance at the screen from time to time. The silver tips of his bolo tie danced around as he spun the cranks. "No... no... no" he repeated as he ran through the first reel of 1971.

Nick fidgeted around and wanted to get out of the storage room. "Where's the men's room?" he asked.

"Down the hall, behind the stairs."

When Nick returned a few minutes later, the old man was staring at the screen. He turned and gave Nick a smile that revealed stained, yellow teeth. "Bingo," he said, and his face lit up. "Bing-O. I'll bet this is what you wanted to see." He pushed his glasses farther up on his nose and leaned closer to the screen, and murmured, "Robert, my friend, rest in peace."

Nick bent over his shoulder and read the brief article displayed on the screen:

SLAIN OFFICER'S SPOUSE BEFRIENDS KILLER'S WIFE

October 8, 1971. Alice Hope, wife of Captain Robert Hope, the 14-year veteran of the Bakersfield Police Department who was killed last month, has befriended the wife of Willie Carter, the man who killed him.

"This woman, Ellie Carter, deserves some sympathy too," Alice Hope told the Californian. "She's not responsible for the death of my husband, she's an innocent person. She has a months-old child, just as I do, and she has no family, she's all alone. I'm asking the press to leave her in peace, let her be. Hounding her won't bring my poor husband back. She didn't kill him."

Alice Hope! Alice HO-PAY. Nick remembered the woman who attended his mother's funeral and told him she was from Bakersfield. The woman whose last name had sounded like "Copay." He tried to picture her face, but all he could recall was that she was dressed in black. The wife of the slain policeman? And she had befriended his mother? Nick was dumbfounded.

"Well?" Harold said.

"That's not the article I was after, but thank you."

"Poor Robert. He went to East Bakersfield High in the early fifties. Those were the glory days—I remember them as if it was yesterday, because I volunteered part time as an assistant coach. We had a great football team, and Robert, he was the best. He was a big strong kid, a fullback. So talented. Everyone liked him. He should have gone to college and become a pro football player, but those were tough times and no one had any money. He couldn't afford college, so he went into the Marines and when he came home, he became a cop."

Nick couldn't believe that the old man had found this tiny article in the time it had taken him to pee.

Harold continued on, "I remember when this happened. The whole town was devastated. His wife, his poor wife, she was expecting her second child and had a miscarriage after he was killed. Some low-life robbed a hundred dollars from a convenience store and Robert got killed in the process. What a waste.

People wanted a scapegoat. They took it out on the scoundrel's wife, and Alice stood up and put a stop to it." Harold pushed his glasses farther up on his nose with his forefinger, and looked at Nick. "What's your involvement in this? You say your mother talked to the paper? Was someone in your family related to Robert?"

Nick shook his head.

"Friend of his?"

"Not really."

"Witness?"

Nick didn't answer. The old man was asking way too many questions. "Excuse me," Nick said. "I'd like to read the article again." He sat down in front of the screen, hoping Harold would leave him alone. The old man lingered, and Nick ignored him.

"Don't forget to rewind," Harold finally said, and left the room.

Nick read the short article once more and sat in the silence of the microfilm tomb for a few more minutes. When he left, he didn't rewind; Nick left the reel where it was, on the reader. He walked out of the storeroom and upstairs into the daylight. The old man was sitting at his desk, fiddling with his tie.

"Thanks for the help," Nick said.

Harold stood up with an alacrity that surprised Nick. "I'm still wondering what your connection is to all this. Are you related to the man who robbed that convenience store?"

Nick stood, frozen in front of the old man.

"Is that it?" Harold asked.

Harold looked at Nick through his thick glasses and Nick felt as if the old man was reading his mind.

"Did someone in your family kill Robert? Was it your father? Did your father kill Robert?"

Nick knew he could never explain anything to the old man confronting him. Silence was his only response.

"Robert should be alive today," Harold went on, his voice rising. "He was cheated out of the rest of his life. Cheated. And his daughter grew up without him. Was it your father?" Harold demanded and stepped closer to Nick. "I can see it in your face. It was your father." Harold was unsteady on his feet, and had to lean against his desk, but he wasn't finished. "I hope he's rotting in prison. I hope he rots in hell," he screamed, and his voice echoed through the building.

Nick didn't say a word. He turned and walked out through the lobby without looking back.

Harold called after him once more, his voice booming. "Was it your father?"

Nick wanted to run. He forced himself to walk.

Outside, the rain had stopped and the gray clouds were moving east. Nick inhaled the smell of heavy crude drifting in from the oil fields that surrounded Bakersfield, and tried to clear his mind. On the other side of the street he saw the Bakersfield police headquarters, a two-story building with half a dozen blue and white patrol cars parked out front. Without knowing why, Nick was drawn across the street, crossing in the middle of the block. He stood at the entrance of the station, glanced down at the sidewalk, and wondered if his mother had ever walked there. He was certain that Alice Hope had.

Nick followed two police officers into the building and thought about the difference between entering a police station and a fire station—it was like night and day. At any fire station, urban or rural, big or small, you were met with a smile and the first question was always, "How can I help you?" Police stations were different, and Nick attributed that to the nature of the job. Law enforcement people were more distant, wary, and less inclined to flash an immediate smile. When you walked into a police station you felt a chill and even if your conscience was clear, you knew you didn't want to be there.

Inside, the reception area of the Bakersfield Police Department was uninviting. The floor was covered with worn, green linoleum. The walls, once meant to be a cheerful tan color, had darkened with age and looked dirty. The air had a faint odor of cigarette smoke. The overhead light was harsh, and Nick's eyes reacted with a brief flash of pain. To one side, a man sat on one of several metal chairs. He looked like a migrant farm worker. His clothes were worn; his boots were water stained. He sat silent and unmoving, staring ahead with a blank gaze. Three other people—a family?—clustered around the watch officer's desk, all speaking at once.

"Don't he get to have a lawyer?"

That had to be a father, Nick thought.

"How long's he gonna be in there?"

Sister? Girlfriend?

"I wanna see my son. I wanna see my son." The mother was in tears.

Nick was glad he had the moment to collect his thoughts and decide exactly how to ask about an officer killed 30 years earlier. "My father murdered one of…" wouldn't be the best way to begin. "I'm a firefighter from Los Angeles and…" didn't seem right either. He edged over to a corner of the room to think, and next to the California state flag, he saw three pictures mounted on the wall under an inscription that said END OF WATCH. He glanced at the photos and the dedications below them.

The first picture showed a man wearing combat fatigues. Nick skimmed the memorial to Bakersfield Police Officer Frank Crosby, 2nd Brigade, 1st Battalion, 1st Cavalry Division… killed in action… Desert Storm… Battle of Wadi Al-Batin… Iraq… 15 February 1991.

The second picture was of Assistant Chief Michael Bennett, an older man with a white mustache, wearing four stripes of gold braid on each cuff of his jacket and gold oak leaf clusters on the visor of his cap. The information detailing Chief Bennett's death in June, 1985 described his murder on the front porch of his home in Bakersfield by a recently released parolee.

Nick's attention was drawn to the third picture of Captain Robert Hope, dressed in a blue uniform with a shining badge. He sat with his hat in his lap, next to an American flag. He looked like a nice, average guy; the kind of person Nick might have shared a beer with. Nick studied the officer's face and thought Hope was looking directly at him with sad, accusing eyes. Nick read his memorial:

BAKERSFIELD POLICE CAPTAIN ROBERT HOPE

On September 3, 1971, Captain Robert Hope, a 14-year veteran of the Bakersfield Police Department was killed when he interrupted a robbery in progress at the Desert Inn Convenience Store on Stockdale Highway. The gunman, Willie Carter, 31, of Bakersfield, ran from the store and fired at Hope when he exited his patrol car. Hope was hit once in the chest and fell to the ground. Carter jumped into his car and ran over Captain Hope as he lay wounded in the parking lot. The fire department and a Bakersfield ambulance responded, but Captain Hope was pronounced dead at the scene.

A California Highway Patrol officer spotted Carter's car traveling north on Highway 99 and pursued him onto Highway 46, where Carter

*stopped near Wasco and exchanged fire with the officer. Carter then fled
with additional CHP units in pursuit, and again exchanged gunfire with
the officers near McFarland. He surrendered and was arrested after
running out of ammunition.*

*Carter was convicted on charges of first-degree murder with special
circumstances, use of a deadly weapon to commit a felony, and flight
to avoid arrest. He was sentenced to life in prison without parole. He
is reported to have stolen $119 during the robbery.*

*Captain Hope grew up in Bakersfield. He is survived by his wife,
Alice, and a seven-month-old daughter.*

In disbelief, Nick reread one sentence several times: Carter jumped into
his car and ran over Captain Hope as he lay wounded in the parking lot. He
backed away from the photo and imagined the scene of the shooting outside
the Desert Inn Convenience Store. He pictured Willie Carter wounding the
officer and then running over him before speeding away, leaving Captain Hope
lying in his own blood, dead in the parking lot. He saw the Highway Patrol in
pursuit and heard the sound of gunfire. He watched his father glaring with his
pale blue eyes at the police as they cuffed him and shoved him into the back
of a patrol car. The next image he saw was his father looking at him through
the glass at Pleasant Valley. "You son of a bitch," Nick whispered.

One his way out of the station, Nick heard the mother telling the watch
officer, "My son's a good boy. He wouldn't hurt anyone."

Dozens of semitrailers labored up the steep Grapevine Grade in the right hand
lane. Nick jammed his foot hard against the accelerator of his pickup and flew
past them, anxious to leave Bakersfield behind, along with the image of Robert
Hope lying dead in a convenience-store parking lot. He rolled his windows
down, turned his radio up to full volume, and listened to the music and the
roar of the wind. When he reached the top of the grade, he kept his foot pressed
to the gas, and tried not to think as he drove south over the rolling highway of
the Ridge Route. Minutes later, he saw the flashing red and blue lights of a
California Highway Patrol car in his mirror. Nick cursed to himself, slowed,
pulled to the side of the highway and turned off his radio.

As the CHP officer approached the pickup, he glanced at the small red fire

159

helmet sticker on the rear window, an indication of Nick's membership in the state firefighter's union. "Afternoon," he said.

Nick handed him his license and registration before the cop could even ask. "Sorry, I wasn't paying attention."

The CHP officer glanced at Nick's license, paused for a moment, and said, "You're a firefighter?"

Nick nodded.

"Well, you were going way over the speed limit. I'll let you off with a warning, but you need to slow down. I just came from a nasty crash north of Bakersfield. Wet road, speeding driver didn't survive. You're a young guy with a long life ahead of you. The trick is to make sure you're around to enjoy it. I'm sure you've seen your share of accidents. Speed will kill you, so take it easy."

"Thanks, I appreciate the warning," Nick said. He watched the officer drive off and sat in his pickup by the side of the road long after the black-and-white disappeared in the distance. The cop was right, Nick thought. In seven months, he would celebrate his thirtieth birthday. He did have a long life ahead of him. He had everything to look forward to and so much he wanted to accomplish. Nick decided enough was enough. He was tired of agonizing about his heritage. After his visit to Bakersfield, he knew more than he wanted to know about his father. He was finished struggling with Willie Carter's past. The old geezer at the newspaper was right—He could rot in prison and then rot in hell. It was time to move on and forget about the man spending the rest of his life at Pleasant Valley Prison.

Nick stayed under the speed limit on the long descent toward Los Angeles. He suddenly felt liberated. A weight he had carried his entire life had been lifted from his shoulders today. Willie Carter no longer mattered. For the first time, Nick felt he was free.

SIXTEEN
June 22, 2014, 1:15 p.m.

T HE SERGEANT MADE SOME NOTES on a pad and said to the officer, "Roll down the center of the street. I'll make the evac announcement." He turned to Nick and Daniels. "You guys want to ride in the back, or just walk?

Nick didn't feel great. The pain was getting worse in his ribs from the impact of the crash. His wrist was throbbing and his head hurt. The dizziness and nausea had returned, passing through his body in waves. He didn't think he could sit in the back of the patrol car; he needed fresh air and thought he would feel better on his feet. "I'd rather walk," he told the sergeant.

"I'm with you," Daniels said.

The patrol car made a U-turn and came slowly out into the center of the street on the first block of Fenton Avenue. The sergeant rode shotgun and began the broadcast using the external megaphone on the front of the car: "THIS IS THE LOS ANGELES POLICE DEPARTMENT. A MANDATORY EVACUATION HAS BEEN ORDERED BY THE COUNTY OF LOS ANGELES. PLEASE LEAVE YOUR HOME IMMEDIATELY AND MOVE ONE BLOCK SOUTH TO WHEELER AVENUE. THERE IS A BOMB THREAT AND THE RISK OF A GAS EXPLOSION. IF YOU NEED HELP WITH A DISABLED OR ELDERLY PERSON, SIGNAL TO US FROM THE SIDEWALK. REPEAT, THIS IS AN IMMEDIATE AND MANDATORY EVACUATION ORDER. IT IS NOT OPTIONAL. PLEASE TURN OFF YOUR CELL PHONES WHEN YOU COME OUTSIDE. NO OPEN FLAMES OR CIGARETTES. REPEAT – THIS IS AN IMMEDIATE EVACUATION."

Nick and Daniels walked along behind the patrol car, and Nick wondered how the residents would react. The few individuals standing outside had retreated into their homes when they saw the Sheriff's car arrive, but by the time it reached the middle of the block, blaring the evacuation message, people began to reemerge. One woman carried a baby, and another led three small children. Two teenage boys came out, one holding a soccer ball. An older man supported a woman on his arm as they descended the steps from their porch. The residents gathered on the sidewalks on either side of the street and began to walk down the street.

Nick looked at his watch, and was pleased to see that the numerals weren't dancing around before his eyes. It was just after 1:00 p.m., on a dry, warm summer afternoon in the San Fernando Valley. In the distance, he heard automobile horns from the traffic backup on the 210 Freeway. He thought he smelled the brushfire in Magazine Canyon, and saw an expanding cloud of ugly smoke rising into the sky from the west. If Sylmar doesn't get blown up, he thought, it'll probably burn down.

More people straggled from their homes, and Nick watched a heavyset man come out of a house wearing a bandana, a sleeveless T-shirt, and gang-banger shorts that hung off his ass. His thick arms had sleeve tattoos that covered his skin from wrist to shoulder. He stood in his yard and watched the police car for a moment before he set off down the sidewalk, walking in the opposite direction, glancing over his shoulder as he walked.

"Did you hear what Morris said?" Daniels asked. They continued to walk behind the car, which was creeping down the street, and Daniels had to raise his voice over the din of the sergeant's evacuation announcement.

"What?" Nick said.

When Cindi got the report about Duane, he sounded like he already knew which twin we had arrested.

"What do you mean?

"He made a funny comment… like he knew it was Duane all along. He said it to himself, under his breath. I'm sure he didn't think anyone was listening, because when he realized I'd heard him, he started playing stupid."

"I don't see how he could have known it was Duane," Nick said.

"I've just got a bad feeling in my gut about Morris. Something's not right, and I don't trust him."

Nick rubbed his eyes, then the side of his head. "All I know is that he speaks to the fire department every year about tunnel safety. Seems like a normal guy."

"You know, we're taking his word for everything. What if that vent was never blocked?" Daniels stopped in the middle of the street and looked at Nick. "Jesus, could someone from the MWD be involved in this? Maybe it's not a coincidence that Morris was on call the day this incident went down. What if he's leading us on, keeping us busy, distracting us from what's really about to happen?"

"Then Cindi shouldn't be down there alone in the storm drain with him."

"She can take care of herself, but I'm gonna go get them. I want to talk to this guy."

They drew abreast of the house with the wolf-dog. The animal paced back and forth along the fence, growling at them. "Hey," Daniels said, turned his head up, and took in a deep breath through his nose. "Smell that? It smells like someone's cooking meth."

Nick inhaled and caught the distinctive smell of solvent.

Daniels walked to the window of the patrol car, and said, "Someone's doing meth in that house with the big dog."

The officer stopped the car, stuck his head out the window, and inhaled. "You're right," he said.

The sergeant got out of the car and took a few steps toward the house. As he approached, the wolf-dog bared its teeth, let loose a round of furious barking and snarling, and hurled itself against the fence. The sergeant backed away and said, "It definitely smells like meth." He walked back to the patrol car and leaned into the window to talk to the officer.

Nick caught a flash of movement out of the corner of his eye and turned to see the animal charging across the street toward them. Somehow it had managed to get out of the yard and was moving with the speed of a greyhound. Its mouth was open and its lips were pulled back to display an even row of white incisors bracketed by sharp, pointed canines. The hair on the back of the animal's neck stood straight up around a thick, chain-link collar. A deep, guttural growl came from the beast's throat—it was in full attack mode. "Watch it," Nick shouted. "The dog's loose!"

The sergeant was still leaning into the open window of the patrol car, his back to the street, when he heard Nick's warning. He turned just as the animal leaped at him and buried its teeth in his thigh. The sergeant screamed in pain, and went down on the ground with the snarling dog on top of him.

Before Nick could even think of how to get the beast off the downed police officer, Daniels pulled his pistol out of the holster on his thigh, pressed the muzzle to the side of the animal, and fired once. The shot tore a hole in the side of the dog and knocked it sideways as a gush of blood burst from its body. Its jaws went slack and it collapsed on the pavement.

The officer jumped out of the car and helped the sergeant struggle to his feet. "Son-of-a-bitch, look what that thing did to me," the sergeant said. The bloody flesh of his thigh showed under the torn material of his tan pants. "Christ, that hurts."

The four men stood by the patrol car, looking at the dying dog, still twitching as its blood drained out onto the pavement. Daniels leaned down and fired another bullet, this time to the animal's head. The shot blew apart its skull and scattered more blood and bits of bone and flesh across the street.

Nick heard another shot—a sharp, loud crack—from a high-powered rifle.

"AAHHH!" Daniels screamed out and fell to the pavement.

Two more shots followed in quick succession and the windshield of the patrol car shattered. Nick's rescue reflex kicked in and he bent to grab Daniels by the arms and to drag him to shelter around the far side of the car. Pain shot through Nick's injured wrist. Daniels was a big man and with only one good hand, Nick could barely move him. The officer joined in to help to pull Daniels across the blacktop, and the sergeant hobbled after them in a half-run, pressing his hand against his torn flesh.

When they reached the protection of the far side of the car, the sergeant kneeled next to the open passenger door and reached inside to unlock the shotgun rack mounted behind the driver's seat.

"My leg," Daniels groaned. He clenched his teeth and his face contorted into a grimace of pain.

Several more shots came from the direction of the meth house and they heard the thud, thud, thud as bullets hit the side of the patrol car.

The sergeant shouted into the radio on his shoulder. "10-33. LAPD emergency. We are under fire and have a badly wounded man. We have an active shooter and need immediate backup and medical assistance. I am at…" He turned to Nick. "Where the hell am I?'

"Fenton and Maclay Streets," Nick spoke into the sergeant's shoulder mike. "In Sylmar."

Daniels tried to sit up and look at his wound, cried out again in pain, and fell back onto the pavement.

Nick leaned over the injured man. "Hold on Rick, we've called for help." He held his small pocket knife in his left hand and cut open Daniels' bloody pant leg. "It looks like you took a bullet in the shin." An ugly patch of flesh and pieces of bone were visible, along with the blood, where the bullet had hit halfway between Daniels' knee and ankle. From what Nick could see, he thought Daniels' shin bone might be shattered. The sight of Daniels' mangled leg was shocking enough to part some of the fog in Nick's brain and allow him concentrate. "Try not to move," Nick said. He eased the pistol out of Daniels' thigh holster and tossed it on the front seat of the patrol car. Working with his injured wrist was clumsy and painful, but he managed to detach the holster and use the belt—it was already in the perfect spot—as tourniquet. Nick loosened Daniels' Kevlar vest and wondered if the shooter in the meth house had intentionally targeted the unprotected part of his body.

"How bad is it?" Daniels asked. "You can tell me." His face was contorted in pain.

"Not good," Nick said, and tried to remember his paramedic training. He tightened the belt around Daniels' thigh and tried to raise both his legs by propping them inside the open door of the patrol car.

Daniels screamed in pain. "No! Don't touch me."

"Look at me," Nick said. "Look at me, Rick, and breathe." He turned to the sergeant and asked, "Have you got a first-aid kit?"

"It's in the trunk, I can't get to it."

More shots came from across the street. The sergeant crawled around to the rear of the car, and returned fire with a loud shotgun blast that blew away part of the wood siding of the house.

The sound reverberated in Nick's ears and brought a surge of pain to his aching head. The smell of the gunpowder brought back a fleeting image of the morning's explosion in the canyon and for a second Nick remembered the sickening feeling of the fall in the helicopter. His memory was playing hide and seek.

The sergeant shoved more shells into his shotgun and swore.

The officer muttered, "I wasn't even supposed to be on duty today."

Daniels moaned.

Nick remembered something else. He pressed his hand against his shirt and felt the two sheets from the JRIC binder—the map of the Jensen plant and the diagram of the water tunnels—folded in his pocket. He pulled the pages out and looked at the tunnel diagram. There it was. He saw what it was he had been trying to recall before, and wondered how he could have forgotten.

Daniels groaned. His pant leg was soaked in red and a small pool of blood was beginning to form on the pavement. Nick thought he was about to go into shock.

Another shot ricocheted off the pavement behind the patrol car, and the sergeant returned fire again with his shotgun. The officer joined in and fired back with his pistol from the front end of the car. The street was completely empty.

"Nick."

Nick turned to see Cindi, crawling across the pavement, keeping the patrol car between her and the gunfire from the house.

"What's going on?" She saw Daniels lying on the pavement, his leg soaked in blood. "What happened to Rick?" She looked around. "And where's Morris?"

"We've got a shooter in that house," the sergeant said, and pointed across the street.

"Cindi," Nick said, "I just remembered, there's another—"

"Your man was hit," the sergeant went on. "He needs immediate medical attention. We've called for help, but I don't know how fast it's gonna get here."

Cindi leaned over Daniels and took his hand. "Hang on, Rick."

"We need a Medivac in here," Nick said. "But not with all the shooting."

"Morris left me in the storm drain," Cindi said. "Where is he? Did he come back here?"

"No," Nick said, "I haven't seen him. Listen, there is another way into the tunnel. There's a big access shaft on—"

"Another way into the tunnel?" Cindi said. "Where?"

Nick held up the page with the tunnel diagram. "About two miles west on Foothill Boulevard. It's halfway between both ends of the tunnel."

"Jesus, we should've been over there." She grabbed the map from Nick's hand. "Where did this come from?"

"I pulled it out of the JRIC binder this morning and stuffed it in my shirt. I forgot I had it. I guess I'm not thinking clearly. I—"

"Why didn't Morris tell us about it?"

"Good question. Daniels was just about to come after you. He thinks Morris may be involved in what's going on."

"Morris?" Cindi's eyes widened. "You've got to be kidding. Did he take off?"

"I haven't seen him. Rick was thinking the vent might not be blocked, and there's really no plan to blow up the tunnel."

"No plan to blow up the tunnel?" Cindi said.

"I'm not sure I can think straight," Nick said, "but I think Daniels is wrong. They are after the tunnel; it all fits together."

Two more shots came from the house, hitting the side of the patrol car. The officer responded with several shots from his pistol.

"Keep your head down," Cindi said to Nick. She looked at Daniels' leg again, and asked Nick, "How bad is it?"

"I think his bone is shattered," Nick said. "The tourniquet will only do so much. The sergeant called for backup, but I think you should call and see if the ATF can do anything. We've got to get some medical help in here."

As Nick spoke, they heard a low-pitched whine coming toward them down Fenton Avenue.

"Yesss, the Bearcat!" Cindi said, and pumped her fist in the air. "About time!"

Nick looked down the street and saw an olive-colored, four-wheel drive armored assault vehicle with gun ports and narrow windows of bullet-proof glass. It rolled up and stopped in the middle of the street, between the patrol car and the gun house. The side door slid open and Nick watched three men in battle gear emerge. They wore Kevlar helmets and armored vests marked ATF POLICE. The front of each man's vest was stuffed with high-capacity magazines, flash-bangs, and other items Nick couldn't identify. Each carried an ugly-looking black automatic weapon with a laser sight, as well as a pistol in a thigh holster. They had tinted goggles pushed up onto their foreheads, wore gloves, knee-pads, and had communications microphones attached to their shoulders. Nick had never in his life been so happy to see three men decked out for total mayhem. "One of your agents has been shot," he said. "He's losing a lot of blood."

The driver of the assault vehicle reached inside and handed Nick a medical bag. Nick pulled out gauze, bandages, a real tourniquet, and did his best with one good hand to work up a pressure bandage. Daniels screamed in pain when Nick touched his shattered leg.

"What have we got here?" a member of the assault team asked.

"There's a shooter with some kind of high-powered assault rifle in that house." the sergeant said. "Second floor, right window."

"I thought we were responding to a bomb threat," the ATF man said.

"We're still looking for our bomber," Cindi said. "Seems we're at the wrong location."

"Take these guys out," the sergeant said, pointing to the meth house, "so we can get a Medivac in here and get your man to a hospital."

The ATF man studied the gun house for a moment, and then said to the other men on his team, "We'll go through the front fence, push in the front door, and make entry. No tear gas or flash-bangs, we've got chemical fumes." He turned to the sergeant. "How about rear containment? Can your officer go with one of my men to the back of the house?"

Cindi pulled out her cell phone and hit the speed dial. "Damn Morris," she said.

SEVENTEEN
April 2008

Morris parked his white MWD pickup on the street and joined the USAR crew gathered around an open manhole leading into a 2-mile storm drain in the San Fernando Valley.

"We're gonna go with six-man entry teams," the training instructor said. "And you'll get a chance to develop some 'mask confidence' with the new four-hour rebreathers."

The firefighters stood sweating in the heat. They wore full rescue gear and carried the bulky new rebreathers on their backs. They had a stretcher loaded with extra lights, air bottles and the medic pack. It had a litter-wheel attached to the bottom, so that the men could roll it along—a necessary feature when they brought out their victim, the 200-pound rescue dummy they called Herman.

The instructor looked up to see Morris, glanced at his watch, and said, "Hey, Gene, what's up? You're here two hours early."

Morris cursed himself. How had he gotten the time wrong and arrived at the beginning of the drill instead of at the end? He could have used the extra sleep. He wasn't feeling his best—in fact, he felt terrible. He could count on the fingers of one hand the number of times in his life that he had drunk too much and had awakened the next morning with a hangover, but this was one of them. He had gone out to dinner with a friend from the DWP—the Department of Water and Power. His friend had brought someone else along, another DWP employee, and over dinner and some beers they talked about the Dodgers and the San Diego Padres. Later, they moved on to a quiet bar on Sepulveda Boulevard. The other two drank Tequila shooters and persuaded Morris to have another beer while the conversation turned to the state of affairs at their respective water utilities.

Halfway through his third beer, Morris was feeling no pain, and warmed to his favorite subject. "You know," he told the others, "California's running out of water and no one seems to care. We're not solving the problem, we're just diverting water from one part of the state to another. Robbing Peter to pay Paul. Pretty soon, there won't be any water to divert."

"You're right," his friend said, "and when that happens, it's gonna be a train wreck."

"If we live long enough to see it happen," the third man said, "we've got front-row seats."

"Live long enough?" Morris said. "Are you kidding? Unless someone starts doing something to cut down on water usage now, it will happen, and soon."

The three men had more to drink while they continued to talk. By the time Morris drove home, he was certain he would be stopped for DWI. After a fitful night of half-sleep, he felt terrible and wasn't in any mood to deliver a presentation on gassy tunnels to a bunch of firefighters.

"Here's how this drill works," the instructor continued, talking to the firefighters assembled around him. "When you get into the tunnel, you'll clip onto the rope-loop in the order I specify. We're pumping smoke, so it's a near-zero-visibility environment down there. You can slide forward or back on the loop as you move, but you can't become detached and separated from the team."

Morris went back to his pickup, sat in the passenger seat, and closed his eyes against the glare of the sun. It was the sixth year, or maybe the seventh—he couldn't remember which—that he had spoken to the men from the County Fire Department about tunnel safety. At this point, he could say what he had to say in his sleep, and today he might just do that. Through the open window of the pickup, Morris half-listened to the instructions for the rescue simulation, and thought about the things he and his friends had discussed at dinner.

"Carter, you're the lead man going in," the instructor said, reading from his clipboard. "Start the search on the right side of the tunnel. Got that? You always start on the right."

"Yessir," Nick said.

"Take high and low gas readings as you move." The instructor pointed to a long metal pole. "Use that to poke the roof. It could help you avoid a potential cave-in if you were in a dirt tunnel. Following Carter is Healy." He looked around for Healy, who raised his hand. "You're the tagger. Mark the wall with iridescent spray paint every hundred feet. If the group comes to a dangerous spot, illuminate it with a glow-stick. Behind Healy is… um…" The instructor checked his clipboard again. "Behind him is Serna. He's the mapper, and his job is to record every unusual feature in the storm drain. The medic comes next." The instructor looked up. "Who's our medic?"

"That's me," one of the men said. "Esquivel."

"OK," the instructor said, "Behind Serna is Esquivel, and behind him is Farmer, the reel-man. Farmer, you're responsible for the communications wire. Don't let it get hung up on anything. If it gets severed, the whole group is cut off from the surface. On the way back, wind it up. Last, Wolfe is the co-captain." He looked at Wolfe. "You bring up the rear. On the way out, you'll lead the group out. Retrace the same route, but on the left side." The instructor looked at the men. "Any questions?"

"Yeah," Healy said. "We're actually gonna find Herman, right? This isn't a wild goose chase?"

"He's definitely in there somewhere, and he needs help," the instructor said. "Your job is to find him and bring him out to safety."

"Are we ready?" Nick said to his crew. "Lower the equipment down after me, then enter in order, and clip on."

"Watch out for rattlers," the instructor cautioned. "They sometimes get washed into the drains."

"On air," Nick called out, as he pulled the breathing mask over his face and climbed down into the open manhole.

After the drill and debriefing was completed, the firefighters gathered on the street curb near the Engines and ate lunch. "Should we let Herman eat, or put him on a diet?" the instructor asked, and the men laughed.

In his pickup, Morris roused himself from his stupor and joined the USAR men. The sight and smell of their sandwiches made him slightly nauseous.

"This is Gene Morris," the instructor said. "He's a tunnel safety expert from the MWD. While you finish your lunch, he's going to talk about gas issues relating to tunnel entry." The instructor turned to Morris and said, "Gene, thanks for coming out today. I'll let you introduce yourself."

"Thank you," Morris said, standing on shaky legs to address the men. "I've worked for the MWD for thirty-two years, I'm a field engineer, my specialty is tunnel safety, and I'm here to tell you what I can in the next hour about entry procedures and underground gas."

What else do they need to know about me, Morris wondered. Would it be important to tell them that my father was a groundwater remediation consultant? Does it matter to them that he was a strict disciplinarian who taught me the value of water? Do any of these firefighters care that when I was a kid, my father wouldn't even let me wait for the shower to warm up? "Get in and get wet," Morris remembered him saying. "Don't waste it, it's precious. Cold water won't hurt you."

Morris had taken his father's admonitions to heart and developed his own interest in water conservation. He planned to become a hydrogeologist and enrolled at the University of California at Davis, known for its water-related engineering programs. One year into his studies, he learned an important lesson—but it had nothing to do with water conservation. When his father deserted his family and ran off to Colorado with a co-worker, Morris couldn't pay for his tuition and was forced to leave school and find a job. He had completed just enough courses to qualify as a lowly engineering intern at the Metropolitan Water District and was lucky enough to be hired. Now, after more than three decades of diligently working his way up through dozens of MWD engineering and administrative departments, he had risen no further than the level of a field engineer and knew this was the peak of his career path. During all the years, Morris had done his job and kept his mouth shut. Now he regretted that he had never found a meaningful way to speak out and express his own ideas about the need for water conservation.

"The tunnels you enter," Morris told the USAR men, "won't be as simple and as safe as this storm drain. The first issue will be the air inside. Most of what you'll encounter will be classified as 'gassy' or 'potentially gassy' by Cal-OSHA. If you go into an underground space that's outfitted with explosion-proof light fixtures, you're on notice of the danger. And if there are no lights at all, be prepared for the blackest black you've ever seen; the darkness in a tunnel will devour the beams from your head lamps." As he spoke, the group of firefighters faded before Morris's eyes and his thoughts drifted to the presentation he had delivered a few weeks earlier to a small group of water conservationists.

It was not Gene Morris the 32-year MWD employee speaking; it was Gene Morris the activist who told the group, "Too many people in the West are living in places where the natural water supply won't sustain them. If they had to survive on God Water—ordinary rain—they'd perish." "God Water" always caught everyone's attention. It was a phrase he had learned from his father.

"You may be going into subterranean passages—tunnels, drains, or old mine shafts filled with toxic and explosive gasses," Morris said to the firefighters. "You've got to expect hydrogen sulfide and some of the dangerous hydrocarbons like carbon monoxide and methane. Some of these compounds were created by decay of marine organisms over thousands of years, but watch out, because it only takes a second to ignite one of them. If you're dealing with methane, a concentration low enough to let you breathe the air can still explode and annihilate you."

The water conservationists had welcomed Morris, and were eager to listen to him. He only wished he were more than just a midlevel MWD engineer. Perhaps if he was a well-known hydrogeologist, his opinions would be more widely publicized. If he was a well-known hydrogeologist, maybe his son would be less scornful and his daughter would love him more. And his wife? That was another story.

"Sooner than later," Morris told the conservationists, "the population in California is going to outgrow the water supply. There's less rain and snow every season, and the levels of the lakes and rivers are beginning to drop. By the time we do run out of water, it'll be too late. We've built all these dams and aqueducts, all these canals and tunnels, and there won't be enough water to feed them."

It was a perfect audience. They were enthusiastic; they cared about the water supply. He saw heads nodding in agreement. Morris was in his element. If only the group was larger, if only more people could hear the message.

The firefighters ate their lunch and fiddled with their equipment while Morris spoke. He looked at them and wondered if they were bored. "Methane is the worst of the gases, because you can't smell it. It's only combustible when it's mixed with air in a concentration of five to fifteen percent. Combinations above or below that level aren't explosive, but if you ventilate and bring more air into the space, you can change the mix and cause an explosion."

The modest crowd pressed around him, and Morris felt a warm flush. This was what he was supposed to be doing—promoting the sensible management of water resources. "Half the people in California are living on arid land, in a desert, and they don't even realize it. One day, when it's too late, they'll look up and the dark clouds on the horizon will be dust, not rain."

"You have to know before you go in to any tunnel or confined space whether there's a ventilation system and if it's working, because that will affect the gas mixtures. A heavy gas like decane will lie on the floor, while methane will float to the top, so use your gas monitors accordingly. You should also know that shift in barometric pressure can cause gas to migrate into a tunnel."

"The answer is to slow population growth and reduce water usage in the dry areas. That includes a large part of Central and Southern California. It also means less water diversion. That'll affect a lot of individuals as well as the big Ag companies. People won't be happy, but it has to be done. Someone has to make it happen. We have to make a start." The crowd applauded and people surged forward to shake Morris' hand.

"Finally," Morris told the USAR team, "be careful and take your time going in. Mind what you are doing underground. Once you get in there, it may be a long distance back to fresh air. If you cause an explosion, you'll be caught in a fiery oven channeling heat and flames right at you, and you won't survive."

A man stepped out of the throng and told Morris, "I wish the politicians screwing around with the Sacramento River Delta would listen to you. Those pumps are already sucking up half our water and diverting it to Southern California. Pretty soon that won't be enough. They won't stop until they've taken every drop of fresh water out of the Delta and let the seawater come in from the Bay. We've got a farm up there, been in our family for three generations, and I know what's coming. If we don't get aggressive and do something, we're gonna lose our water. When that happens, we'll lose our land and our livelihood. We'll lose everything we've ever worked for. The problem is, we have no leverage. Somehow we've got to get the attention of the State Water Authority, the MWD, and the Department of Water and Power. Those bureaucrats have got to start listening to us." His face turned red and he scowled as he spoke.

"It's true." Morris said. "Southern California is using water at an unsustainable rate. Something has to give." He studied the man wearing high boots and work clothes, with the tan, weathered look of a farmer, and decided he liked him. The two boys standing next to him resembled him so much that they could only be his sons. More remarkable was the fact that the two were mirror images, identical twins.

"My name's Darrell," the farmer said, and shook Morris' hand. "These are my sons, Dwight and Duane. Maybe you could come up to the Delta sometime and speak to the landowners. We're planning on organizing some demonstrations."

Morris immediately forgot which son was which. The only difference he could detect between them was that one averted his eyes when he shook Morris' hand, while the other engaged him with a direct stare. They were both tapping their left foot, in unison, to some unknown beat. Someone had once told Morris that if you get to know them, identical twins are distinguishable. Could he ever tell these two apart?

Morris told the farmer, "As long as what you're planning is peaceful, I'd be happy to come up and talk." He was flattered.

"You could really help us," the twin with the direct gaze told him.

"Just remember," Morris said, "tunnel entry is dangerous. Being well prepared is your ticket home."

The firefighters clapped their hands politely, murmured thank-you's, and began to load their equipment on the Engines.

Morris shook hands with the instructor, grabbed a bottle of water, and walked to his pickup. It was now early afternoon and the hot Southern California sun was bearing down, raising the temperature, lowering the humidity, and sucking the moisture from the earth. Morris stopped for a moment and thought how ironic it was—he'd spent his entire career working for the MWD, the biggest diverter of water in the United States.

EIGHTEEN
June 22, 2014, 2:05 p.m.

"T HAT'S RIGHT." CINDI SPOKE INTO her cell phone while they crouched behind the Sheriff's cruiser, which was now riddled with bullet holes. "You are hearing gunfire. We have a problem with a shooter in a meth house. Daniels has been hit in the leg, and we need a medical response immediately. He's bleeding big time. The Response Team just arrived. As soon as they stop the gunfire, they'll notify you. Can you have a Medivac on standby?... Wait, that's not all. The MWD employee who's been helping us, Morris, may be involved in the threat.... Yes... he led us on a wild goose-chase and now he's disappeared. There's nothing here at the East Portal, but it turns out there is another entrance to this damned tunnel... uh huh... an access shaft on Foothill Boulevard... yeah... did you get any response yet from the MWD?... What's wrong with those people? Keep trying, I need whatever info you can get.... I'm headed over there, it's about two miles away.... Can you get someone to airlift in some backup to help me? Captain Carter's with me, but he's injured... OK?" Cindi disconnected and grabbed Daniels' hand. "Rick, hang on, you'll make it. Help's coming." She turned to the Special Response Team. "I need help at the access shaft. Can anyone come with us?"

"We can't take down that house without a full team," the leader said. "We'll be along as soon as we can, but first I need both my men with me here. We've got to neutralize whoever's in there before Rick can be evacuated."

Nick gave him the map from the JRIC binder. "Here's where we're going." He pointed to the spot where the access shaft was marked. "It's about two miles west on Foothill."

Cindi started to crawl away from the patrol car. "C'mon Nick," she said.

As the ATF men climbed into the Bearcat, Nick said, "Have someone contact Command and Control at L.A. County Fire. Tell them Captain Carter wants the USAR Task Force and a HazMat unit at the Sylmar Tunnel access shaft on Foothill Boulevard. Got that? Tell them the tunnel may be full of methane." He turned and followed Cindi as best he could on his hands and knees.

When they were out of the line of fire, they stood up and ran to Cindi's SUV, parked by the embankment. "No wonder Morris left his truck down the street," she said. "He didn't want anyone to see him leaving."

Nick had barely closed the door to the SUV when Cindi accelerated out of the cul-de-sac. "I hope we can get through on Foothill," he said.

Cindi sped three blocks along Fenton Street. When she turned onto Foothill Boulevard, they hit the mass of vehicles still exiting from the 210 to escape the closure. Cars and trucks were barely moving, packed bumper to bumper in both directions. "This is impossible," she muttered.

Nick sat in the passenger seat, rubbed his head, and tried to remember what he knew about the Foothill Boulevard access shaft. It probably had a steep metal stairway hung inside the circular wall, much like the old fire escapes on the sides of buildings. He knew for certain that it would be deep and dark.

Cindi swerved, hit the gas, accelerated through a small gap in the traffic, and slalomed between cars down the center lane of Foothill, reserved for left-hand turns. She leaned on her horn, lowered the tinted window and screamed at other drivers, "Move! Drive, dammit." The SUV's flashing red and blue lights had no effect—the other vehicles had no way to move aside. She wove back and forth, honked furiously, and managed to travel a couple of blocks before they came to a complete halt in a sea of cars jamming the street. She hammered the steering wheel with her fist and shouted, "Damn," then leaned back in her seat, closed her eyes, took a deep breath and blew it out. "I will remain calm and in control at all times," she said. She repeated it, then slammed the steering wheel again, and shouted, "Shit!"

Nick gazed out through the windshield. The traffic gridlock on Foothill extended far as he could see. Black smoke and embers drifted through the air toward them from the direction of Magazine Canyon. "The brush fire," he said.

"What about it?" Cindi said.

"It's moving this way. This isn't just traffic from the freeway. Foothill Boulevard may be closed because of the fire."

"Is it really possible Morris is involved?" Cindi said. "None of this makes sense. If he was working with them, why would he even mention the covered gas vent? Wouldn't he just let us flounder around without saying anything?"

Nick wasn't listening. He was thinking that it was Sunday. Cindi was by his side, and they were spending the day together, just as he had planned it. "Cindi," he said.

"He could have just kept his mouth shut and we probably wouldn't have even thought about the tunnel as a target. It doesn't make sense," she repeated.

"Cindi."

"What?"

"I was going to ask… I want you to… uh… will you marry me?"

She looked at him for a moment with a startled look on her face, and then began to laugh.

"What's so funny?"

"It's just… you're proposing to me? Now? In the middle of this shitstorm? You almost died this morning in a copter crash, there's a bomber running loose, and everything is in total chaos. I've been waiting for months for you to pop the question, and now you decide to ask me to marry you?"

"I had a ring. I was going to give it to you today, but it went down with the helicopter. It's probably just a blob of melted gold now."

"Yes."

"But first, there's something I have to—"

"I said yes, Nick. Yes, I'll marry you. Yes, yes, yes."

"Yes?"

"Yes. And I think I know what you want to tell me. About your father? What he did. Right?"

They were less than two feet apart in the SUV. Nick looked at Cindi's face. It still had the dried blood and scratches from the pursuit through the brush. For an instant, she was a blur. "How long have you known?" He felt dizzy.

"A couple of months. Maybe it's just my nature, but once I got really serious about you, I had to do a background check. I'm a cop, remember? So I already know your father killed a police officer in Bakersfield—and I figured when the right time came, we'd talk about it." She turned to look at him again. "Christ, Nick, you look so pale; your face is covered with sweat."

Nick sat in the passenger seat of the SUV and tried to concentrate on what Cindi was telling him. He watched her lips as she spoke. They were dry and cracked. His head throbbed. He wanted to lean over and kiss her. They were going to be married. A wave of nausea washed over him. He heard the sound of horns from the traffic jam on Foothill Boulevard. The smell of the explosion in Magazine Canyon still lingered in his nostrils. His ribs and shoulder hurt. His wrist throbbed. "You knew?"

"Yes, and I know there was a different Willie Carter who was killed in the Sylmar Tunnel. I think I understand about all that, and someday, any day but today, you can tell—" Her emergency tone sounded. "Burns," she answered. "On the south side of Foothill?" Cindi said aloud. "A circular cement structure, off the street, behind a fence. Got it."

Nick nodded. "Sounds familiar."

"Two separate entry doors," Cindi continued, repeating out loud what she was being told. "An outer door, and an airtight inner door at the top of the shaft. A metal staircase down… Good, that helps. Do we have anyone on scene? Eyes on the outer door?... No?... There's a brush fire out here and we're stuck in traffic.… I think I'm going to have to walk. Captain Carter's here, but he's suffering from a concussion.… Get me some help." Cindi put her phone away and looked at Nick. "You look like you're about to pass out."

"I don't feel right," Nick said. He leaned back against the seat.

"What do you think Dwight has planned?"

"Planned?"

A small gap in the traffic opened and Cindi moved three car lengths down Foothill Boulevard. "What exactly are we trying to prevent him from doing?"

"I think he's going to ignite the methane in the tunnel." Nick squeezed his eyes closed and tried to clear his head. Images flashed through his brain—Cindi walked naked into her bathroom—the explosion in Magazine Canyon rose up in a black and orange cloud—the fire paramedic said, "You could have a concussion"— Daniels lay on the ground, writhing in pain.

"But how does he ignite it? Can he just toss a flame in from the top of the shaft? Does he have to leave a device in the tunnel to set off the gas?"

"Yeah, sure. But maybe not."

"What does that mean?" She started to maneuver the SUV toward the curb.

Nick rummaged through his memory. "If he ignites it from the top, just the gas in the shaft will explode. You'll have a big… uh… vertical explosion, blowing up out into the air. But if he…" Nick fidgeted in the seat and released the safety belt.

"But what, Nick?"

"I'm trying to think how it works." Nick paused and rubbed his eyes. "Yeah, OK. If he ignites it from the top, only the gas in the shaft blows, but if he sets it off it from inside the tunnel, from the bottom, the explosion will move horizontally." Nick paused again. "Yeah, then the whole tunnel will blow up. Sorry, I've got such a headache."

Cindi managed to get into the right-hand lane, and drove the SUV over the curb onto the sidewalk. "Nick, listen, you're not in any shape to do anything. I can get to the access shaft on foot and I'm leaving you here, OK? You can't—"

"Leave me here? No, I'm fine, I'm coming with you. You're not going by yourself."

"No, you're not fine. I'll be back as soon as I can, or I'll send someone to get you. Do you understand? Are you listening to me?" She shook Nick's shoulder. "You stay here and wait." She shook him again. "Tell me you understand what I just said."

"Yes, I hear you. I'm OK, don't worry about me."

Cindi leaned over and kissed him. "Good. And yes. Yes. I want to marry you, as soon as this is over. See you later. I love you." She got out, closed the door, and disappeared in the crowd of people on the sidewalk.

Nick sat in the car, thinking about what Cindi had just said. He wanted to explain to her about his father. He was in prison at Pleasant Valley and… he closed his eyes and leaned back against the seat.

"Hey you moron, get this car off the sidewalk."

Nick opened his eyes. A man was pounding on the windshield. He glared at Nick through the glass before he turned and walked away. Nick looked out at the plume of smoke rising in the sky. He blinked his eyes. Had he dozed off or lost consciousness? Whatever had happened, he felt a little better. The clock on the dashboard indicated it was 2:25 p.m. He remembered. Cindi left him in the SUV. She was on her way to the access shaft—alone. The woman he loved, the woman he planned to marry, was by herself, risking her life, heading to a confrontation with a terrorist. She had asked for his help this morning. She needed him now. He was a captain in USAR Task Force 103. He was the one who knew about tunnel entry and all the gas risks. He should be with her. What was he doing sitting in the SUV?

Nick opened the door and felt unsteady as he got out. He held onto the outside door handle for a moment until his head cleared. The air carried the odor of automobile exhaust and the burning scent of the nearby brush fire. He stood on the sidewalk in front of a Mercado with a sign in the window that said, WIRE MONEY—ANYWHERE!!! People streamed past him, moving away from the oncoming flames. Bright flashes of light pierced his eyes. On the corner, dozens of chrome wheel rims and hubcaps hung suspended from the roof of SAL'S AUTO PARTS, a gaudy little gold and purple building. The wind blew, and each disk became a twisting mirror, reflecting light in all directions, shining into Nick's delicate eyes, blinding him.

Nick looked away and started west down Foothill Boulevard. Between the two and three story apartment buildings lining the street, he saw the traffic jam on the 210. He walked past a drive-through fajita restaurant and inhaled the smell of cooking. He hadn't eaten all day, but still he wasn't hungry. In the parking lot of the restaurant he saw Morris' empty white MWD pickup truck. It still had ash on it from the fire in Magazine Canyon. Nick started to run down Foothill Boulevard, toward the access shaft, against the tide of people.

NINETEEN
September 2010

N ICK STOPPED AT THE STARBUCKS on Sierra Madre Avenue. It was a Saturday, and the early crowd had swept through the shop, picked up their coffees, and disappeared. The place was deserted. He took his double espresso outside and sat down on the empty deck, resting his feet on the wood railing. Behind the store, the foothills of the San Gabriel Mountains began their gradual ascent into the Angeles National Forest. Before him, the city of Los Angeles stretched out below, partially obscured in a blanket of haze and smog.

Nick pushed his chair back onto its two rear legs and let his mind wander. He didn't like the path it took. Suddenly he was thinking about the trip he had taken to the Pleasant Valley Prison a decade ago. After all the years, he still recalled each detail of his father's face and it was a memory he did not want to revisit. He tried to clear his mind and checked the time. It was only 8:45 a.m., but the air in the foothills was already hot and dry. He had 30 minutes to kill before driving on to Manooshian Park, where the Foothill Caving Club met once a month. Nick had joined years ago. The members, a small group of enthusiastic and expert cavers ranging in age from 20 to 50, regularly explored the caves that honeycomb the mountains in Los Angeles and Ventura counties. In the last year, Nick had lost some of his enthusiasm for the club and thought this might be the last meeting he would attend. By now, he had already seen the inside of most of the caves in Southern California, and if he needed thrills, his USAR activities provided him with more than enough excitement.

While he finished his coffee, a faded red Jeep Cherokee pulled into the parking lot. Nick recognized it immediately. The battered old Jeep belonged to an attractive woman who had recently become a member of the club. Since she had begun attending the explorations, Nick had admired her trim, compact body and the confident way she crawled through the underground passages. They had said hello a few times and chatted once, briefly, about caving. On several occasions, he had looked up and met her eyes.

Cindi Burns knew exactly what she was doing when she stopped for a cup of coffee. Her "accidental" meeting of the handsome firefighter wasn't a coincidence at all—she had planned it for weeks. In the past, the first thing she did with any man she met was look at him as a suspect—Cindi was a cop, and she couldn't help it. She was determined that this time would be different. She would simply get acquainted and enjoy his company. If he ever turned out to be a serious love interest, there would be plenty of time to find out everything there was to know about Nick Carter, USAR Captain at the Los Angeles County Fire Department. "Morning," she said, as she walked up on to the deck. "Want some company?"

"Sure," Nick said.

She went inside and returned in a moment with a large, black, iced coffee. She pulled up a chair next to Nick, sat down and extended her hand. "We've never really met. I'm Cindi, with an "I." Cindi Burns."

For the first time, Nick was able to look at her up close, in bright daylight. He thought she might be 40. She had light brown hair, beautiful skin, and dark, intense eyes. When he shook her hand, it was wet and cold from the plastic cup. He felt rough, calloused skin and a strong grip. "I'm Nick."

"Hey, Nick. There a last name attached to it?"

"Carter, Nick Carter."

"What do you do?" she asked. "You look pretty comfortable underground."

"I'm a firefighter. Search and rescue. You?"

"I'm a special agent with the ATF."

"ATF?" Nick raised his eyebrows. "Someone named Cindi with an "I" works for the ATF?"

"My real name is Lucinda, but no one calls me that. If they did, I'd break their neck. I transferred down from the San Francisco field office two years ago."

"You don't look like a cop. You're too good-looking."

"Yeah, and I can walk and chew gum at the same time." She flashed a broad smile. "My father was in law enforcement, I'm just following in his footsteps."

Nick looked at her left hand. She wasn't wearing a wedding ring. "I've always wondered, do female cops just date other cops?"

"It starts out that way, but the problem is that with male cops it turns into a rivalry. They begin to play mind games. Pretty soon they're interviewing you, trying to analyze you, sizing you up, and getting competitive. Stuff like that. It's enough that I have to out-macho the men at work and compete with them in physical fitness training, I don't need a performance evaluation in bed. A long time ago, I was married to an FBI agent. That lasted less than two years, and it was a big mistake."

Nick felt a strong attraction to this woman. "Well, I'm sure there are plenty of civilian men who would like to go out with you."

"I haven't dated much lately, can't find the right guy," she continued. "Civilians love the idea of going out with a chick that carries a gun, but that gets old fast, and then my erratic schedule drives them off. They expect me to be at home cooking dinner every night when they come home." She met his gaze. "You know, you have beautiful eyes."

"You're embarrassing me."

"That color is very rare. I think it's called convict blue."

"Convict blue?" Nick tensed up. "I've never heard anyone describe my eye color as convict blue."

"Did you ever have an aquarium when you were a kid? Remember the angel fish? With the black stripes, like a prison uniform? Their real name is Convict Cichlid, and the color of their bodies is convict blue." She gave him a dazzling smile. "That's the color of your eyes."

Nick relaxed. "Never heard that before. So what's it like to be an ATF agent?"

"We deal with a lot of slime—nuts with explosives and gangs trafficking in guns. Every day's a shitstorm. I worked undercover for a while. If we dated, you could tell your friends you went out with someone who spent a year with the Sons of Silence." She gave him another broad smile.

Nick liked her openness, and her insolence. "A motorcycle mamma, huh? I happen to love motorcycles."

"So do I, but I have to tell you, I spent a winter on a bike in Wichita. The snow and rain sucks. I'll take Southern California any day."

"Have any biker tattoos?"

She laughed and said, "Well, I only have one, and it hardly sees the light of day." She looked at her watch. "You know, I'm not sure I can take the cave group today. Want to do something else?"

"You must be reading my thoughts," Nick said. "What do you have in mind?"

"C'mon, you'll find out."

Nick followed her Jeep up San Gabriel Canyon Road for several miles. After they passed a large reservoir, she turned off onto a dirt road that ran into the dry, dusty hills above Glendora. She barely slowed when the road narrowed and then became two dirt ruts. It finally disappeared altogether and she stopped in a clearing surrounded by chaparral and shrub. By the time Nick pulled up behind her, she was already out of her Jeep, pulling a small pack out of the back. A few hundred feet away, a granite wall of one of the San Gabriel Mountains rose up abruptly.

"We're here," she said.

"We are?" Nick glanced around. They were somewhere on the south edge of the Angeles National Forest. "Where's here?"

"Come on," Cindi said. "I'll take you somewhere you've never been."

"What gear do I need?"

"Just your helmet and headlamp. I'll bring my small pack, just in case."

Nick heard the enthusiasm in her voice and, in turn, felt a wave of excitement wash over him.

"Where are you from?" she asked.

"I grew up in Fresno. You?"

"Sacramento," she said. For a moment, she looked at Nick in a strange way and he wondered what she was thinking. The serious look faded and she gave him a quick smile. "We're not going far," she said, and set off through the shrubs toward the wall of granite.

Nick followed close behind her and after a short walk, they emerged at the base of the huge outcropping of rock. A two-foot wide crevice split the face.

"This is it," she said

"It is?" Nick looked at the crack in the stone.

"C'mon." She was already heading toward the opening.

Nick put on his helmet and secured the headlamp with the Velcro straps.

Cindi slipped on her own helmet and light, slung her small pack over one shoulder and disappeared sideways into the crevice.

Nick followed her and found himself pressed between two walls of stone. He had learned long ago that the narrowest possible squeeze for a caver is the distance between the tip of his thumb and the tip of his little finger, spread wide. This space was not much bigger. He exhaled to make himself thinner and inched sideways for several feet in near darkness, the rough sides of the rock rubbing against his back and stomach. He emerged on a stone shelf jutting out from the wall of a vertical passageway, looked up, and saw only black space where the beam of his headlamp ended. He looked down into a similar hole of darkness. A cable ladder, secured with rivets set in the stone, provided a descent. Cindi stood waiting on the small ledge, less than a foot from him. In the cool air of the cave, Nick could feel the heat coming off her body. "This place is unreal," he said. "You know where you're going, right?"

She turned toward him and the light from her headlamp shined directly into his eyes, causing him to squint. "I know this place like the palm of my hand. I worked one summer for the Bureau of Land Management and helped map it." She grabbed one of the cables and stepped onto the ladder. "Like this? One of my assignments was to anchor it into the wall. I know every rung." She began her descent and the beam from her headlamp bounced against the side of the shaft as she climbed down.

Nick followed her and counted the rungs. At 44, he touched ground. Down in this pit, the air was moist and even cooler, a dramatic change from the near-desert conditions they had left behind.

Without saying a word, Cindi sank to her knees and began to crawl through a twisting, three-foot diameter passageway. Nick crawled along behind her. His headlamp reflected off her backside and he marveled at her perfect ass, outlined under her green coveralls. He had the urge to reach out and grab her, and wondered what would happen if he did. If she had her gun, she might shoot him and leave him for dead. Or, she could just give a swift kick backwards, hit him in the face and break his nose. Most likely, she would just be pissed, and it would ruin the beginning of what seemed to be a promising relationship. Nick lowered his eyes to the bottoms of her soles and concentrated on following her.

He guessed they had crawled about 25 feet when they emerged into an underground grotto. Nick stood up, looked around in the light of their headlamps, and was overwhelmed. Somewhere, in the dark recesses of the cave, he heard the distant sound of running water—an underground stream—and wondered how many centuries it had taken to sculpt the space in the stone around them.

"Here we are," she said. She put her gloved hand lightly on his arm. "I don't know how many men would just follow me without freaking out and asking a million questions. You passed the first test."

The walls of the chamber disappeared up into the darkness. In places, their headlamps illuminated white pillars of calcite, created by centuries of dripping water, rising up against the sides. A pool of black water covered most of the floor. Cindi sat down, and when Nick joined her, he realized they were sitting on fine, black sand. "Amazing," was all he could say.

"Now let's try this," she said, and reached over, took off his helmet and turned off the headlamp. "Lie on the sand." She turned off her own headlamp.

Nick had been in the dark in dozens of caves, but this was the most absolute black he had ever experienced. His irises expanded to their maximum, but eyes open or shut, it made no difference. The darkness pressed against him, a thick, heavy feeling as though he was under a bulky blanket. He lay on his back, felt the soft and accommodating sand, and wondered what it would be like to spend the night in this non-light, with this woman next to him, wrapped in a sleeping bag and the darkness, oblivious to the passage of time and the sun.

Cindi moved closer. Along with the distant sound of water, he heard his own long, slow respiration, and her shorter breaths. He lay motionless, imagining the weight of the entire mountain pressing down on him. "I passed the first test?" he said. "What's the second?"

"You'll find out."

He felt her lips brush his face. He thought if he ever wanted to marry this woman, he would have to tell her his father was a cop killer.

TWENTY
June 22, 2014, 2:40 p.m.

NICK WAS STILL MORE THAN a block away from the Foothill Boulevard access shaft when he heard the piercing, high-pitched sound of an alarm. As he came closer to the windowless cement dome that covered the shaft, the noise became deafening and penetrated to the center of his brain. The gray structure was set back from the street, surrounded by an 8-foot-high chain-link fence; the entry gate lay on the ground, twisted and bent. People fleeing the brush fire streamed past on the nearby sidewalk and the vehicles caught in the traffic gridlock moved a few feet at a time, but no one paid any attention to the shrieking alarm. Nick looked in vain for any law enforcement personnel, and he would have been overjoyed to see the big red trucks from USAR 103, but the area around the shaft was deserted. More important, there was no sign of Cindi.

He pressed the palms of his hands against his ears, walked partway around the structure, and saw an empty white Ford van. The driver's side door was open, and when Nick looked in the back, he saw old newspapers, a couple of dirty sleeping bags, empty plastic water bottles, and a half-eaten bucket of Kentucky Fried Chicken. What he didn't see was a pile of fertilizer or anything that might be an explosive device. A Southern California Thomas Guide street atlas lay on the front passenger seat, open to the grid that included Sylmar. Nick looked at it more closely and saw the location of the access shaft on Foothill Boulevard circled in blue ink. On the floor he saw an MWD business card that belonged to Gene Morris, Field Engineer. A telephone number—Morris' cell number?—was written at the top of the card in the same blue color. "Morris, you bastard," Nick said to himself.

He continued on around the cement structure to the half-open steel door that was bent where someone had used a crowbar on the latch to gain entry. He glanced at the warning sign—NO TRESPASSING – $500 FINE OR 6 MONTHS IN JAIL—and pushed the door open as far as the hinges would allow, hoping to start venting whatever methane gas had accumulated inside. The alarm sound continued to drill into his brain and the pain was excruciating.

Nick stepped inside and took a tentative breath. He inhaled musty, damp air, but didn't smell any gas, although without a sensor it would be impossible to detect methane. He thought of the Draeger meter, packed in his equipment bag, somewhere in the wreckage of the 412. The empty chamber was lit by a few dim fluorescent lights mounted high on the circular wall. A thin layer of dust on the floor had been disturbed, and Nick saw several sets of footprints and scuff marks leading to a steel stairway. Had Cindi ignored everything he told her and gone into the shaft after Dwight? And where was Morris? Was he down there with them? Nick glanced at his watch—2:46 p.m. How long had they been in the tunnel? He fought back anxious thoughts about Cindi as he followed the trail to the stairs. Was a huge gas explosion—like the one that annihilated the miners 40 years ago—about to come blowing up the shaft? He stopped to let a wave of dizziness pass, and then descended two flights to a small cement platform and another steel door, one with an air-tight seal. The sign on this door said TEST AIR BEFORE ENTERING. That's not an option at the moment, Nick thought, and struggled to release the pressure latch with his left hand. He pulled the heavy door open and stepped onto a steel grate suspended at the top of the 25-foot-wide shaft. He saw the first flights of metal stairs winding around and down the circular wall into the black hole leading to the bowels of the Sylmar Tunnel. How deep was the shaft? One hundred seventy-five feet? Two hundred feet? He had no idea. The explosion-proof light fixture mounted inside the doorway was dark; the bulb was burnt out. As soon as Nick let go of the heavy door, it swung shut, extinguishing the fluorescent glow from the other side and leaving him in total darkness. He pushed it open, and again it swung closed when he released it.

Nick stood in total darkness on the grate and screamed, "Cindi?"

Silence.

"Cindi" he shouted again, held his breath, and listened for a response, any sound, however faint.

Silence.

Nick opened his eyes wide and hoped his pupils could adjust and gather some light, but the darkness was absolute. He reached into his pocket, pulled out his truck keys, and grasped the tiny, ultra-bright LED flashlight attached to his key chain. On a whim, he had once purchased it for $2.99 at a gas station, but had never used it. Now the device, the size of his little finger, was a godsend. He pressed the button, and a thin ray of blue-white light penetrated a few feet into the heavy night surrounding him.

He yelled "Cindi," once more. This time, he thought he heard the faint sound of water somewhere far below. Nick pointed the tiny light down toward his feet, held the rail with his good hand, and began to descend the metal stairs into the black abyss.

The luminous dial on his watch showed 2:49 p.m.

Twelve stairs down, a small steel landing, and 12 more stairs. Nick's USAR training told him to keep a count.

Around and down.

His rubber-soled shoes barely made a noise against the steel tread of the steps, but the heartbeat in his chest sounded like thunder. Nick felt light-headed and dizzy. He continued step by step, descending as fast as he could. The total blackness swallowed him.

"Cindi?"

Silence.

Nick soon lost track of how many steps he had descended. Did it matter?

He checked his watch again. It was 2:51 p.m., and he thought these could be the last minutes of his life. He continued down, then paused, and stood motionless on the metal stairway. Nick held his breath and directed his puny light into the darkness below. He sensed he wasn't alone. A presence loomed somewhere nearby. Were the ghosts of the dead Sylmar miners waiting for him in the shaft?

A disembodied voice floated up to Nick. "Get out."

The voice sounded familiar. Nick went down another flight.

"Go back, there's gas. It's going to explode."

Nick descended a few more stairs.

"Don't come down here. Save yourself."

His penlight illuminated a face wearing wire-rim glasses on the landing below. "Morris," Nick exclaimed. "What are you doing here? Where's Cindi?"

Morris looked up at Nick and turned on a high-intensity, hand-held emergency light. He pointed the powerful beam directly at Nick's face.

Nick was blinded. He held up his hands to shield his sensitive eyes from the light. "Jesus," he exclaimed, "turn that off."

"This wasn't supposed to happen," Morris said. The light jittered back and forth, and the beam raked across Nick's face.

"Where's Cindi?" Nick took a couple more steps down. "Is she down in the tunnel?"

"We planned a demonstration," Morris said, ignoring Nick's questions. "Here at the shaft. A big rally. Peaceful. People from the Delta were supposed to come. Hundreds of them." The words spilled out of Morris, he wasn't even talking to Nick. "I tried to do something good. We're running out of water. I tried to help." His voice rose as he spoke.

"Where is she?"

"They lied. I should have known." The beam from the emergency light cast Nick's shadow against the smooth cement lining of the shaft. "They were always edgy. They came back from the Army... their father died... and everything changed."

"Morris, listen to me." Nick descended another step and squinted into the light, trying to see. "Where's Cindi?"

"When I heard about the explosion in Magazine Canyon, I knew something was wrong, but I... I didn't realize what they were planning... until I saw the blocked gas vent. It wasn't supposed to happen like this."

Nick stepped down onto the landing next to Morris, reached out, and shook Morris with his bad hand, sending a sharp pain from his wrist up through his arm to his shoulder. "Stop babbling. Is Cindi in the tunnel? Is she down there with Dwight?"

Morris was hysterical. "The device didn't work. I tried to stop him, but he went back... into the tunnel. He's trying to fix it."

"Did she go after him?" Nick shouted, even though Morris was only a few inches away. "Answer me."

"Yes," Morris said between sobs. "She came down looking for him. And she said I was under arrest. I'm supposed to wait outside... Arrest?... Prison?... I can't go to prison."

Nick exploded. "Give me that damn thing." He grabbed the emergency light from Morris. The two men stood face to face, and now it was Nick's turn to shine the light in Morris' eyes. "Damn you," Nick said. He pushed Morris aside. "Get out of the way."

"I had a bad feeling...." Morris moved to the edge of the small steel landing. "I'm sorry, I didn't mean—"

He was a shadow that went over the railing and melted into the blackness. His hoarse shriek faded as he plunged to the bottom of the shaft.

Nick heard the soft but solid impact of Morris' body, and then there was a hush. All that remained was the sound of his own breathing.

2:53 p.m.

Nick descended as fast as he could, shining the emergency light ahead of him. His feet barely touched one step before he was on to the next one. He paid no attention to the pain in his body or the ache in his head. He ignored the danger of slipping and falling into the shaft. He forgot about the gas. He didn't think about an explosion. His only thought was to find Cindi and bring her out.

After what seemed like an endless descent, Nick reached the bottom and stood panting on the last metal step. He gazed down at the murky water on the tunnel floor, illuminated by the beam from the emergency light. A few feet away, Morris lay crumpled and broken, face down, one arm under his body, his legs splayed apart. His shattered wire-rim glasses were nearby.

The air at the bottom of the shaft was thick and damp, and it reeked of some kind of petrochemical. Nick stepped down into several inches of cold water on the invert of the 21-foot-wide tunnel, and it began to seep into his shoes. The passageway ran off in both directions; he stood halfway between the East Portal and Magazine Canyon and had no idea which way to go.

2:55p.m.

"Cindi?" Nick screamed several times, and the effort left his pulse throbbing in his skull. He pressed one hand against his forehead, trying to drive away the pain of his headache. At the base of the shaft, his shouts were muffled and diminished. There was no echo; his voice melted into the cement lining of the tunnel. Nick pointed Morris' light in one direction, then the other. All he saw were white circular stains and deposits of calcium on the cement, left by water seeping in through the cracks. The beam seemed weaker. Were his eyes beginning to fail?

Nick's training told him to always start a search to the right, which he did, and headed off into the tunnel. He hadn't taken 10 steps before the emergency light flickered and went out, plunging him back into the terrifying darkness. Nick shook the light and pressed the switch several times, but he remained in the dark. He dropped it, pulled out his tiny LED flashlight, and continued on. At that moment, he would have given anything to have a complete USAR team with him; outfitted with rebreathers, helmet lights, and a rope linking them together.

Nick sloshed along through the water. Every few steps he screamed, "Cindi," then paused and listened for a response. He shouted so many times that his throat felt raw. His wrist hurt. His bruised ribs ached. He was exhausted and although he didn't want to admit it, he was frightened. The darkness pressed against him. Nick tried to steady himself. His head was spinning and he thought he might faint. The ground underneath him was moving. The overwhelming hydrocarbon odor—Kerosene? Gasoline? Oil?—was suffocating him. He wasn't getting enough air in the unventilated tunnel. Nick tried to take shallow breaths, but the smell and the taste filled his mouth and sank into his lungs. Suddenly his empty stomach convulsed and a surge of bitter acid rose in the back of his throat. Nick bent over and spit into the tunnel water. His eyes began to tear. He closed them and leaned against the circular wall, trying to gain control of his senses.

When the earth stopped whirling, Nick opened his eyes again and tried to get his bearings in the darkness. How far had he come? Could Cindi be somewhere behind him, on the other side of the access shaft? He decided it was time to turn back; he was certain he had gone the wrong way. Nick flashed his tiny light in both directions and was totally disoriented. He stood in the middle of the invert and felt the cold water in his shoes. USAR Captain Nick Carter of the Los Angeles County Fire Department was lost in the Sylmar Tunnel.

3:03 p.m.

He took a few tentative steps.

"Turn around, Nick."

Nick peered into the darkness.

"You're going the wrong way."

It was a deep voice. Nick stopped and stood still while the tunnel again spun around him.

"You're heading toward the East Portal. The access shaft is behind you."

Nick stared into the darkness. "Who—"

"Shine your light on the side of the tunnel."

Nick pointed his feeble LED at the cement lining.

"See that brass disk with the number on it?"

"Willie?" Nick heard himself say.

"That's a tunnel station marker. They're mounted on the wall every 500 feet."

"Willie Carter?" Nick remembered the story Rainwater told him about entering the burning tunnel. He remembered the pictures from the archives. He thought of the charred bodies, and of the men who had been blown to pieces, their remains brought out in buckets. "Did you know your friend Ralph Brissette survived the explosion? He made it out. He's alive. I talked to him, and he—"

"The numbers get smaller as you head back toward Magazine Canyon. Nick, you're going the wrong direction."

"… he went to see your wife and daughters as soon as he got out of the hospital."

"The station number at the access shaft is 894."

"Lockheed shouldn't have let you go to work in the tunnel that night."

"Go."

"But at least your family received a payment. A lot of money. It must have helped"

…

"Willie?"

…

The darkness had nothing more to say, and Nick turned and started back, holding his pathetic little light. On his way to the access shaft, he realized Willie Carter's daughters were now older than Willie was when the methane explosion killed him.

TWENTY ONE
June 22, 2014, 3:14 p.m.

NICK ARRIVED BACK AT THE bottom of the access shaft where Morris' body still lay in the water at the foot of the stairs. He shined his LED on the side of the wall and saw it—the brass disk with tunnel station number 894. He tried to think clearly about Cindi. What if he had somehow missed her? While he had gone off in the wrong direction, had she already left the tunnel, expecting to find him waiting on the surface? Yes, Nick decided, that was it, she was already at the top.

He climbed the first flight of stairs, but stopped on the landing and reconsidered. How long had he been in the tunnel? It seemed like hours. He looked at his watch. It was only 3:14 p.m. Wasn't it just before three o'clock when he was descending the stairs? He had been inside less than half an hour. Maybe Cindi was still in the tunnel, chasing after Dwight. Nick changed his mind. He had to search in the other direction. He retraced his steps down, stepped over Morris' body, and splashed off through the water.

"Cindi? Hello?"

He continued on, stopped, and thought he heard a barely audible noise.

"Cindi?" he shouted in desperation.

This time, he was certain he heard a faint sound, a muted response. Nick began to run, as best he could, down the center of the pitch black tunnel.

He thought he saw a flickering light in the distance. He strained to see it more clearly.

It disappeared.

It was visible again.

Nick ran toward it.

The small, square glow grew brighter as Nick approached it. Soon he made out the dark outline of a person.

"Nick? Nicky?"

She stood in the middle of the tunnel, holding the cell phone in front of her. The screen was lit up. "Thank God it's you. I thought I heard someone shouting, but couldn't tell which direction it was coming from. I got so disoriented down here; I'm lost, I don't even know which way it is back to the stairs."

"Why are you here in the first place? I told you not to come in here." Nick wrapped his arms around her.

"And I told you to stay in the SUV." She hugged him back. "I saw Dwight going in up at the top. I was sure I could stop him."

"And you came down here without a light?"

"No," she waved her cell phone. "I've got my flashlight app."

"Oh, great." Nick shined his small light on her face. Cindi was a mess, but he thought she looked beautiful. "Is he still down here?"

"I think so. He flew down the stairs and took off before I even got to the bottom. I could barely see. On the way down I ran into Morris. He was just standing there on a landing, in the dark. He mumbled something about Dwight and an ignition device. That it hadn't worked. He was almost incoherent."

"Let's go, Cindi." Nick grabbed her hand. "I don't want to be down here to find out if he fixed it."

"I came down here to stop him."

"You did your best. C'mon."

"And I let him get away."

Nick started to pull her back toward the access shaft. He had never felt so tired.

She followed him through the water. "At least we got Morris. I arrested him."

"It doesn't matter."

"Why?"

"He jumped off the stairs."

"No!"

"Give me your phone, I need the light." Nick took the phone from her hand and continued on. He tried to run, but the best he could do was stagger. Cindi followed behind him, and it seemed forever before they reached the bottom of the steel stairway. Nick kept looking back, expecting to see Dwight, or even worse, the flash of an explosion.

They stepped around Morris' lifeless body and began to climb. The stairs seemed to ascend forever. On the way down, Nick hadn't thought about how hard it would be to climb back up.

"Remember when I took you into the cave?" Cindi said behind him. "I think I fell in love with you that day."

Nick was one step ahead of her; pulling her up with his left hand. He was exhausted, drawing on a reserve of energy and adrenaline he didn't know he had. He looked up and saw nothing but the darkness.

"Still want to marry me?" she asked, beginning to struggle for breath.

They were going surfing. Nick had a picnic in his truck. Then he would take Cindi to sit on the motorcycle. He had a ring. They just had to get to the top of the shaft.

"Nicky? I said, 'Do you still want to marry me?'"

"Before he could answer, Nick heard shouts and looked up. Far above them, the door at the top of the shaft was open. Now he saw light—a lot of light, shining down on them from huge fire department emergency lamps. Through the glare, he saw a group of yellow angels descending from heaven—it was a USAR team, starting down the circular stairs. "Cindy," he said. "They're here."

The sound came from somewhere in the bowels of the tunnel. It was a distant clap of thunder. Nick felt it as much as he heard it; a change in the air pressure that hit his eardrums. He felt it in his chest. Then the concussion hit him hard and knocked him forward against the stairs. When his head hit the metal, he lost his grasp on Cindi's hand.

The roiling, angry cloud of smoke and flames blew up the shaft. Nick didn't experience anything in slow motion—it happened in the blink of an eye. Before the heat and smoke engulfed them, Nick Carter remembered that he hadn't done his laundry.

TWENTY TWO

LOS ANGELES TIMES - July 9, 2014
WEDDING ANNOUNCEMENTS

Lucinda Hope Burns and Nick Carter were married on July 1 at the UCLA Medical Center Hospital. The ceremony was conducted by Los Angeles County Fire Department Chaplain Paul Thornburg.

The bride and groom are both recovering from multiple injuries sustained during the recent terrorist incident in which a California man protesting water diversion from the Sacramento River Delta was killed after igniting methane gas trapped inside the Sylmar Tunnel. The explosion damaged several homes along Fenton Street and forced the evacuation of part of a Sylmar neighborhood. After the incident, the Metropolitan Water District reported that the water delivery infrastructure had not been compromised and that service was functioning normally.

The bride, 43, is a special agent in the Los Angeles field office of the Bureau of Alcohol, Tobacco and Firearms. She is the daughter of Alice Hope and the late Robert Hope of Bakersfield and Sacramento. Her father, a Bakersfield police captain, was killed in the line of duty during a convenience store robbery in 1971.

The groom, 43, is a fire captain with the Urban Search and Rescue Task Force of the Los Angeles County Fire Department. He is the son of the late Ellie Carter, of Fresno. Captain Carter placed a slightly misshapen ring on the bride's finger. He lost the ring when he was involved in a helicopter crash near Sylmar. It was subsequently found in the wreckage by members of Captain Carter's USAR team and returned to him in time for the wedding.

The bride's mother joined them at the hospital for the wedding, along with Ralph Brissette, the only survivor of the first explosion in the Sylmar Tunnel in 1971.

PHOTOGRAPHIC ARCHIVE

Figure 1. Sylmar Tunnel – East Portal. A group of investigators and trainmen prepare to enter the Sylmar water district tunnel hoping to find survivors from the early morning blast.
June 25, 1971. Los Angeles Public Library Photo Collection.

Figure 2. View From Inside the East Portal.
June 25, 1971. Los Angeles Public Library Photo Collection.

Figure 3. Foothill Boulevard Access Shaft. Rim view, looking down into the opening of the 250 foot deep Foothill Boulevard access shaft. June 26, 1971. Los Angeles Public Library Photo Collection.

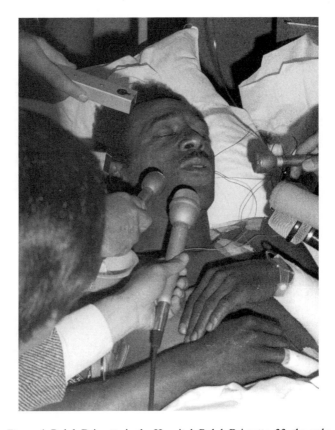

Figure 4. Ralph Brissette in the Hospital. Ralph Brissette, 33, the only survivor of the Sylmar Tunnel blast, is interviewed in his hospital bed. June 26, 1971. Los Angeles Public Library Photo Collection.

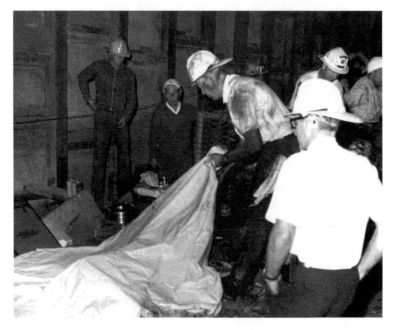

Figure 5. Members of the Los Angeles Fire Department Cover a Body
Inside the Tunnel.
Photo source unknown.

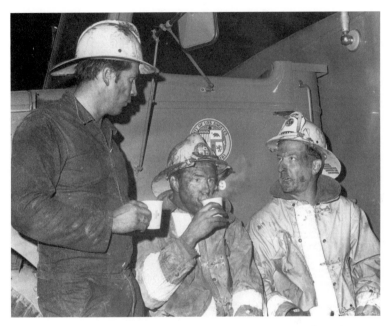

Figure 6. Los Angeles Fire Department Rescue Crew Members. Fire Department rescue team, Ross Rauh, Kenneth Thompson, and Frank Fasmer, have coffee and talk after reaching the surface.
June 25, 1971. Los Angeles Public Library Photo Collection.

Figure 7. Bringing Out the Bodies. Four Metropolitan Water District
tunnel explosion victims are brought out.
June 26, 1971. Los Angeles Public Library Photo Collection.

Figure 8. Tools Left at the Mouth of the Tunnel. A missing worker's safety hat sits on a pile of recovered shovels.
June 26, 1971. Los Angeles Public Library Photo Collection.

ACKNOWLEDGMENTS

I wish to thank all of the following for helping me in the preparation of this novel:

Captain Dave Norman, Captain Dave Chapman, Engineer Rich Meline, and the other members of Los Angeles County Fire Department USAR Task Force 103.

Battalion Chief Larry Collins, Los Angeles County Fire Department, Urban Search & Rescue, California USAR Task Force2/USA-2.

Senior Pilot Thomas Short, Los Angeles County Fire Department Air Operations.

Los Angeles County Fire Department Captain Tony Duran.

Jennifer Cicolani, Special Agent, and Roy House, Explosives Enforcement Officer, from the Los Angeles field office of the Bureau of Alcohol, Tobacco, Firearms and Explosives.

Senior Federal Air Marshall at Homeland Security Mickey Kopanski.

Finally, special thanks to Ventura County Fire Captain Mel Lovo and the men of Station 54, who graciously allowed me to stand in a cold, wet, dark storm drain to observe a tunnel entry and search and rescue drill.

ALSO BY KURT KAMM

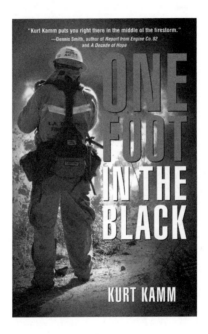

ONE FOOT IN THE BLACK – A Wildland Firefighter's Story

"Kurt Kamm has been there with the firefighters, step by step, and you will feel in the pages of this book that you are right there in the middle of a firestorm as well."
—Dennis Smith, author of *Report From Engine Co. 82* and *A Decade of Hope*

"With *One Foot in the Black*, Kurt Kamm has used the tools of popular fiction to shine a light on the inner workings of the wildland fire service. The tortured main character, who tries to pull a brutalized life together by joining Cal Fire, the Golden State's fire protection agency, takes us on a journey from training ground to fire ground that vividly captures the sense of family, of pulling together, of physical challenge and mortal danger that go with this increasingly vital occupation."
—John N. Maclean, author of *Fire on the Mountain* and other fire books

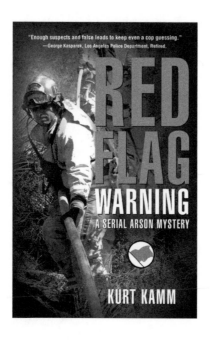

RED FLAG WARNING – *A Serial Arson Mystery*

"NiteHeat is memorable—another lunatic out setting fires."
—Mike Cole, CalFire Battalion Chief, Law Enforcement

Red Flag Warning has won two FIRST PLACE
national mystery competitions:
The Written Art Awards – Mystery/Thriller 2010
Royal Dragonfly – Mystery Category 2011

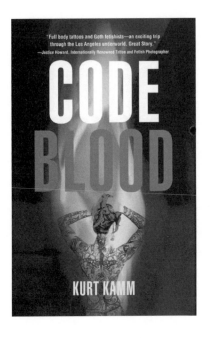

CODE BLOOD

An edgy L.A. Noir thriller! Kamm takes the reader into the world of emergency medicine, the science of stem cell research, and the unsettling world of blood fetishism and body parts.

Code Blood is the winner of three FIRST PLACE
national literary competitions:
2012 International Book Awards, Fiction: Cross Genre category
National Indie Excellent Book Awards® – Faction (fiction based on fact)
The 2012 USA Best Book Awards, Fiction: Horror

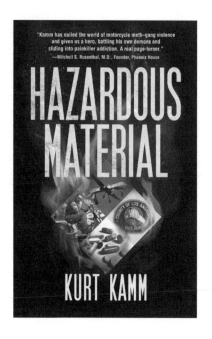

HAZARDOUS MATERIAL

A firefighter battles painkiller addiction and the Vagos outlaw motorcycle gang.

Hazardous Material won several literary awards:
Best Novel 2013 – Public Safety Writers Association
2012 Hackney Literary Award for best novel of the year
Reader's Favorite 2013 – Finalist – Urban Fiction
The 2012 Dana Award – Finalist

All books available on Amazon.
Visit Kurt Kamm's author/firefighter website at **www.KurtKamm.com**

ABOUT THE AUTHOR

Malibu resident Kurt Kamm has used his contact with CalFire, Los Angeles County Fire Department, Ventura County Fire Department and the ATF, as well as his experience in several devastating local wildfires, to write fact-based firefighter mystery novels. He has attended classes at El Camino Fire Academy and trained in wildland firefighting, arson investigation and hazardous materials response. He is also a graduate of the ATF Citizen's Academy. He is currently riding with Los Angeles County Fire Department's famed Urban Search & Rescue Task Force 2/USA-2, and is working on a USAR mystery.

One of the Malibu fires, the 60 mile-per-hour Santa Ana wind-driven Canyon Fire, burned to his front door and destroyed the homes of several neighbors. Kamm said the lessons he learned from the County Fire Department while writing his first book helped him save his home.

A graduate of Brown University and Columbia Law School, Kamm was previously a financial executive and semi-professional bicycle racer. He was also Chairman of the UCLA/Jonsson Comprehensive Cancer Center Foundation and is an avid supporter of the Wildland Firefighter Foundation.

For further information on Kurt Kamm visit his first responder/author website **www.KurtKamm.com**.